Rift

A novel

by

Todd Robert Petersen

ZARAHEMLA BOOKS

Provo, Utah

ISBN 978-0-9787971-8-8

Published by Zarahemla Books
869 East 2680 North
Provo, UT 84604
info@zarahemlabooks.com
ZarahemlaBooks.com

Cover photo and design by the author.

For Pete Peterson and Marlow Imlay,
two of the last great American barbers

Part One: The Feud

Chapter One

THE SCREEN DOOR AT THE BACK of the Thorsen home blew off its hinges, flipped once in the air, and crashed in the gravel behind a white Ford pickup. The sound ricocheted around the yard and barn and carport, sending a pair of thrushes rocketing through a gap in the cottonwoods. The report died in the open before it could reach the mountains. Thorsen paused for a moment in the doorway, his arms stiff and his palms out, his overalls heaving, his forehead stippled in sweat. He was an old man in good health; his fingers were thick, his hands broad, the width of his shoulders was half again the width of his waist. His white hair was full, and combed ineptly.

Thorsen was used to the secondary clap of the door as it cracked against the siding before clattering shut. It helped him punctuate his sentences, but this time his property was filled with silence. He firmed his lipless mouth as he examined the door on the ground in front of him. When he heard his wife's feet on the linoleum, his tight eyes swiveled around, then he lurched down the steps and made for the barn.

Lila stopped in the open entry, a mason jar in one hand and a paring knife in the other. She was wearing a yellow chamomile print apron over a white-collared blouse and denim slacks. Her sleeves were rolled to the elbow. She wore two steel-shot earrings. Her wedding and engagement rings hung around her neck on a thin silver chain.

"Jens Thorsen," she shouted, her eyes settling on the unhinged door. "That doesn't look like self-control."

Thorsen ignored her. When he reached the barn gate, he unlatched it and pulled it open. The horse lifted its head and exhaled. Thorsen squeezed through the opening and pulled the gate shut. Lila pointed to the door with her knife, then gestured to the split and hingeless rectangles spaced along the open jamb.

Thorsen hooked his arms across the gate and hollered, "I put the door in, so it's within my rights to take it out."

"Half that corn is still on the stalks."

"Your harvest can wait. It's the end of month, and you know what that means."

"If you have to run off and do your church work, then I might as well leave that field to the hogs. I won't bottle day-old corn, Jens Thorsen. I might as well buy it in a bag."

Thorsen disappeared into the barn and began parceling a flake of hay into the horse's stall. "Don't look at me. She's the one put it off until now." The horse whinnied and lifted his head toward the house. Thorsen stroked the side of his face and watched the large black eye close once and open. "Calm down," Thorsen said, scowling. "It's just a door."

Enoch lowered his head and continued to eat. Thorsen tisked

once and snuck a look back at the house. Lila was still there, jar and knife in hand, her apron dark against the white of the house. He cursed once and looked away. When he looked back, she was leaning the screen door against the house. Enoch chewed dully and exhaled through his nose as if laying out premises in an argument. When Thorsen looked back at the house, Lila was standing in the doorway with the phone in her hand.

Thorsen rushed to the gate of the barn. "What do you think you're doing?"

"Calling someone."

"Hellfire, woman. If you bring that so-called bishop out here, we're through."

She put the phone to her ear and began speaking. Thorsen undid the gate and burst through. He didn't run, but crossed the open ground in a bearlike lope that was faster than it appeared. By the time he was at the base of the stairs, he heard Lila say, "Thank you, Brother Pearson," and then she hung up. "We'll be having some help from the elders," she said.

Thorsen was two and a half feet lower than his wife, which made it even harder to look her in the eyes.

"The minute you lost control of yourself, this became none of your business," she said and strode through the mudroom and into the kitchen, pivoting right before disappearing into the house. Thorsen considered the refrigerator and the edge of the kitchen table and the long rug that ran to the open inner door. "Well, dang it," he said, then maneuvered his way to the doorjamb and plucked a few coarse slivers from the wood and threw them on the ground. He went to his truck and returned with a tape measure, which he used to gauge the size of the door and jamb.

Then he left.

On the drive to town he tried the radio, got disgusted, and switched it off.

Things had been building up. His retirement hadn't quite been what Lila was expecting. He'd spent much of his life building highways, work that didn't keep him home much. He spent the first few retirement weeks at home, then he'd drive out to job sites just to see if he could help. He'd run his old D9 for a while, give the young folks some pointers, and then beg off, saying he had to get home, always some project or someone to look in on. He told Lila once that she would never understand why he kept going back. He told Lila that her daily routine was at home, in the kitchen and the yard. "Mine," he said, "starts with two eggs over easy in some diner outside of some town on the way to nowhere. I'm not used to being bolted down, Lila, and now that I am, I get a little lost."

As he drove into town, Thorsen rolled down his window. The Sanpete Valley was ringed on all sides by mountains. It had no interstate and no quick way to get to one. Other towns in the valley had junior colleges or BLM offices, but the town of Sanpete was frozen in a time somewhere between 1965 and 1972. It was unclear whether the shops on Main Street were open or closed. The service station on Main and Center had two pumps. A sheet-metal sign hung on old wires between two light poles made from twenty-foot lengths of painted pipe. The image of a winged horse was barely visible on the north side of the building. On the other side was a steel-doored ice cooler with a hasp and no lock.

Three years ago most of the activity in town had been diverted to the Wal-Mart built on the south end of Sanpete, where the old roller mill had been. Thorsen thought the blue building was a blight, and as he passed it, he extended his arm through the window and raised his middle finger.

A kid in a blue vest, who was edging the lawn by the store entrance, looked up and recoiled, sending a mist of geraniums into the air. Thorsen honked, pumped his finger up and down a couple more times, and drove on. He turned off Main and came around the old bishop's storehouse with its compact brick walls and high foundation and came into the parking lot on Second West behind Frisell's Hardware. He went in and returned in a few minutes with a carton the size of a sheet of plywood cut in half the long way. He placed the box in his truck bed and headed home.

As he passed the library, Thorsen heard the loud whoop of a police siren, and he turned around to find a sheriff's patrol car following him. Its lights were on, but he ignored them. *"Jens, pull over,"* a voice said over the loudspeaker.

Thorsen drove on.

"Come on, I'm serious."

Thorsen drove past the Sanpete Hotel and the boarded-up dry-goods store. He looked in the mirror and then poked his head out the window. The police lights throbbed red and blue, and the siren whooped again and then a third time. Thorsen sighed and clicked his turn signal and drifted to a stop.

Spencer Kimball got out of the car and unfolded to his full height of six and a half feet. He was the son of a man Thorsen used to go to high school with, Vernell Kimball, second cousin to a prophet. Spencer was one of a handful of kids who never left the valley except for the two years he spent preaching the gospel. As he approached the truck, Spencer removed his sunglasses and folded them gently and slid them into the pocket of his uniform.

"Brother Thorsen, you got a brake light out, passenger's side."

"The other one working?" Thorsen asked, his head tilted down.

"Sure, but you should hose the mud off it."

"I'll get right on it, Spence," Thorsen said, shifting his weight and grabbing the ignition.

"Hold on," Spencer said, opening his citation book. "Law's the law."

"I ain't out for a Sunday stroll, son. I've got my home teaching to wrap up. Return and report or so says the man behind the pulpit."

"They got this thing called a phone, and you can call it in on that. I actually make my reports on e-mail, Jens. You don't have to drive around with a broken brake light to serve your neighbors. It's the twenty-first century."

"Phones are for suckers."

"You don't like phones?"

"Almost as bad as computers."

"You can't do anything without computers, Jens."

"We beat the Japs without computers," Thorsen said. "Used Navajos."

"Look," Kimball said, agitated.

"Listen, Spencer. If you could tell one of my lights was working, what's the problem? It's not like half my truck is going to stop while the other half keeps driving."

"'Course not, but the law . . ."

"Then what's the big deal? I got bulbs at the house, but I also got to get my home teaching report to that no-account Andy Pearson before the month rolls over—now, you wouldn't want me to be out of compliance with the Lord, would you, Spencer? You wouldn't want to keep me from my sacred duties of watching over the church, and making sure needs are getting met?"

"That's not it—the law says."

"Scripture says to render unto the Lord."

"Okay, well . . . that part also says to render unto Caesar. Okay, so . . . render yourself a new brake light. And quit trying to give me the runaround. You and your buddies are always running me around. If I keep calling in and not citing people, sheriff's gonna think I got no spine."

"You gotta make a report, and I gotta make a report, and we're both just sitting around here not making 'em. Spence, you know how that Andy Pearson can be. He's stuck on the numbers, doesn't really care about the people part of the work. You're not stuck on the numbers, are you, Spencer?"

"Come on, now," Spencer said, writing. "Andy's all right."

"He's on a high horse. You played ball with him, so you know. He runs off to get an education on the backs of the tithe payers. Comes back with this trashy-looking wife from Arizona, both of them living in the house his grandfather built. He jumps on the city council like a tick on an open wound. Now we've got dark-sky laws and a park for thirteen-year-olds to roll around all night in with their undershorts hanging out of their pants. He's got no sense of history. He makes changes just to see what will happen."

"Jens."

"You know, that son of a gun gave me a new assignment, just waltzed in and handed me a slip of paper full of names I didn't recognize. I've been going to my families for twenty years, some of them, and he just scatters my responsibilities like it didn't matter *who* looked after them. Karl Ramke's got emphysema and can't get around. I know what he needs done, and his wife tolerates me. Deloy Meeks is down for a nine-year stint in Gunnison for that gun trouble, and Noreen Hafen's been dreaming that her husband comes to her in visions and has his way with her while she's asleep. It's taken me most of Pearson's life to earn the right to know that, and this organ grinder waltzes into town and reminds me to teach out of the church magazines. I'd rather cut my arm off."

"That's a pretty thorough report," Spencer said.

"I'm gonna give that jackass a piece of my mind."

"And you don't want to do that on the phone?"

"Dulls my blade."

"And this—what we're doing here—this is the rehearsal?"

"Maybe." Jens spat on the ground and looked across the valley.

"Okay then," Spencer said, folding up his book and slipping it in the back pocket of his pants. "Get it fixed. If I see that driver's side light out again, I'll cite you."

"Very good, deputy."

"And why don't you teach Andy how to live in Sanpete instead of just tearing him a new one? One day you old guys will be gone, and we'll be all that's left."

"God help us if it comes to that, Spencer. God help us."

Thorsen fired up his truck and started off. Spencer followed until Thorsen pulled into the NAPA. Spencer kept to the road and drove a hundred yards before pulling a U-turn and passing slowly in front of the store, leaning over the passenger seat with his finger pointing at Thorsen. Thorsen gave Spencer a small salute and got out of his truck and went into the store. He browsed among the floor mats and vinyl restoration formulas, said hello to the kid at the desk, and then told him he forgot his wallet and got back in his truck and drove home.

From the road in front of his house, Thorsen could see four or five vehicles scattered between the house and barn. He only recognized two of them. One was Pearson's and the other belonged to Bishop Darrell Bunker. When he saw Bunker's truck, he cursed and jammed his foot on the brake just as somebody disappeared into the open hole where the screen door used to be. Thorsen burst from his truck and trundled past the barn and glared down the draw to the garden. Half a dozen men were down in the corn, their heads appearing and disappearing in the midst of the trembling stalks.

"H'lo, Jens," a voice said. It was not Bunker's.

Thorsen whirled about to find Tom Leavitt making his way from the house back down to the garden. Tom was in his thirties, a welder. Thorsen knew him from church. As Tom disappeared into the corn, Andy Pearson appeared, red-faced, his immense body draped in a dark nylon tracksuit. He was a big man for his age, paunchy, with long legs and massive feet. He was whistling "Born in the USA" as he walked.

"What's this about?" Thorsen asked.

Pearson stopped whistling but kept walking. "Lila called, said she needed a little help with the canning. BYU game's over, so what the heck."

Thorsen swore another oath, scratched his cheek, then craned his neck toward the house melodramatically.

"Come on, Jens," Pearson said. "It's a blessing to serve. Bishop's here." There was a gleam in Pearson's eye.

Thorsen spat on the ground and then got over to the house. He reached it just as another man was climbing the stairs. "I've got a door to replace, and I can't have you people coming in and out while I'm doing it."

Without waiting to see if his instructions had been followed, Thorsen took the broken door and set it lengthwise across the opening and went back to his truck to get the new door. When he returned, another man Thorsen barely knew was stepping over the old door with another basket of corn. "Quit using this door," Thorsen called.

"Oh, you're back," Lila sang as she passed briefly into view.

" 'Course I'm back. Why wouldn't I be back?"

"Lord knows," she said, stopping briefly so she could see the door. "That can go on the table, Brother Allison. Thank you." Allison came through the mudroom and stopped at the old door, which was now doubled up with the new one in its carton.

"Go around," Thorsen growled. Allison's mouth twitched, and he lowered his eyes and backed up and went to the front door.

Lila took his place at the opening. "I got some help," she said.

"Did you know he was here?"

Lila shrugged. "He who?"

"He, that no account, that's who,"

"Oh, him," Lila said, glancing for exactly one second at the sky.

"Doesn't look good," Thorsen said, lowering his voice. "What do you think I am? A gospel-moocher? He's laying up ammunition against me."

"I think this feud of yours with the bishop is disgraceful. And I think you should let these people come through, so they can get back to their families and enjoy the rest of their Saturday."

Thorsen's face drew tight, and he breathed heavily through his nose. After blinking four or five times he placed both hands on the jamb and leaned into it. "Tell them to go around," he instructed and turned to find another young man with a load of corn approaching the steps. Thorsen pointed to the front end of the house and said, "She'll take that corn at the front."

A few more loads came up from the garden while Thorsen fetched his tools. He watched as they went straight to the front without veering. While he was opening the new door, Pearson appeared suddenly over his shoulder and said, "How's that new home teaching route working out?"

Thorsen shrugged, then cut a plastic strap with his pocketknife, freeing some cardboard. "You'll get your stupid report," he said, tossing the cardboard aside.

"I'm excited to hear about those new families of yours and how they're doing."

Pearson headed down to the garden. Thorsen waited until he

was a hundred feet or so away, then he took a piece of cardboard from the ground and tore it into a rough square. With a stubby pencil he wrote for two or three minutes, holding the cardboard in midair like a clipboard. When he was finished, he went over to a black Dodge pickup and lifted the wiper blade long enough to slip the cardboard underneath.

After the blade dropped, Thorsen turned around to see if there were any witnesses. Across the yard, the blockish form of Darrell Bunker appeared, his arms taut under the load of a half-bushel of corn. He nodded once and then smiled.

"Keeping the place a little more natural these days," Bunker said, casting his eyes around. "Don't blame you at all. Who wants the trouble?"

"Bishop," Thorsen said, "I paid my tithing last week, so make sure the whole hundred percent of that corn makes it to the kitchen."

Bunker frowned and began to examine the box. After a while he shook his head and said, "Looks like the earworms got past you this summer. Don't think they'd take it at the store house."

Thorsen centered his weight and drew a breath, then caught sight of Lila out of the corner of his eye.

"Oh, Bishop," she said, "we're glad you could come help."

Before he had the chance to respond, Thorsen pointed his finger at Bunker and said, "You're proof of something," then he turned away from Bunker as if he did not exist. He walked over to the house and picked up the new door. Lila saw him coming and retreated into the house. "Don't talk to me," he hissed at his wife. "Don't say a word."

After a moment, Thorsen could feel a gathering force behind him. He looked over his shoulder and noticed the corn gatherers congregating in the drive. Pearson spoke to them for a couple of minutes, then gave Bunker a chance to speak, which he waved off.

Soon, they broke their huddle and began backing, one by one, down the drive. Pearson climbed into his truck and reached out the window to snatch the cardboard. He read it and stared at Thorsen for a few seconds. His face was throbbing. Thorsen smiled and waved. Pearson put his truck in gear, swung around, and headed home. The bishop followed.

Thorsen waited for their dust to settle, then went back to work on the door. He tested it a couple of times, made a few adjustments to the air piston, and cleaned up his mess. Carefully, he took out his knife and cut the old screen from the broken door, rolled it, and took it into the barn. He returned with a short handsaw and cut the old door into a dozen pieces and stacked them on the woodpile. On his way into the house, he paused with his hand on the new door and cast his eyes skyward for a moment, then took a breath and dropped his head.

He mumbled something to himself, then went inside.

Lila was zigzagging about the kitchen, pots boiling, jars everywhere. Nearly two bushels of corn lay about in boxes and baskets. Thorsen went to the table, picked up an ear, sat down, and began shucking. Lila's eyes flashed once toward Thorsen, then she got a glass from the cupboard and filled it from the tap. She set it on the table next to Thorsen, and as soon as she let go, he took the glass and lifted it slowly to his lips and drank.

Chapter Two

Sunday morning. The slippery twitter of a green-tailed towhee somewhere beyond Thorsen's pickup. The air still but for the illuminated motes that sailed crosswise through the light. Thorsen slammed the door of his truck and stomped through the back door, shedding his canvas coat in the mudroom. "Looks like summer's just about done for this year," he said, working a toothpick from one side of his mouth to the other. He rubbed his hands and rumbled into the kitchen. Lila was humming to herself, packing jars of corn into a cardboard box.

Without looking up, she said, "There's a flash of yellow in the cottonwoods—doesn't mean a thing. We haven't seen a frost yet, and I don't guess we will for a few more weeks."

"Look like big snow this year?" Thorsen asked. He got himself a glass of water, leaned against the counter, and drank. When it was empty, he poured himself another.

"Almanac says by Thanksgiving," Lila said. She walked past Thorsen with her eyes on the glass and the toothpick, then closed the flaps on the box and turned with it and set it on the kitchen table. "There won't be much to it down here until the middle of December, I should think."

Thorsen drained the second glass of water in a series of five glugs, then he smiled. "Mamma, you've got a knack—"

"It's fast Sunday," Lila announced, drying her hands on the front of her apron. Thorsen froze with his hand on the toothpick. He blinked and let his eyes drop to the floor.

"Jens!" she brayed.

"It was Phyllis—when I got done with her chores she cut me a slice of coffee cake. What was I supposed to do, turn her down? She's about to come around, Mamma. You want me to throw that out on account of some fast I can do tomorrow as easy as today?"

Lila was unfazed. She kept staring at Thorsen, who didn't know what to do with his glass of water except to dry the rim on his shirt and clap it decisively on the countertop.

Lila tugged the bottom of her apron and smoothed the rest of it down, starting at her collar and moving down across her bosom and belly. "We were fasting for Brandon's mission call," she said and gave a sign of exasperation with her left hand, then plopped into a chair.

"I'll start up again this afternoon and go for two days," Thorsen said.

"I don't want you going over there anymore if all Phyllis is going to do is compromise your convictions."

"Karl'd be out there working if he didn't have the oxygen. Besides, those animals got to be fed, and Phyllis is in no shape to do it. You have to have some mercy, Lila."

"I'm not getting into this again, Jens Thorsen. You putter around in people's lives, then leave loose ends all over the place around here. I asked you to fix the gutters three weeks ago, and they're still hanging off the corner of the house. My compost still needs turning, and yesterday—I'm not even going to talk about yesterday."

"It was the end of the month, Mamma," Thorsen said, backtracking. "And besides you called in the stooges and their king."

"Don't *end-of-the-month-mamma* me. From the minute you retired, you haven't been able to stand it here. Don't think I can't see what that means."

Thorsen waved her off and headed down the back hall.

"Don't you give me that geezer hand either," she called after him.

Thorsen did it again, then gripped the banister and began climbing the stairs. "I'm going to clean up," he called out. "It's still Sunday, even though it don't feel like it down here."

Thorsen came back wearing a white shirt and bolo tie, his scriptures under one arm, and a small white triangle of toilet paper stuck to his neck on a single rivet of blood. "You look nice, Mamma," he said, smiling, sizing up Lila's backside. Her legs were straight and the calves still rounded. She was stout but not boxy, and her hips still slanted in toward the waist, unlike other women her age whose lines ran parallel from shoulder to floor. Thorsen smiled. "Pull off that apron, and let's go."

There was a clatter of silverware, and Lila turned suddenly, her mouth full.

A grin stretched across Thorsen's face, and he started laughing. "Ain't you the picture of temperance?"

Lila exhaled through her nose and continued to chew. As she did, Thorsen shook his finger at her. Her face flushed, and she swallowed. "I guess we're both gonna get tossed out of the garden, ain't we?" Thorsen said.

"We're starting over tonight. It's for our grandson," she said, fuming, her hands rapidly brushing crumbs from the shelf of her bosom. She stepped past Thorsen, grabbed her bag, and marched right back past him. She lifted a sweater from a hook in the mudroom, then went out the door. Thorsen followed.

"We're going to be late," she said.

"We'll just miss the chitchat and the song. No loss." Thorsen fished a single silver key out of the ashtray and slipped it into the ignition.

"I wish you wouldn't do that," Lila complained. "One morning you're going to wake up and find this truck gone."

"Why would somebody come all the way out here to steal this piece of crap?" Thorsen asked, cranking on the ignition.

"That's not my point."

The starter ground for a few revolutions, then the engine coughed and flared alive. "There she goes," Thorsen said, gunning the throttle, causing the truck to backfire.

Lila glared at him. "It could be kids out at night looking for trouble—"

Thorsen gunned it again, drowning her out. He hunched over to scrutinize the tachometer and the gas gauge, which he tapped a few times with the back of one knuckle. The needle was pegged at full. He tapped it again and it fluttered. "Ain't no kids in this town anymore," he said. "They're just foreclosures in embryo."

"My point isn't that something might happen. It's just good to be prepared. It was your father who said, 'Trust in the Lord but close the gate.'"

Thorsen grunted.

"I'd think with your upbringing, you'd be more apt to take his advice," Lila said.

"How much gas did you put in here?" Thorsen asked.

"I filled it—are you listening to me?"

"I hope you reset the odometer."

"Of course I did. It's got eight miles on it—you haven't heard a thing I've said."

"I heard you. Eight miles."

They fell silent, their voices giving way to the hum of tires and pavement and the rattle of loose compartment panels. Occasionally Lila would arrange the folds of her dress and move her scriptures from her lap onto the seat beside her and then, after a few minutes, move them back. Thorsen drove, listening for strange sounds in the vehicle and watching the temperature gauge the way some people watch the tip of a fly rod.

They climbed up the road that led from their property and crested the bluffs east of town near the brick remnants of old pioneer homes and barns that had slowly crumbled and blown away. Lila turned her head out the window and watched the jagged graph of the mountains play out along the edge of the sky. Trees at the top of the mountains were, in fact, beginning to turn, but it was early, too, and against the juniper and pine the yellow of aspens and orange of scrub oak punctuated the fault line like panels in a quilt. A jackrabbit caromed into their lane, pivoted, then darted back into the sagebrush. Thorsen drew a deep breath and exhaled, then repeated the process with more noise.

"If I'm not going to be listened to, it doesn't really serve me to talk, now does it?" Lila said.

Thorsen shrugged, then polished the underside of his nose with his forefinger. "Since when do you care about who listens to you?"

"Jens," Lila exclaimed. She turned and pointed a finger at him. "With other people, I don't care, because I can assume they don't care either. That's easy. But you and I have a different arrangement. Once you and I get threadbare, everything else is going to break down. If we can't be at least decent to each other, then we've wasted this life on the devil, Jens. You're at my disposal and I'm at yours. Always. That's what little Paul taught us, or should we waste his sacrifice, too?

"I haven't forgotten about him."

Thorsen knew his wife was in uncharted territory. She did not speak of Paul. He regripped the steering wheel and tried not to look at her. The clouds above the mountains were low and thick, so many shades of gray it was easier to let them bleed into one. Lila was breathing through her nose. The sound of it made Thorsen want to shrivel.

They were still not talking when they pulled into the church parking lot. Lila would not let Thorsen hold the door for her.

Once she was inside, she sped up, putting half a hallway between them.

By the time Thorsen had made it a third of the way to the chapel, he had been greeted twice. While he was shaking hands with one of the greeters, Andy Pearson turned the corner, his wide shoulders crammed into a grayish-green suit coat. His stride was rapid and forceful. He moved with the certainty of a football coach. His hands twitched as they swung from his sleeves, weighted by a massive class ring on one side and his stainless-steel dress watch on the other. He was clean-shaven, with a receding hairline cropped down to nothing on the sides, which made him look like an immense toddler in wedding clothes. He did not seem so absurd on Saturday.

Thorsen was not sure that Pearson had seen him, and he wasn't interested in finding out. He turned and stiff-armed the door to the men's room and disappeared inside. Fearing that Pearson would follow, he rushed past the urinals and locked himself into a stall. The door opened, followed by a dozen thunderous footfalls and the long metallic buzz of a zipper, followed by a slight but intentional sigh.

"Jens," Pearson said, his urine trickling in the background, "I found something strange under my windshield wiper yesterday." The echo of Pearson's voice against the tile made him sound villanous.

"You talking to me?" Thorsen answered, his hand on the toilet paper roll.

There was a pause. "I'm sorry. I'm wondering about the report you *filed* yesterday. I found this sheet of cardboard with some numbers scribbled on it and a note that says, 'NRA pamphlet'—but, you know, I didn't recognize any of the families." Remarkably, Pearson's urination lasted the whole of his monologue.

"I don't talk to those contraptions," Thorsen growled. "It's not dignified."

"What contraptions?"

"Answering machines."

The faucet turned on, and Thorsen listened to the slick sound of Pearson washing his hands. The glutinous slap and pop of his hygiene made Thorsen's stomach turn. "What do answering machines have to do with the fact that there are three families this month who haven't been looked after because you've ignored your assignment?"

"They aren't mine."

"I assigned them to you."

"I take my assignments from the Lord."

Pearson said nothing.

"You've got a lot of gall, son. You haven't spent more than eighteen months in Sanpete as an adult. How can you know these people? How can you have a handle on what they need?"

The door opened, and Pearson said hello to the bishop. Bunker said hello back, and they spoke in vague tones about a good solution to a certain situation. Pearson said that he thought everyone had given good counsel, and Bunker agreed. A pause followed, punctuated by intermittent splashes. For a moment, Thorsen considered lifting his feet to avoid detection. He cursed to himself and made a series of short contortions with his lips as he decided on a course of action.

"Thanks for coming out yesterday, Bishop," Pearson said, his volume rising. "It was good to see everyone working together like that. Nothing brings the guys together faster than a little service."

Bunker didn't answer right away. Thorsen stared at the inside of the stall and made a list of the things he'd like to do to Pearson and then immediately dismissed them as too soft-hearted.

"I had my reservations," Bunker said after a while. "You want to leave people to their agency, but you also want to make sure everyone's doing okay. I worry a lot about the women of the church, President."

"Must be a load off to have Angie back home, then," Pearson said.

"Sister Bunker and I are relieved."

"You guys work so hard. Our oldest is six. I don't even want to think about what we'll be dealing with when she's twenty-one."

"Little kids don't let you sleep, and big ones don't let you rest," Bunker said. "We're blessed she's back. Teach them while they're little, and they'll come back to you."

Thorsen had begun to wedge himself into the stall to keep himself from blowing his cover. The isometric resistance was sapping his strength. There was another pause and then the flushing of a urinal and then the rush of a faucet. "Better get this show on the road," Bunker said, and then there was the sound of hard soles on the tile. Thorsen emerged from the stall to find Pearson leaning against the wall with his arms crossed.

"He's gone," Pearson said.

"Thanks for the screen."

"Key to a good offence is your defense."

Thorsen looked up at the kid. "Well, thanks anyway." He washed his hands and shook them on the floor.

He crossed the foyer, shaking his head and swearing again under his breath, then he heard a commotion in the chapel. As he peered through the door, he saw a mob quivering between the front row and the stand. Briefly, through the ring of suits and dresses, a young girl's face appeared. She tried to smile, but it seemed fruitless.

Lila was sitting by herself along the right side, and Thorsen slipped in beside her. He hung his head and rested his elbows on his knees. "That Angie Bunker is back from wherever it is she went," Lila said.

"Her old man was bragging about it in the john."

"I'm surprised."

"Not me."

"Oh, drop it," Lila said.

Thorsen glowered while people drifted to their pews and settled in. Bunker invited Angie to sit next to him on the stand by pointing to her and beckoning with a strangely adolescent series of hand gestures. She rose and went up slowly. The bishopric shuffled around and made room while Angie stood waiting. When a spot had been cleared, she hooked a piece of loose red hair behind her ear and sat down in a way that began with grace and ended with collapse. Bunker looked pleased and proud, and when the music stopped, he gave no thought of rising, but kept on beaming like he was alone in the world. A minute or so passed, then Angie nudged her father to his feet. He took his spot at the podium and opened the meeting with the normal hymns and announcements.

During the meeting, Bunker's eyes drifted periodically to his daughter, then back out to the congregation. He was a dutiful shepherd, his eyes mechanically scanning the room. Thorsen dropped his head as Bunker's eyes swept the chapel and came past. His neck bristled, and he wrung his hands dryly as if washing them. Thorsen's distaste for Bunker grew more sour as the seconds passed. He tried to tell his wife that a prodigal child needs to be given a bed and hot meals, and people need to leave her alone until she's ready to go public. Lila nudged Thorsen with her arm and passed him the silver tray of sacrament bread. He took a piece, ate it, lifted his eyes to the ceiling for a second or two, and returned to his thoughts.

Eventually he said that with a track record of kids turning south as bad as Bunker's, you'd think he'd be a little more careful with the baby. Lila hushed him, and Thorsen said that putting her on parade would make it harder to bring her around, if that is, in fact, what she needed.

"With that attitude, you might as well spit out the sacrament onto the carpet before it turns to damnation on your tongue," Lila whispered.

"Since when did telling the truth ever get somebody crosswise with the Lord?"

Lila's eyes sliced toward her husband. "Grandma Glynnis used to say that most truths keep better as secrets—quit digging your nails into the bench and forget this insanity. You know, elephants just kick the males out before they get territorial. I'm starting to think that's a good idea."

Thorsen looked up and noticed that his hands were clamped onto the rounded top edge of the pew, the tips of his nails caught in the grain of the oak. "You siding with him now?"

"How can I pick sides when I don't even remember how it started?"

"I loaned him that hammer drill in good faith, and you saw what he did to it."

Lila's eyes rolled back in her head, and she clutched a green hymnal for support. "I didn't mean I wanted you to remind me."

"It's that bishop up there who burned out the motor on a good Porter Cable—the same one who left it on the back porch like nothing in the world was wrong with it. The last thing this church needs is bishops that don't know their scriptures. Deuteronomy twenty-two and fourteen, Mamma—and if a man borrow aught of his neighbor and if it's been screwed up, then the owner shall surely make it good. I don't think leaving the damn thing on the porch is making good. Do you?"

People in the next row glanced back.

"Well, it doesn't make him a thief either," Lila whispered, "and you were probably off somewhere home teaching, or whatever you want to call it. So, can you blame him for just leaving it where he did?"

"He could have left a note."

"It did have a short to begin with."

"I told him about the short."

"*After* he brought it back."

"All you have to do is shake the cord. It's not rocket science—"

"Look at him now," Lila said, lifting her chin.

Bunker raised his arm and slipped it around his daughter, who continued to sit, slumped in her seat. His pallid face was beaming, his cheeks like hubcaps, the hole of his mouth dark but for the line of small white tiles appearing from behind his lips. His whole face was blooming in creases, his neck packed into the collar of his shirt.

"Jens, this is not about some hammer drill, and you know it."

"I don't care what it's about. He keeps throwing fuel on the fire, Mamma, fuel on the cotton-picking fire."

After the sacrament had been passed, Bunker stepped up to the podium, adjusted the microphone, and cleared his throat three or four times. "Well," Bunker said, "I'd like to thank our priesthood boys for their reverence. And I forgot to mention that we're putting together a ward basketball team, and Charlie Davenport is the guy to see about that." Bunker paused and glanced over toward his daughter, who was still looking sheepish and trapped. Thorsen, his patience overtaxed, cradled his forehead in his hands.

"Brothers and sisters, it's my honor to lead you in this testimony meeting with some thoughts and feelings of my own. Hopefully they'll help you with your own testimonies, which you are welcome to bear up here, until ten after." Bunker gestured to his daughter, who looked mortified. "My prayers have been answered. I'm reminded of the parable of the ninety and nine. Christ said that even if a man had a hundred sheep and—" Bunker paused, a troubled look on his face. His right eye twitched, and the sound of his breathing rasped through the microphone and filled the chapel. "I'm not going to make it without crying, I guess," he said.

"Me neither," Thorsen whispered, and Lila scowled at him.

"What I mean to say is, wouldn't anybody go after that one sheep that's missing, go and look for her and call her name? Jesus says, of course you would, and that sure put those Pharisees on edge. But brothers and sisters, wouldn't you? Of course you would. And that's the gospel. I know this church is true. I know that the Lord answers prayers." He glanced down at Angie, who was slumping in her seat like an empty coat.

"He's not answering mine," Thorsen groused again.

"That's enough," Lila said.

"If he loved that kid, he'd stand down."

Bunker dragged the back of his hand across one eye, then pushed it across the other. "The time is now yours . . ."

During the service, as people came to the stand to speak briefly on their faith and trials, Bunker nudged his daughter lightly and nodded to the podium, and every time he did, Thorsen would groan until Lila nudged him.

People bowed their heads and listened, off and on, the way people listen to the news while they are cooking dinner. As the meeting went on, people could see that their testimonies were robbing Angie of her opportunity to rise and speak. Eventually no one rose at all. They cast their eyes upon their bishop as Angie steadily twined a lock of red hair around her index finger, a gleam flaring on each of her five rings as she turned her hand again and again, knitting and purling the hair with her fingertip.

The chapel was filled with silence except for the objections of bored children and the stray rustling of thin scripture pages. Bunker leaned over and whispered to Angie, who shook her head. Bunker kept whispering to her until she looked like she might vault the stand and break for the rear doors.

"Well, Mamma," Thorsen said, grabbing hold of the pew in front of him, "here comes the cavalry," then he hoisted himself up with an audible grunt and eased into the aisle.

"Holy heck," he heard someone behind him say, but he didn't turn around. Bunker dropped his chin scornfully, which caused his cheeks to flex and crowd his mouth and nose. "Cover your heads," another voice said. Thorsen hitched up his pants and stabbed along stiff-legged up the stairs. He caught Angie's eye and winked. A wrinkled smirk unspooled across his face. Her head bounced girlishly, then she winked back. He installed himself behind the mike and signaled Bud Miner, the bishop's counselor, to raise the stand. Bud leaned over and tripped a switch that raised the podium like a pneumatic car lift. Halfway up, the podium hardware screeched and everyone flinched.

"Sounds like my back," Thorsen said. The congregation laughed, but the laughter tapered off quickly. Wayne Blitch made a barely audible turkey call. The congregation laughed again.

Bunker was livid, his eyes shrunken to points, one hand cupped over his mouth, his legs crossed.

"I've been listening to you all here for most of forty-five minutes, thinking about how when I was a kid, I used to spend my summers working on my grandad's ranch over to Mount Nebo. My old Grandpa Thorsen was an ornery old Dane so thick-tongued with the old country that you could barely understand him. He was hard but fair. He never talked about hearing angels or miracles. That kind of thing might have happened to him, but he never talked about it. Once I asked him why he joined the church and came over from Copenhagen to live with people he couldn't talk to. He told me it was because it felt like the right thing, and there wasn't anything for him in Denmark anyway. He'd never even read the scriptures because he couldn't read, in either language."

Thorsen took hold of each side of the podium with his thick-fingered hands and let his eyes pass once from right to left to take stock of his audience. Many heads were tilted down in an attitude of reverence, but Thorsen knew that it was just as likely an attitude of exhaustion. Those with their heads up looked like their bellies were about to explode.

He glanced down at his watch: three more minutes.

"I used to work on that old ranch," he continued, "when they'd bring a whole herd of horses down from the high pastures at the end of summer—" Blitch made the turkey call again, and Thorsen stopped, squinted toward him but kept his hands on the podium. "As Brother Blitch can surely tell you—I think he's heard this one—my granddad would have his hands build up this big old V out of fence rails and surplus Army net, and he'd have them put it up on the front of the corral to funnel those horses into the gate when they came a-running.

"I must have been around twelve and getting a hot spot in my britches to prove something, so I nagged my granddad to let me help bring in the horses. He took one look at me and knew I was more likely to kill myself or a couple of his horses than I was likely to be of any use, but he put me on gate duty. All I had to do was shut that gate once all them horses got inside. He ran me through the paces, but I was so full of wind that I didn't hear anything he said. I told him 'yes sir' and 'no sir,' and he nodded once and rode off to bring those horses down.

"So there I was, sitting up on the fence there, watching that horse dust rise up into the sky like a bonfire, then I heard this turkey clucking behind me—"

Blitch gobbled again, and laughter spilled over the edges of the congregation.

"All right, Blitch, you're welcome to come up here and share your wisdom with the group," Thorsen barked. Blitch laughed and shook his head and then waved Thorsen off and kept on laughing and shaking his head. Thorsen continued.

"So I've got my granddad's horses and my grandmother's turkeys set to cross paths at the mouth of that corral. Those crazy animals were all out there laying in the dust, trying to beat the heat and keep clear of the bugs. If I didn't get to work, there was going to be a mess I didn't want to stick around for. So I climbed off that fence and went trying to herd up those turkeys, and I tell you, there's nothing in this world like trying to get a dozen turkeys headed in the same direction. I was picking those birds up with both hands and throwing them over the fence, their wings flapping and stirring up dust and smacking me in the face and ears. I'd dump them over the fence and they'd just run back under and I'd pick them up and toss them over, till I'd thrown them all two, three times apiece."

The ward members were stupefied and still as boulders.

"Those horses were coming full bore, and I could hear their hooves, and I realized I was right there at the neck of that V with this flapping basketball in my hands, its legs just running in the emptiness. Before I'd really realized I was in for it, my grandmother came running with her entire clothesline full of laundry and hooked one end to one arm of that V and strung it across the whole open mouth. Those sheets and shirts hung down like a white wall between me and the turkeys and those horses. I didn't think it would work, but those horses split and ran around the corral like creek water around a stone. I dropped the one turkey I was still holding onto, and they all just milled and pecked around and then dug back into the loose dirt and went back to clucking.

"I caught a tan hide for that one, boy. And I deserved it."

Thorsen looked at his watch. "I can see that we're just about out of time, so let me say sorry to Angie for me taking up her share of the meeting, but I suspect she'll get another shot before too long. Amen."

The congregation said amen as well, but with a gasp, the way people end a breath-holding contest. Thorsen turned at the waist and winked at Angie a second time and clambered down the short flight of stairs. Bunker went to the stand and stood there propping himself on the podium. He looked like he was having a heart attack. After a few heavy breaths, he announced the hymn, his eyes following Thorsen as he crossed the front of the chapel and slid into a pew next to his wife.

"Oh, Jens, we should have come fasting," she said as the first notes of the organ sounded.

Thorsen hunched over and leafed through his hymnal, then felt a light tapping on his back. He turned around to see Lois Murty, ninety years old, smiling. She said something he couldn't hear and then smiled again, the slight tremors in her hands and head granting her a very specific kind of authority. Thorsen thanked her and gestured with a knuckle in the air and returned to his hunch. The rest of the men on the stand were singing, but Bunker stared across the congregation, his eyes fixed on a point in the same direction as Thorsen but farther in back. During the prayer, Thorsen snuck a look, and Bunker's eyes hadn't moved. In fact, it seemed as if he hadn't blinked.

At the conclusion of the prayer, people milled about the chapel longer than normal. Thorsen and Lila rose. "I'm not sure whether to be proud of you, or ashamed."

"So it's a normal morning for you, isn't it?" Thorsen said.

As they turned to leave the chapel, Thorsen caught Angie's eye. She looked right at him and mouthed the words *thank you*, then placed the palms of her hands together and bowed slightly. As she did, her father grabbed her by the arm and stepped in front of her. He stabbed his finger at Thorsen and said, "That takes a lot of nerve, Thorsen." The congregation froze, even the children, but Lila continued on, weaving through the people like they were so many highway cones. Thorsen placed the palms of his hands together and bowed to Angie, the strings of his bolo tie hanging plumb, then dropping back against his shirt.

"Blessed are the peacemakers, Bishop," Thorsen said. "I think that part of the bible is correctly translated."

Chapter Three

Downtown Sanpete was devoid of cars, except for those of shop owners and people passing through town to jobs at the school or city hall. The trees still held their leaves, and the snowless caps of the twin ranges on either side of the valley hunched upon one another like the withers of a string of horses. Thorsen turned onto Second South, as a flock of birds pulsed behind the storefronts. The grainy mass of wings swelled once against the faded bricks, then turned sharply and rematerialized in rows on the power lines. The morning shadows reached halfway up the buildings, and the blue sky above them was heaped with clouds.

Only a day had passed since Thorsen's showdown with Bunker, but in that time, talk volleyed furiously across back fences and shopping carts and checkout counters. It had come to restaurant tables on serving trays, and it left the hardware store in bags of concrete and roofing nails. Women and children in parks told their versions. Teachers shook their heads and told of it again as they poked at their lunches. Dispatchers made queries over the airwaves. By sundown, the valley had been slathered in gossip.

Thorsen unfastened his seatbelt but didn't immediately leave the truck. Instead, he watched the dawn light weld the sky to the mountains. After a few minutes, he backed across the street and hauled himself out of the truck. Through the greenish window of the barber shop, Thorsen saw Lewis Stucki, who owned the shop, standing behind the farthest chair. He was reedy, with a Gallic nose and weak chin. His white hair was close-cropped, a wide path of waxy baldness catching the light. Stucki stooped to reach the head of Wayne Blitch, who sat in Stucki's chair with nearly half his small, square head shorn down to the skull. Tufts of wooly hair leapt to the floor as Stucki deftly nudged his clippers about. The other half of Blitch's head was slicked back. Ernest Passey sat in the closest chair in gray coveralls, the cuffs of which were frayed and discolored, an issue of *Bowhunter* magazine stretched between his massive grease-tarnished hands. Passey's brother-in-law, Glade Smith, the youngest of the four, sat in one of the side chairs, facing the television. As Stucki spun Blitch's chair around, he caught sight of Thorsen standing on the sidewalk. Blitch motioned wildly and began speaking to the others in the room. Glade pointed the remote at the television, and Passey pulled his magazine to his chest and turned himself toward the window.

Thorsen placed his hand on the door and pushed. Before he could stop himself, he was inside. The silence was crystalline, each man frozen in his sphere, his eyes on Thorsen, his breathing stopped. Thorsen nodded to each, then pursed his lips and scanned the shop, satisfied by the plainness of it. Nothing but the calendar photo had changed in a dozen years: the stack of newspapers and magazines, the cardboard display of palm-sized travel hair brushes, the bank of mirrors behind the chairs, and the mirrors on the wall opposite them. Though there were three red leather barber chairs in the shop, only one was backed with clippers and cylinders of scissors and combs steeping in blue antiseptic. This was a one-man show.

"So, they excommunicated you yet?" Passey said.

Stucki's clippers clattered back to life. Passey waited for the answer for a few seconds, then returned to his magazine once he realized Thorsen was ignoring him. Glade unmuted the television and remuted it to silence a commercial for cholesterol medicine. Blitch's hands appeared from under his maroon smock as he gripped the arms of the barber chair.

"You should have seen him," Blitch said, shaking his head in disbelief. Stucki reached out with both hands, caught the sides of his head, and jerked it straight. Blitch threw his eyebrows up, ignoring Stucki. "You know, Thorsen," he said, "before too long that grudge of yours is going to turn into an episode of *America's Most Wanted.*"

"You know what, Blitch, you need to quit being my deputy," Thorsen said, then he took the middle chair between Blitch and Passey. "Whatever you fellas heard ain't true," he continued. "Blitch has got a flawed perspective."

"It ain't flawed!" Blitch protested. Thorsen shrugged. Glade unmuted the television again, and the barber shop filled with the screeching of a chimpanzee.

"Truth is in the eye of the beholder," Passey mumbled. "You

gave a bishop the high hat during fast and testimony meeting. Back in the day, they'd have sent Porter Rockwell after you."

"Well, that's always the trouble, isn't it?" Thorsen coughed once into his fist and then eased back in his chair. "Truth ain't things, it's the knowledge of things. It's hard to get that point across in this valley sometimes, especially when people's knowledge of things is spotty."

"My knowledge of things is that you and Bunker squared off in a sacrament meeting," Passey said. "That untrue?"

"Nope. We squared off all right."

Blitch leaned forward in his chair. "It was the pure love of Christ, fellas," Blitch said. "Bunker kept trying to shanghai a testimony out of that poor runaway."

Stucki told Blitch to sit still.

"He dang near put a gun to her head," Blitch said and then relaxed again into the chair.

Thorsen nodded. "I was thinking about putting one to mine."

"I love you like a brother, Jens," Stucki said, "but one of these days you and Bunker will be swinging baseball bats at each other in the church parking lot. I don't see what you get out of it. You two have been at it for twenty years."

"Ain't a feud," Thorsen said.

"Why not?" Passey asked.

"A feud doesn't have grounds. It just happens," Thorsen answered. Stucki shook his head, chuckling. He set down the clippers and comb and began to apply hot lather to Blitch's cheeks and neck.

Under his breath, Stucki said, "What he's got is hatred."

Thorsen hoisted himself in the chair. "What *I've* got is hatred."

Stucki lifted one eyebrow and continued to work the lather.

"And your hatred is founded on the rock of what?" Passey asked.

"It's founded on the rock of he's a sidewinder, always looking to get the advantage, always living whichever half of the gospel suits his business practices," Thorsen said. "You can see it with our current situation. That girl of his ran off, and now she's back, and he's putting on a show to make us think that girl was up north coming to Jesus."

"She might have been," Stucki said.

"Looking holy and being holy are two different things," Thorsen said.

"I thought this had something to do with Bunker making more money building roads than you did," Glade said. Passey glared at his brother-in-law, then dragged a finger across his throat to kibosh him.

"Bunker doesn't build roads, Glade. He hires people to build them. He doesn't know a backhoe from his backside. If God told Bunker to build a ship, he'd drop to his knees and ask, 'Whither shall I go to hire illegal Mexicans?'"

Laughter came like the whoop of a siren. Blitch snickered convulsively and then jumped. "For crying out loud, Stucki," he shouted, lunging out of the chair. "What the heck is going on?" Blitch leaned toward the large mirror and lifted his hand from his neck. A rosette of blood the size of a silver dollar clung there just behind the curve of his jaw.

"I'm sorry, Wayne," Stucki said, the straight razor quaking in one hand. A thin sheen of blood coated the face of the blade, and the lather spread across the forefinger of Stucki's opposite hand was likewise damasked and trembling. "I'll clean it up and put some styptic on it."

"I think I'm done," Blitch said, struggling to unfasten the smock.

"All right, then," Stucki said, letting his hands drop to his sides. He looked scared. "It's on the house, Wayne. You shouldn't have to pay me to cut your throat."

Blitch balled up the smock and tossed it in the chair. He kept the paper collar and brought it to his neck to stanch the blood. Passey looked past Blitch to his brother-in-law, who held up the palms of his hands. He then swung his eyes over to Thorsen and set his face firmly and shrugged. Passey pursed his lips and then looked at his boots. Blitch, cursing under his breath, pushed past Jens, his hand clamped back on his neck. He snatched his cap from the hat rack and went out into the street. The bell on the door clanged twice and fell silent.

Blitch paused on the sidewalk, lifted his hand again, and then dropped it. He turned at the waist to look back into the shop for a moment, and Passey waved him along. Blitch nodded and crossed in front of the window and disappeared.

Stucki turned and began to rinse the razor, carefully, letting a full stream of water wash over his hand and the handle and the blade stem and the blade. Then he dried the blade on a towel, removed it from the stem, and tossed it into the trash. "Must have been all the commotion," Stucki said. Passey turned a page in his magazine. Glade turned back to the television. Thorsen dug at his fingernails.

"You ready, Glade?" Stucki asked.

They both rose and set things back in order. Glade set the remote control back on the mute television, and Passey slipped his magazine back into the rack. "It's getting late," Glade said.

"You fellas take it easy," Stucki said. "I'm headed down to Fish Lake next Monday."

"If things work out at the shop, I'll see about it," Passey said, checking for his keys and wallet. "Can't make you any promises. See you around the block."

"Yeah, see you," Stucki said, folding up the empty razor and slipping it into his pocket.

"You all take care," Glade said, following Passey. They both shook hands with Thorsen on the way out. Thorsen told them that everything was going to be all right.

The bell on the door clanged again, and then the shop was silent. Thorsen thumbed the seam of his Levis and coughed to make it seem like he was only marginally interested, but Thorsen knew what it was all about. Stucki had been looking strange the past few months. His face looked a little dead and rubbery, and he looked tense lately, tight. Thorsen had noticed that Stucki was speaking more softly, but he passed it off as a fault of his own hearing.

Thorsen crawled into the chair Passey had left empty, while Stucki shook out Blitch's smock and grabbed the dust mop from the corner and started to sweep. Thorsen followed Stucki with his eyes as he robotically swept the gray and black hair into a pile and pushed it into the corner. His old friend's face had a strange oiliness to it that Thorsen hadn't noticed before, an odd condition for the dry desert air that dusted everything in this valley. Stucki crossed to the window, flipped the sign to closed, and twisted the lock on the door, then crossed back to the far chair and lowered himself woodenly down.

"What's all that about?" Thorsen asked.

"Jens," Stucki started, scrubbing the back of his hand under his nose a little, perhaps to buy some time. "I guess I have to come clean. Violet's the only one knows any of it."

"Let's just sit here a minute and enjoy the quiet," Thorsen said.

"You saw them," Stucki said, lifting his hand heavily and gesturing with mechanical resignation to the empty chairs. "That was old friends, Jens. I can't have people think I'm careless, not them. This town's too small for that."

"What I meant was, let's just sit here so I can think up something to say that isn't stuipd."

Stucki deflated further into his chair and stroked the palms of his hands up and down the length of his slacks. Thorsen adjusted his weight and coughed to signal that he was ready. Stucki just nodded and drew a breath. "Looks like I got Parkinson's," he said.

Thorsen winced but said nothing.

"Doctor says it's sort of like my nerve cells are rusting. Might could be from all that spray I got into when I was crop dusting. Lots of chemicals could do it to you, I guess. But they don't know. Could just be that I just got it. It can happen like that, you just get it and that's . . . they . . . well, they don't know."

"How long?" Thorsen said.

Stucki appeared to be nettled by the question. "You're about as sensitive as a chain saw," he said.

"How long *since* you got it?"

"I know what you meant." Stucki grinned. "I've known something was going on for about a year. Vi caught it first, noticed my handwriting was getting kind of spidery. She told me I was walking kind of stiff, kind of hunched over, she said."

"You getting the shakes yet?"

"It's not so bad, only starts when I'm not thinking with my hands. They've just got to be out there doing nothing, then they shake. I can still cut hair and tie flies. It's not like it keeps me from doing anything. But if people are scared, I don't blame them."

"What happened with Blitch, then?"

"He did it, laughing at you."

"Glad I could help ruin your reputation."

Both men lapsed into silence. They looked around the shop: at the other chairs, worn and empty, and the greenish linoleum of the floor. In the waiting area, Glade had left the television on but muted. Tarzan dove silently into a river. He came out of the water on the back of a crocodile and wrestled it away from a woman and small boy, who were crouching in the water along the riverbank. Thorsen turned his head and looked outside. The sky above the buildings across the street had darkened slightly, though they could sense no shift in the color because of the polarizing film on the window. The granular wisps of high cirrus clouds extended at a tangent to the phone lines like clouds in a photograph. "Looks like we got a front coming in," Thorsen observed.

"Yep," Stucki said.

"So what about the shop?" Thorsen asked, twisting a finger into his ear.

"I don't want people talking. I knew a barber once in Texas who got Parkinson's. People called him Shakey. He never cut a soul. I'll bet dollars to donuts I'll lose folks to Bill Chamberlain over this."

"Decent folks don't want a guy like that touching their heads. They won't sell you out."

"Only one way to leave the planet, Jens," Stucki said, frowning. "We all go down that road."

"Maybe you should just clam up," Thorsen said. "Nobody's dying. Not today, at least."

"What's going to happen when these tremors start taking hunks out of people's necks? Maybe I should just close the shop. I got my pension and the social security."

"You haven't cut hair for the money in years," Thorsen said, returning to the chair. Stucki threw up his hands, and Thorsen matched the gesture. "Why don't you put out an ad—get somebody in here to help out?"

"Somebody from Sanpete?"

"Why not?"

"Maybe I'll call Bill and have him send over one of his wives."

"There's gotta be someone looking. Maybe from Ephraim or Mount Pleasant. It's not like work is growing on trees around here. Maybe you'll get lucky and one of those Cannon girls will break off her engagement again and run home for a semester."

"I don't see what kind of sense it makes to keep going."

"You're the only one in here. You get someone else, and the nervous ones can go where they want, and you can go fishing whenever you want. Least it'll keep you from folding up and quitting like everyone else in this county."

"You're a hard man, Thorsen."

"I ain't hard. I'm right," Thorsen said, winking. "Before I head home, I need to get things cleaned up back here," he announced, stroking his hand across the curve of his sun-wrinkled neck. "You'd be doing me a favor."

"Lila onto you again?" Stucki asked, climbing out of the chair and dusting it with the smock he held in his fist.

"Let's just say we aren't seeing eye to eye on a few things right now," Thorsen said. He crossed the room and picked up the remote control, then parked in Stucki's chair. "And I wouldn't mind the distraction of wondering if you're going to cut my throat or not."

Stucki swung the smock around him, tucked the paper into place, and fastened the collar. "You should have been a doctor, Thorsen," he said. "You really know how to put people at ease."

Thorsen unmuted the television and waved at Stucki to be quiet. *Tarzan* was over and *The Rockford Files* was on. Stucki chose a set of clippers and made a few deft moves around the back side of Thorsen's head. On the show, a cop came into the lockup and let Rockford out of his cell. "Listen, Jimbo, I can't keep pulling favors for you like this," he said. "You're a good man, Dennis," Rockford told him, "a good man." Stucki worked steadily, not asking how Thorsen might like the cut. Stucki switched to a pair of finely tapered scissors when the scene cut to Rockford's trailer at the beach. He slammed the door of his gold Firebird, which drew his old man to the front door. Rockford went into the trailer and changed clothes and checked the bullets in a .38, while the answering machine squawked about some characters who'd been "nosing around the place."

"All right, before I carve up your neck," Stucki said, leaning over onto one side so he could dig into his hip pocket. "I want you to take a look at something. I sort of wrote up this little ad. I figure I might could run it in the paper and see what I get."

Thorsen took a quick look at it. "So you *have* been thinking about it."

" 'Course I have. Thinking and doing are two different things."

"Worst thing that could happen is nobody'd come by, then you'd be no worse off than you were before."

Stucki smiled woodenly and nodded his head.

"Well," Thorsen said, rising stiffly from the chair, "let's take a look at yer grammar."

Stucki extended his hand gingerly, the small packet quivering in his hand. Thorsen unfolded the paper, looking up at Stucki a couple of times as he did. Stucki's eyes were skittering all over the place and they made Thorsen nervous, so he looked down at the paper and turned slightly away. His letters looked like bent fragments of baling wire.

Wanted : Part–time barber. Come down to the shop to pick up application. Stucki's Barber Shop #2 S. 400 W. Sanpete

While Thorsen was reading, Stucki said, "Still not sure I'm going to run it, but I figured that maybe I'd . . . I don't know . . . see what it looked like."

"You're not too worried about qualifications, are you?"

"Well, I don't want to scare them off."

"Don't they have laws for this kind of thing?"

"Sure, but like I said."

"Well, it's your ad." Thorsen looked up at Stucki and gave a little nod and handed him back the ad. "How's the cut? You got me looking orthodox? I've got enemies in high places, you know."

"You look okay for an old fart."

"Okay is pretty much all I can manage any more."

"About this war of yours with the bishop," Stucki said. "You can call it what you want to, but you know you're just beating the devil around the bush."

Thorsen stared into the mirror. "Maybe," he said, "maybe I am."

Chapter Four

Sunday again. Thorsen had been up since before sunrise. Rain had been hammering Sanpete since Friday, and it continued when he slipped out of the house into the morning. Water beaded up on his slicker almost immediately, and the cold shot through his knuckles and lanced up the length of his arms. Silently, Thorsen milked both his cows and fed them, set a flake of hay in Enoch's stall, ground oyster shells, and fed the hens. In an old towel, he carried eight eggs from the coop and set them on the back porch next to the steaming pail of milk. Then he ran twelve sheep down into the lower pasture, nailed three planks back into place on the far corner of the barn, and listened to the wind in the cotton-woods and the rain on the roof. Despite the wet, he drove around the section road to check a fence, found that it was only slightly torn up, hammered the wire back into place, and continued to Karl and Phyllis Ramke's place.

Thorsen fed the Ramkes' horses and saw to a cut on a draft horse's foreleg. He fed the chickens, topped off the water trough in the corral, and went up to the back door, knocking lightly on the glass. Phyllis appeared, sipping her coffee. She did not open the door. Thorsen glanced down at his muddy boots, and he stepped back. The knob rattled and clicked as she struggled with it, then the door opened inward, the sudden sharp odor of coffee filling Thorsen's nose.

"I got those animals up and going, Phyllis. You need anything else here?" Thorsen said, stuffing his hands shyly down into the pockets of his work pants.

"Need the kitchen garbage took out to the burn pile."

Thorsen nodded.

"Don't want you tracking up my floors." Still in her robe and slippers, she stepped back and let the door open. Phyllis paused at the table, where she set down a mug of coffee. She grabbed the garbage bag and brought it back. Struggling somewhat, she handed it to Thorsen, who took it without speaking and hobbled out of the house and through a gap in the backyard fence to the burn pile. A few stray wires stuck out of the black cone of ash. Large pieces of charred wood and a few bedsprings were mixed in. Thorsen dumped everything out of the bag and returned to the house. He hung the limp bag on a hook, and knocked again. Without waiting for an answer, he opened the door.

Phyllis was scrambling eggs.

"I got your garbage all out there, but there isn't anything going to burn on that pile," Thorsen remarked. "It's too wet."

"Don't you drag nothing in here," Phyllis said without turning around.

"Karl doing okay?" Thorsen asked.

"Same as always. Maybe a little worse. I don't know." She turned the eggs over with a rubber spatula. "He just keeps talking about some old fossil he found on the plateau. All I hear is how he ain't worth a dime to no one anymore."

"You want me to talk to him?" Thorsen said, scratching at the back of his neck.

"No," she said, and Thorsen felt relieved. "He'll start milking you for some religion, and you know how I feel about that."

"That Belgian's got a nick on her forelock. I put some Merthiolate on it and bandaged it up. Tell Karl she'll be fine," Thorsen said, fussing with a hangnail.

"I'll tell him."

"I got to get going," he said, glancing sideways into the kitchen, making sure to stay in the mudroom.

"It helps," Phyllis said after a few seconds. She kept her eyes on her work. Thorsen froze mid-turn and then slowly came about. "When you come, it's no strings," she said, plating the eggs and turning off the stove. "With your people it's always some kind of strings attached, but not with you."

"I appreciate that," Thorsen said. He kept it at that. "Keep an eye on things. Been raining a lot this week. I bet Thompson Wash is going to be a mess."

"We ain't had no trouble from it," Phyllis said.

"Good," Thorsen said, then he nodded and left, closing the door behind him. He took a couple of steps and then the door opened again.

"Jens," Phyllis said. "One more thing, if you don't mind."

"Sure."

"Karl's been talking about getting himself a haircut. Doesn't want me doing it. You ever cut hair?"

"Nope, but I know someone who does."

When he pulled up to his house, Thorsen saw lights on downstairs. He glanced at his wristwatch; it was eight o'clock. He grimaced and coasted to a stop, set the parking brake, and dumped the key into the empty ashtray. He pulled off his boots on the back steps and hung his slicker on a wire hook in the mudroom.

Lila was washing dishes in her church dress. Her hair was still up in curlers, and she padded around the kitchen in her house slippers. Without turning, she gestured to the oven.

"I got some omelet in there for you. Toast is dried up. Milk's back in the fridge."

Thorsen nodded. "We're gonna get some trouble from Thompson Wash if we don't already have it."

"You're gonna get some trouble from me if you aren't dressed and ready to go in a half-hour, Jens Thorsen."

"Well, now listen, it isn't like Karl Ramke went and got emphysema on purpose."

"The Ramkes have family like everyone else on this earth. I imagine they've got to take some responsibility for their own. Besides, a man that spends his whole life walking around behind a cigarette's got what's coming to him."

Thorsen stopped listening to her and opened the oven. He bent down and took out the plate and immediately stood up, waving his hand. "Dammit!" he shouted.

"Can't you control that septic tank of yours one day in seven?"

"I burnt my fetching hand, Mamma."

"That's going to happen, pulling things straight out of the oven. A body'd think you'd have something to show for all your years."

"I need the sink," Thorsen said, pushing past his wife.

Lila danced out of the way. "Mind you don't mess up my Sunday clothes."

Thorsen ran the water full on and thrust his hand under the stream, turning it over and over.

"Church starts at nine o'clock, not when the Thorsens decide to show up. I've got responsibilities, Jens. I can't be waltzing in whenever the urge strikes me."

Thorsen had shut off the water and was already halfway up the stairs before Lila went silent and returned to the dishes.

Lila came into the bedroom as Thorsen was snugging a bolo tie under his collar flaps. "It's time to leave," she said. Thorsen walked right past her into the bathroom and splashed some Old Spice on his hands and rubbed it into his neck. "Jens," she called.

"You know where the truck is, Mamma, right where I left it. Key's in the ashtray."

"You think I was born yesterday? If I leave you here, it won't be ten minutes before you're off fishing."

Thorsen looked up at her in the mirror and raised his eyebrows. "Fishin' in the rain, Mamma?"

"Don't you fishing-in-the-rain-mamma me." Lila turned and left the room.

"You got my scriptures?" Thorsen called after her.

"I don't see how it matters," she called back.

Once they were on the road, Thorsen asked, "What do you have those women doing today, Mamma?"

She looked over at him slowly, disbelievingly. "Having a lesson," she said, eyeing him.

Thorsen nodded and kept driving.

"You know, Mamma, we haven't had fall rain like this in three, four years."

Silence sat static in the truck cab while wet shrubby junipers flickered by on either side of the road. "Okay, what do I have to repent of this morning?" Thorsen asked.

"Jens Thorsen," Lila accused. "I don't think I know a man so half-hearted about things as you."

"What's bringing this on? Can't be me doing Karl's chores. That's just service."

"It isn't." Lila sat taller and braced her hand on the window.

"What then?"

Lila paused and watched the wire frames of the cottonwoods whisk by.

"You can't start in on something like that and then quit," Thorsen complained.

Lila turned suddenly and fused her eyes back onto her husband's. Thorsen snapped his head forward and tried to ignore her. "When's the last time you sat next to me in church without galloping off to the rescue?"

"You mean like *when* when?"

"I mean you're always off on some errand instead of with me."

"I respect that, but oxes keep slipping into the mud around here, Mamma. I can't help that."

"You're so busy with everybody else's oxen, you don't know when your own are in distress."

Thorsen let the truck drift slowly to a stop and sat in the road, watching his wife. She rearranged her scriptures, planner, and purse and stared straight ahead into the rain, which beaded up and raced to the sides of the windshield. Thorsen was waiting for a further explanation, but Lila did not give one. A car came up behind them, slowed, and stopped. Thorsen cracked the window and shook his fist. The car pulled around and continued on.

"I'm sick of showing up to church a widow," Lila snapped

"Don't you worry. If you ever end up a widow, I'll make sure I come back and check on you."

"Jens, they're worried about you."

"Who, Bunker?"

"There's plenty of people been concerned about you for a long time."

Thorsen stepped on the throttle and brought the truck back up to speed, his lips tight as radial tires, his eyes fixed on the road ahead. Lila was likewise rigid. As they came over the rise, they saw the town doctor out in the road in front of his house in a yellow slicker. He was waving them down.

"What's that quack want now?" Thorsen muttered to himself.

Lila glanced down at her watch and fumed. Thorsen slowed and rolled down his window.

"Dr. Wizenberg," Thorsen said cordially.

"Creek's rising. It's about to crest and flood my house," the doctor said, huffing. "I'm not sure what to do."

Thorsen shook his head and cursed. "I told Everly not to put any lots at the mouth of that wash."

"Jens, we're going to be late," Lila whispered.

Wizenberg noticed and said, "I don't want to be any trouble, I just don't know what to do."

"You got a truck?" Thorsen asked. Wizenberg nodded. "All right then, Mamma, can you get yourself to church all right?"

Silence.

"Well, slide on over. I'll see you later."

"I don't want to impose on you, Jens," Wizenberg said.

"You aren't," Thorsen said as he opened the door and slid out of the truck. "Charity never faileth. Ain't that right, Mamma?"

Lila lowered her head and began to draw deep breaths.

"When you get there, send fellas back, and we'll have this thing wrapped up by closing prayer." Without a word, Lila rolled the window back up and drove on.

After an hour of waiting in the garage, taking periodic surveys of the land and the conditions, Thorsen decided that no one was coming. Sondra Wizenberg had come out twice with coffee, but Thorsen refused. "Those hypocrite sons a bitches," Thorsen muttered, and he spat off into the grate at the side of the driveway and scratched at the back of his neck.

"What?" Wizenberg asked.

"It looks like it's going to be the two of us today, Doc," Thorsen said. "Let's go." Thorsen hobbled over to Wizenberg's vehicle and got in the passenger's side. Startled, Wizenberg jumped in and started the engine. "Take me up to Bunker's," he said.

"He won't be there. He's a bishop or something, isn't he?" Wizenberg answered.

"That's the idea."

At Bunker's, Thorsen got out of the truck and went up to the house. Without knocking, he opened the door and went into the kitchen, tracking mud across the vinyl flooring. There was a rack of keys on the wall above the telephone. Thorsen pulled them all down and walked back out of the house, past Wizenberg in his vehicle, to the backhoe parked behind Bunker's barn. He climbed up into the rig and started trying the keys until one slid into the starter. He pumped the choke and cranked the machine alive. After it had idled for a few seconds, Thorsen put it in gear, engaged the throttle, and drove past the doctor, turning imprecisely onto the road.

Thorsen drove straight down toward the creek. At Wizenberg's, and about ten feet from the waterline, he began digging a trench. He only went down the depth of the bucket, and he moved, quickly repositioning the outriggers and inching backward as he dug, swinging the fill out into the water and dropping it there. Wizenberg and his wife watched as Thorsen continued to dig. As he worked, Thorsen wondered if Lila had said anything at all when she got to church. It wouldn't have been strange for her to show up to church alone, so no one probably took thought to ask. If they had, she'd have made something up anyway. She'd be in Sunday school by now. He didn't put it past her to keep quiet about his helping to save Wizenberg's house. He knew he'd just made her case, and he didn't blame Lila; he just took note.

After about forty-five minutes of hydraulic work, he had fashioned a sloppy canal all the way back to the road. When he broke through to the ditch, runoff from the road flooded back into the new passage until it met the water from the wash and reversed itself. Satisfied, Thorsen shut off the backhoe and climbed down stiffly. He was frozen to the bone and sort of wished that Wizenberg's wife would offer him the coffee again. He hobbled up to the smiling couple, thinking that it would be nice to be full of the future again. Wizenberg reached out and clapped Thorsen on the shoulder.

Thorsen said, "It's not over till the fat lady eats."

"Mr. Thorsen, I don't know what we did to deserve your help," Sondra said.

Thorsen waved her off.

"We didn't think to buy flood insurance out here in the desert, Jens. We'd have been ruined."

Thorsen turned and looked down on his handiwork. The brown waters in Thompson Wash were spilling over the edge of his ditch in a thin foam and had filled it about a quarter of the way. Thorsen imagined that there would be room for another day or so and then the ditch itself would start cresting. "You'll have to get some sandbags if this rain keeps up. You can pick up your bags at the co-op and get sand at the gravel pit. I'll round up a few of the fellas if we need to, and we'll get you set up."

"Can we take you up to the church at least?" Wizenberg asked.

"Nah, I'll be all right. Somebody needs to keep an eye on things here anyway, see that I didn't make things worse." Thorsen turned and headed down toward the backhoe. His steps were slow and measured. When he had gone only a short ways, he stopped and turned around.

"Maybe there's one thing, Doc," he said.

"Anything."

"Could you go on down to Karl Ramke's place and check on him? He's back there on 1200 South, last house. It's the only house, really."

"What's wrong?"

"He's got emphysema and could use some sensible talk."

"I can pay him a visit, just so long as you're not asking me to pull a Kevorkian," Wizenberg said.

"He's got his mind set on giving up the ghost," Thorsen said, scrubbing a finger under his nose. "He's been fighting his lungs for the better part of three years now, but he won't talk about how bad it is."

"Isn't he in your church?" Wizenberg asked. "Wouldn't someone from—"

"He's been in the church at one time or another," Jens interrupted, giving Wizenberg and his wife a slight nod, "but like I said, he's got his mind set. Maybe he could use some advice on getting his other leg over the fence, if you know what I'm saying."

Wizenberg was dumbstruck.

"Doc, he just needs an honest opinion that isn't cluttered up with gospel," Jens said, then he climbed stiffly into Bunker's backhoe and started it up. With the exhaust cap flapping, he turned onto the highway and crept on to church.

Thorsen rolled into the church parking lot and maneuvered the backhoe between the few cars that remained. Most of the way there, Thorsen had been concocting some way to damage the backhoe and finally get even with Bunker, but after a few plans centered mainly around the puncturing of hydraulic hoses and tires, he simply pulled the backhoe around to the south side of the building. He looked around for Bunker's car, a black Continental, which was parked next to the air conditioning array. Its front tires hugged the curb. Thorsen motored in behind the vehicle and turned it around so the shovel was facing the back of the Lincoln. He scuttled the machine forward a few feet and then spun his seat around. There was a roar in the idle as Thorsen worked the boom, which jerked and twitched as it extended, mantis-like, the bucket still curled under. Thorsen then crept the machine back until the boom swivel was almost but not quite touching the bumper. The boom hung suspended over the whole length of the car, quivering slightly because of the engine. Thorsen then extended the outriggers and proceeded to tip the bucket down so a slight trickle of mud dripped from the blunt alloy teeth onto the windshield and pooled in the cowling, then drained into the engine.

Thorsen swung himself down from the backhoe, his knuckles numb with cold. He made his way into the church, stopping at the base of the low flight of stairs. Bunker's Continental looked humiliated. Though he wanted to drink in the glory of it, Thorsen turned away and entered the church, savoring the deliciousness of being right.

The building was empty or nearly so. A few souls wandered about with their faces vacant and ghost-like, the men with loosened ties, the women with faded lipstick and creases in their skirts. Jens felt his body stiffen. His mind grew opaque. His vision tunneled. Somewhere in the back of his head he heard a whisper saying *Vengeance is mine*. His right eye twitched once when he heard it, and he stopped in the hallway, surrounded on either side by accordion doors, and he listened for more. All he could hear was his own breathing, the muscles of his forearms wound tight.

Alone, off to one side, the thought that this was a failure in Lila's errand sat quiet like iron in a stove. It was common enough for her to refuse him, something she did often in protest, something she did often to make a statement, but she had known that the doctor was in dire straits, and it was common enough for men to be dismissed from church and dispatched. Every few years some story like this would float around Zion: a broken dam, the flooding of a lake.

As Thorsen roared around the corner, he saw his wife, alone on a couch. She was knitting, her eyes half-lidded and heavy looking and a strand of orange yarn extending from her hands to the open bag at her feet. Her needles ticked softly.

"What happened to you?" Thorsen growled. Lila looked up. "I was down there all morning with my fingers in the dike, waiting for the goddamn brethren to peel their butts off a church pew and lend a hand—"

"Jens," Lila whispered.

"I don't want to hear anything about the Lord's name. That Jew down the road is more Christian than anyone in this building—"

"Jens."

"No one showed up. Not a single man. Makes me think maybe you were trying to teach me a—"

"Jens, I told the bishop," she said quietly. "I told him the whole thing. I was late, and the meeting had already started. I sent a note up to the stand, but that man barely even looked at it. He put it in his pocket and went on with the meeting. I went up afterward and told him the whole thing again. He asked who we were talking about, and when I told him, he just mumbled and said he'd talk to the high priests. Then we got interrupted and the bishop disappeared into his office. But nothing happened—we just kept moving from meeting to meeting. I went up to him afterward and tried to talk to him, but he ducked into that office. People have been going in and out for the last hour. He'll have to talk to me sometime. He's got to go home eventually, and I'll be here."

Thorsen smiled. "I expect he'll have some trouble there, too, Mamma."

"So here I sit," she said. "Your being right about this doesn't make me wrong."

A long silence ensued, during which Thorsen and Lila stared alternately at each other and at Bunker's door. Lila continued to knit. Thorsen laid his coat over the far end of the couch and warmed his hands, trying to release the tension. The organ churned on in a low coil of the same phrases and bars, but eventually it stopped, and whoever was playing left anonymously through the far doors.

"Who's in there?" Thorsen asked, looking again at the bishop's door.

"Diane Perkins," Lila said.

Thorsen nodded.

"She's been in there a long time."

Thorsen nodded again.

The silence continued. The furnace fans switched on and blew for a few minutes. Lila knit two more rows and then massaged her hands for a minute before continuing on.

"It was wrong to lay into you like that," Thorsen said, his voice failing.

Lila paused in her knitting, looked at Thorsen, and then continued on. "You had to get rid of it somehow," she said. "Doesn't make it nice, but still . . . you had to get rid of it."

"It was wrong," he said.

"To forget a wrong is the best revenge," she said, then she smiled slightly, purled, and then smiled again, more broadly this time. "It is nice for you to know you're right this time, isn't it?"

"It's easy to be right around that no account."

The door to Bunker's office opened, and Diane Perkins came out. Even at a distance they could see that she had been crying. Bunker's hand was on her shoulder, and he was speaking to her with a soft smile on his face, his eyes tiny under his brow. Diane looked suddenly nervous when she saw the Thorsens. She said hello but shuttled herself quickly down the hall and toward the door. Thorsen and Lila bristled, and Bunker stood there in the doorway. Faintly, in the distance, they all heard a door swing shut.

"You," Thorsen boomed, leveling a finger at him.

"Jens," Lila said, "remember where you are."

Bunker moved the door slightly, as if to close it, then stopped as if realizing that it would make him look cowardly.

"Close the door on us if you want to, Darrell Bunker," Lila said, "I've waited this long for you, but I can keep waiting. You've got to leave sometime."

"Lila and I can take shifts," Thorsen said.

"I'm not going to justify my decision to you two," Bunker said.

Thorsen and Lila looked at each other.

"His failure to plan doesn't mean we're supposed to call off the Sabbath," Bunker said. "You think they'd call off synagogue if one of us were broken down over there?"

"Where's over there, Darrell? New York or Jerusalem?" Thorsen asked.

"If we let all the brethren go, then who'd fill in for the children's classes? Who'd be with the young men? Who'd drive all these people home if everyone is down the road at somebody else's house?"

While Bunker was talking, Lila put her knitting away and stood.

"Darrell, you won't get to heaven on other people's sins. That is all I have to say to you. You will not get to heaven that way." Then she turned to her husband. "It's time for us to go." Thorsen took his wife's arm, and they turned down the hall and left the building. They did not look back.

As Lila stepped outside, she saw the monstrous, coital arrangement of the backhoe and the Lincoln, and she burst out laughing.

The bucket hung over the roof of the car, nearly kissing the top edge of the windshield, which was coated now in a dry brown residue that looked like a mixture of paint and mop water. The boom extended back across the whole of the car, the outriggers spread lewdly to each side. Thorsen took the backhoe keys and jingled them next to Lila's ear, then he made a beeline for the backhoe, opened the cab door, locked it, threw the keys on the seat, and slammed the door shut. "Let's go home and get some chow," he said, slipping his arm around the small of Lila's back.

Chapter Five

Thorsen and Stucki came out of the *Patriot-Examiner* offices and walked to Thorsen's truck. "Not bad for two weeks," Thorsen said.

"Never hired anyone before," Stucki said. "Been hired, been fired, but not this."

"Maybe nobody will even call, then you can curl up in the road and wait until a truck drives over you."

"I'm just saying it's different," Stucki said.

They split to their sides of the truck and got in. " 'Course it's different. New things'll keep you out of the bone yard."

"Or put you right into it—Thorsen, I gotta quit letting you talk me into things."

"If you were smart, you would have made that promise in high school." Thorsen cranked up the truck. "I can't help you out of this relationship now."

"All I really want to know is how come you're not telling me where I'm taking my barber kit?"

"It's a surprise."

"For me or for him?"

"Both, I guess."

"I don't know if I'm going to like this. One minute I'm putting an ad in the paper and the next I'm heading out into the boondocks on a house call—you know, in the old days a barber used to basically be the doctor, in charge of amputations and bloodlettings."

"You got any leeches wrapped up in that towel?"

"Nope."

"Then I think we'll be okay," Thorsen said.

They drove out of Sanpete northward, parallel to the mountains. Once they were on the highway, Stucki cracked his window and poked his nose into the breeze. He gulped the air like it was lemonade.

"If you want to ride in the back and stick your head around the side of the cab, you're welcome to it," Thorsen said.

"Vi don't like the windows down. Ruins her hairdo."

Thorsen shook his head and kept driving.

"We're going to Karl Ramke's, aren't we," Stucki said.

Thorsen nodded. "Good guess."

"He's the only one lives out here. I heard he came down with lung cancer or something."

"Emphysema."

Thorsen nodded and watched fence posts flicker past, punctuated by the occasional tree flash. Thorsen rapped the window with the knuckle of his forefinger, trying to distract himself. The last time he thought about it, the condition of being dead didn't match his ideas of dying, of going out of this life suddenly, the way a person leaves a room. What he saw for himself, he imagined for Karl Ramke: something like an old balloon, the string growing slack as it sinks to the floor.

"Must be from the cigarettes," Thorsen said.

Stucki nodded. "Easy to get smug about that."

Thorsen adjusted the rearview mirror. "Our people are smug about everything."

"You don't have to preach to me—"

"That's right," Thorsen said, pointing a finger toward a mailbox perched on a question mark welded from links of heavy chain. RAMKE was painted on the side in crude black letters. Thorsen swung off the road and headed up the drive. "Phyllis is tough. She's bound to have her back arched. Just grin and tell her she's got a good point. And whatever you do, don't say anything about church. We're giving a haircut, not a sermon."

"Why would I preach? They're not members, are they?" Stucki asked.

"Karl quit going when he was five—never got baptized. People got their freedom. It isn't up to me to do anything but drop by and help out." Thorsen parked the truck. "Still, it's obvious that Phyllis isn't going to join the church, so neither is Karl. So we just talk, which is pretty much the only thing I'm interested in anymore anyway."

They got out of the truck and walked through the carport to the side door. Thorsen knocked three times on the door and stepped back to leave room for the screen to swing. Phyllis appeared in the dim space, followed by the acrid smell of burnt bacon. She wore no makeup. Her hair was halfway between yellow and gray and was bound up in an array of pink foam curlers. She wore a gray sweatshirt with a stretched-out neck. She held a cigarette in one hand and a small disposable lighter in the other, which she fingered constantly.

"Was that today?" she said, her voice arid and slow.

"That's what you asked for," Thorsen said. "But we can go, if you want to put off looking at him for another week."

Phyllis lit her cigarette and blew smoke through the screen. "He looks like a lunatic," she said without a change in her voice.

"Hi, Phyllis," Stucki said.

"Y'all can visit Karl, but I don't want no testimonies. You hear?"

"Phyllis, you haven't heard one word of testimony from me ever. What makes you think I'm gonna start now?" Thorsen asked, slipping his fingers down behind his belt and grabbing hold.

Phyllis smiled dryly, her cigarette drooping slightly as the corners of her mouth crinkled. She snatched the cigarette away with a quick gesture and exhaled the smoke with a kind of chugging laugh. "That's how it should be." She returned the cigarette to her mouth and drew so hard that her eyes narrowed. The tip of the cigarette glowed red-hot, then Phyllis's hand floated for a second in front of her face, and the cigarette disappeared as she dropped the hand alongside her leg. "You all have a lot of nerve. Got yourselves packed into this state like sardines. And you look past people, but that ain't strange for Christian folks— why I don't cotton to them. You've got your own talk and your own look and your own vans full of brats, and then you're off to the Cub Scouts or to the temple, and you think everyone else is along for the ride. Well, not everyone wants to be a drone in your little beehive, but come on in." She pushed the door open and then disappeared into the kitchen. Thorsen and Stucki followed.

"Karl's mother left your church after his dad run off to Alaska or wherever it was he went," Phyllis said without looking back at them.

"Alabama," a weak voice called from the other room. "He went to Mobile in thirty-nine." A series of pathetic, persistent coughs followed.

Phyllis turned her head slightly and hollered, "Hold your horses." She took another drag on her cigarette.

Stucki pointed clumsily through the kitchen toward the voice. "You think maybe we should go outside . . . you know . . ." He then gestured to the cigarette. Thorsen cringed and began scratching behind his ear, and with the other hand he tried to nix Stucki by dragging an index finger across his throat.

"This?" Phyllis lifted her hand and looked down at the cigarette. "We ain't anywhere near his oxygen."

"Stucki's kind of a prude," Thorsen interrupted. "He's just here to cut hair, isn't that right, Lewis?"

Stucki smiled and lifted his towel roll to show her he meant no ill will.

"I know you all probably think I'm going to hell—halfway through my first pack, and I ain't even cleaned up the breakfast dishes. There's a pot of coffee on the counter and beer in the fridge. I shop on Sunday when the parking lot is clear—and by the way, some of you all are in there too with your pantyhose and your white shirts. Say what you want, but I don't believe in hell. I don't even believe in the devil. And even if there was a devil, I say it's just God with a hangover. But I don't believe in him neither—never give me any cause to. He's just like every other pink elephant in the world. I know what you've got in mind, what we've got right now is misery, but a body'd best behave, because there's greener pastures tomorrow. Fine, go on in and tell that to Karl. Tell him you people got a way for him to die in peace. Better yet, why don't you lay hands on him and command him to rise and go to the temple and start baptizing dead people? See how he takes to that."

"Phyllis, you know what I'm here for," Thorsen said.

"Well, you got the both of you now," she said, gesturing to Stucki. "And I know what that means."

"Stucki's just a barber."

Stucki gave her a quick salute.

"Don't you get his hopes up with nonsense. You can live it all you want, but leave that evangelizing outside."

Suddenly, Karl appeared in the entry, unshaven, wearing a T-shirt and threadbare flannel pajama bottoms. His chest was distended, pulling the T-shirt tight across his swollen ribs, although he was gaunt in the face. His white hair was riotous and leapt from his scalp like it had been barbered by a stroke of summer lightning. A thin transparent tube ran over his ears, across his cheeks, and under his nose. He had a slender, green oxygen tank strapped to a lightweight chrome dolly in his left hand. When she saw him, Phyllis stubbed out her cigarette. Karl's eyes darted around the room from face to face. "Jens," he said weakly. He gestured to Stucki. "This geezer still cuts hair?"

"Good to see you, Karl," Stucki said. "Been a while."

"Been going to the polygamist. He don't complain when I forget to tip him." Karl laughed, but the laughter was shallow. When he saw that people were concerned, Karl stopped laughing and continued to simply stand in the doorway. A long silence filled the room, ruptured after a few seconds by the hum of the refrigerator's compressor pump. Karl made a few attempts to breathe deeply through his nose, and he brightened a little. "Well, y'all are burning daylight," Karl said, turning, and he disappeared down the hall with his oxygen in tow.

"Mind what I said," Phyllis told them. Thorsen made some brief acknowledgement to her warning, and then he motioned to Stucki and they followed Karl down the hall.

"I sure appreciate you doing this," Karl said. "These tubes in your way?"

"No," Stucki said, fastening the smock around Karl's neck, then turning down the paper strip. "You're just fine."

"Don't mind Phyllis. She just gets a little tired—you know, being stuck out here with you all." He made frail quotation marks in the air with his fingers when he said *you all*.

"I don't blame her," Thorsen said.

"She's got ideas about things."

"Show me a woman who doesn't have ideas," Thorsen said, taking a seat next to the television.

"What are we doing here, Karl?" Stucki asked.

"Just a regular haircut, and leave the ears," Karl said.

Stucki looked down at his hands, then he swung his head toward Thorsen with alarm. Thorsen shrugged. "I didn't say anything," he said, picking up a *Reader's Digest*. "I didn't hear anything either."

"How's that?" Karl asked.

"Nothing," Thorsen said. "I just told my sidekick that he was hearing things."

"I don't hear nothing I don't want to," Karl said. "It's a fringe benefit of everything else going down the toilet."

"You don't want me to take a little of this gray out, do you?" Stucki asked.

"Don't—they'll yank my Social Security."

Stucki laughed dully and pistoned his arms a little to loosen them up. "Well, we'll leave you a redhead then."

"You draw for bucks this year?" Karl asked.

"I pretty much stick to elk anymore. Vi won't eat the venison."

"Women aren't generally much for game—but she'll eat the elk?"

"She'll eat elk, trout, and duck, but she won't dress the elk, gut the trout, or cook the duck. She's had enough of picking shot out of the meat."

Karl laughed pathetically, which sent him into coughing spasms. Stucki pulled the comb and clippers away from his ears, and Thorsen looked up from his magazine, his lips compressed and his eyes narrowed. Karl waved to indicate that he was okay, drew a couple of deep breaths through his nose, sighed weakly, and then collapsed back into the chair. "I'm okay," he wheezed. "We're going to have to keep our poker faces here for a while or you'll run me out of oh-two."

"This'll sober you up," Thorsen said, folding the cover of the *Reader's Digest* back on itself. "Says here that twenty-two percent of Americans who put up a Christmas tree last year went for the fake ones. You know how much those things cost? It's five bucks for a permit at the BLM."

"It makes sense to me," Stucki said. "Isn't so much of a fire hazard with those fake ones."

"And you don't have so many needles to sweep up," Karl said.

"You two wouldn't know Christmas spirit if it popped out of the privy."

Stucki and Karl abandoned Thorsen and continued their discussion of fish and game. "Back in ninety-five, Vi lost a crown on some duck meat I shot. I heard it crack from across the table. So we're off duck unless I strangle it with my bare hands."

"I got a brother-in-law," Karl said, "that loads his own shells so he'll know how many shot he's got to pick out of the meat."

Thorsen snorted. "He shooting them in the driveway?"

"What are you talking about?" Stucki asked.

"Any further and those buckshot would be every which way."

"I didn't say he was smart. I just said he counted shot. I'm not sure I'd know what to do in a world without ignorant brother-in-laws." Karl started to chuckle and cough.

"You choke yourself, and you won't be getting any mouth-to-mouth from me," Stucki said.

"We'll get Phyllis in here to do it," Karl wheezed more vigorously.

The room was large, but it felt compact. It was full of windows, but the shades were drawn, and light poured in only along the edges. In those places where it did, planks of dust swirled and cast strange reverse shadows across the carpet and furniture. The room was warm and soft and cluttered with a lifetime of newspaper clippings and yellowed children's drawings. In the far corner, a low couch was made up into a bed, and the coffee table next to it was strewn with an assortment of drugs and empty glasses and tissues.

A microwave sounded dimly in the kitchen, followed by the dull thud of its door. Stucki shook out his arms and continued to comb Karl's hair and get it ready for the scissors.

Thorsen flipped a page and then snorted to himself.

"You and your magazines," Stucki said.

"Looks like some pastor in California passed out hundred-dollar bills to folks in his ward and told them to go invest it in the poor," Thorsen said, turning the magazine over on his knee. He stretched, then picked up the magazine again.

"Do pastors even have wards?" Karl asked.

"Well, congregations . . . maybe," Stucki said.

"Which church has pastors anyway?" Karl asked.

Thorsen squinted and adjusted himself in his chair as he thought about it. "Lutherans. I think it's the Lutherans."

"Maybe it's the Methodists," Karl said.

"I think they're just reverends."

"They're *all* reverends, even the Catholics," Stucki said. "The Methodists got ministers."

"What about the Presbyterians?" Karl asked.

"Hell, I think they're *all* just pastors when you get down to it," Thorsen said.

"Baptists got deacons," Stucki said. "But they aren't twelve years old. I'll bet that pisses them off."

"That and a million other things. How'd you get so up on your Protestants, Stook?" Thorsen asked.

"Went to Texas on my mission. So watch out, boys, I haven't even started with the Unitarians and Congregationalists."

"Religion gets me crazy," Karl said. "Some bishop gives me a hundred bucks to invest in the poor, I'm gonna invest in some groceries.

"The Lord loves those who help them—" Stucki started to say.

Thorsen glared at him. "Whatever it is, it's just plain dumb to parcel out cash like that. Sounds like a publicity stunt."

"The best way to be poor is to not want anything," Karl said.

"Only way *that* works is if you're a hermit," Thorsen said.

"Me, I never wanted a cabin in the Sevier River Valley or a handmade bamboo fly rod," Stucki added, "or a Weatherby. Man, I sure would not like a Weatherby."

"Or a boat or new snowmobiles or a Lincoln Continental with white leather seats—not me," Karl said. "Never wanted anything like that either. Can't stand luxuries."

"Make you soft in the belly," Thorsen said. "Karl, you been down to your property lately?"

"Not since the summer before last. Oxygen bottle doesn't fit on the four-wheeler too good."

A long silence filled the room as Thorsen read on and Stucki went back to the hair cut. He worked slower than he normally would, sometimes not even cutting the hair at all, just snipping back and forth with the scissors. Karl relaxed somewhat, and his breathing, though still labored, seemed to ease slightly. His hands unclenched, and he let them rest, palm up, in his lap.

When the cut was finished, Stucki said, "There's no mirrors around, so you'll have to take my word for it."

"I don't see it but once a week. There's all kinds of rubble on the floor around here, so I'll call it good."

"You ready for a shave?"

"I got a brush and lather in the bathroom," Karl said, pointing to a door just inside the hallway. Stucki walked into the room and returned, churning a wood-handled shaving brush into a coffee mug. He picked up his razor from the towel and opened it and set it back down on the towel. Then he picked up the mug and brush and lathered Karl's face carefully around the oxygen tube and proceeded to shave him. When it was done, Karl smoothed both hands along his cheeks and jaw, breathing through his nose and nodding. "You've got a gift, Stucki."

"Well, she ought to let you stay in the house now, won't she?"

"Should just leave me out in the snow like an Eskimo. You know, once one of those fellas starts falling apart, he just parks it in the snow and waits."

Stucki glanced over at Thorsen, engrossed in his magazine.

"Don't worry about it," Karl said. "It don't get cold enough around here. Plus, Phyllis would just keep finding me. Probably just end up with my toes amputated." Karl looked around the room, breathing shallowly but evenly. "I don't know where we go once we leave, Stucki, but that's where I'm headed."

"We all are."

"My stop's about here, and I'm not sure what I think about that anymore. Phyllis says dead is dead, but I don't think I'm with her on that one. A couple of years ago I was up on the Kaiparowits around the north end of Fiftymile Mountain. I found this saber-toothed tiger skull, petrified. I got down and stared that thing in the face. You see rocks all the time, and it don't do all that much to you, but this thing just locked there in the rock makes you think about time. Once you're on that track, eternity comes next, then you start wondering who's right and who ain't. Is it Phyllis or you all or the Eskimos? I don't know."

Stucki set down his scissors and looked over at Thorsen, who was leaning over to pick up another magazine, then he looked back at the door to the hallway, which was closed. A single line of white light ran straight across the bottom of the door and the threshold. Shadows flickered there for a moment.

"You know what I think, Karl," Stucki said.

"I know what your people think, but I don't know what *you've* got to say on the subject."

"Same thing."

"I know Phyllis says you all think alike, but fact is . . . you don't. So where am I headed, Stucki?"

The door swung open, and Phyllis stood in the opening, back-lit, an ashtray at the end of her left arm, clamped in place with her fingertips. "He looks presentable. Shaven and everything. You people really *can* work miracles."

Jens snorted.

"The big question is who's going to clean up the hair."

"Oh, Phyllis, we'll get it," Stucki said.

"The hell you will," Karl said. "You've done more than enough coming out here. Phyllis, we got any lunch for these fellas?"

Phyllis looked momentarily alarmed.

"Don't worry about us," Thorsen said, hoisting himself out of the chair. "Stucki here's got to get going."

"That's right," he said.

"Are there that many people in Sanpete need charity?" Phyllis asked.

"You'd be surprised," Stucki said.

Part Two: The Shop

Chapter Six

Angie Bunker stood along the north side of Stucki's shop, clear of the window. A copy of the *Patriot-Examiner*, folded into thirds, was jammed under her arm. She drew heavily on the tail end of a cigarette, then tossed it to the sidewalk and ground it out with her toe. It had rained the whole night, so the streets were glazed, and the air felt colder than it really was. The sky was a single unfurled bolt of gray, low feeling, like an attic. The air was full of sage and juniper. Things in general seemed bright, waxen, and clean.

Angie opened the paper and scrutinized it. She was pretty, red-haired and freckled. Her face was wide from the front and sharp from the side, her lips thin. She wore blue eyeliner, silver shadow, and her nose, tapered and slightly turned at the tip, looked like an inverted "seven." Her left ear was triple-pierced, and the right carried two more earrings—all hoops. Various cheap silver rings cluttered her hands, a wide flat strap banding her thumb to the first joint. Her denim jacket was turned up at the cuffs, and her western jeans were tight and striped in a repeating pattern of pink, blue, white, and black. She was nervous, her boots squirreling on the sidewalk as she approached.

Suddenly the door to the barbershop swung open, and Ernest Passey burst onto the street in his gray coveralls, a cap in one hand and a small paper sack in the other. He noticed Angie and saluted her with his cap and then snugged it down onto his head. "H'lo Angie. Good to see you," he said.

"Good to see you too, Brother Passey," she said.

Passey kept on heading toward his truck, and Angie didn't want to seem like she was just standing outside a barber shop at nine o'clock in the morning, so she walked on and headed inside. Stucki was just starting on a haircut for Wilmer Anderson, a man Angie recognized but did not know well.

"Angie," Stucki said, preparing Wilmer's neck, "what brings you here?"

She held up the newspaper.

Stucki flashed her a nervous look. "Oh, I've got all those old things bundled up in back," he said, gesturing to the door. She was confused, stunned for a second. Stucki ticked his head toward the back of the shop. Slowly Angie moved across the room, skirting the far chair where Stucki was working.

Wilmer drummed his hairy fingers on the armrests of the chair and smacked his lips as Angie passed. "Your dad's pretty excited to have you back in town," he said. Angie nodded. "Been talking about it pretty much every time I see him at the hardware store."

"That's my dad," she said, then lifted her head a little to address Stucki. "Do you want me to go see about those . . . *papers* . . . in the back?"

"If it's not too much trouble. I'll just give Wilmer here a towel and be back in a minute—you don't mind, do you, Wilmer?"

"You're not getting paid by the hour," he said.

Stucki pointed Angie to a door next to the bathroom, which led to a narrow hallway that ended in a small square room completely lined from floor to ceiling with cardboard boxes. A small table was nestled in the center. A single light bulb hung from its socket on a length of lumpy cloth-insulated wire. In one corner of the room a waist-high refrigerator hunkered down, napkins and paper plates heaped on top. The table was covered in outdoor magazines and several sketches of what looked like inventions or structures of some kind. A jar full of sundry spoons and knives sat on the far edge of the table, an open box of combs on the near side. Three vinyl-clad chairs crowded against the table. Angie pulled one out and sat down.

"Don't mind the mess," Stucki said. "I'm not back here all that much." He closed the door carefully behind him. Angie grew nervous. "Sorry about all the hocus-pocus, too. Don't really want people to know I'm looking."

"But you put an ad in the paper," Angie said, confused.

Stucki scrunched up his face. "Listen, the thing is, I'm not sure I really need somebody—"

Angie rose suddenly, "I don't have time for this, Brother Stucki. Thanks for your time and all, but not being sure isn't going to help me out all that much." She started to leave.

"Don't go," Stucki said. "Let me get Wilmer wrapped up."

Angie looked around the room, drummed her fingers on the table.

"Five minutes?" he asked.

Her fingers stopped. "All right," she said.

Stucki disappeared into the front of the shop, and Angie could hear muffled voices. The entire room smelled of after-shave lotion, and she read the titles of the boxes under its ether-like influences. The boxes were all full of paper toweling, cartons upon cartons of it. A cornice of smaller boxes ran about the top, combs in one, lotions of some kind in another, then a series of boxes marked with black ink: extension cords, Christmas lights, clipper parts, receipts, and the like. In one corner, the handle of a push broom leaned in at an angle. In the other corner a mop and bucket rested. Angie picked up one of the magazines and thumbed through it until it bored her, then she tried an-other. She heard a pair of clippers snap on. She slumped over and dropped her head into her arms. A vacuum switched on somewhere behind all the boxes. The whine of the motor rose and fell, and then in a few seconds it switched off again. Angie massaged her temples and cracked her knuckles and fidgeted with her rings.

She heard scratching footsteps, and then Stucki appeared again in the doorway. "Sorry about that," he said. "I hung up my fishing sign, so we won't be bothered for a while." Stucki pulled out a chair and sat down with a sigh. "So, can you cut hair?" he asked.

"Not fancy," she said.

"That's okay. No one around here is going to pay for fancy. You can run a pair of clippers?"

"I used to cut my brothers' hair back before they got married—

crew cuts and flat tops mostly. One time a Mohawk, but that was for football. Besides, I've got three hundred hours from the Sugar House Cosmetology School up north."

"I'll have to call licensing on that." Stucki stroked his chin.

"I'm almost there."

"We can work it out—probably just some forms."

"It's not like I can't do it."

"I know. I just got to keep things on the up and up."

"I understand." She was upset, her lips tensing.

"Mostly we just give regular haircuts. Not much call for any beard trimming, but we do give shaves. You know how to handle a straight razor?"

Angie paused and looked around the room. She took her arms off the table and folded them in her lap. "Yeah," she said. "I'm not great, but I'm not going to cut anyone."

Stucki's eyes narrowed. "We don't get all that many people in here asking for shaves—it's just there's no one wants to pay for it, really. Once upon a time, that's what you did, come down to the barber for a shave and a haircut. You know, like the song."

"Two bits?" she asked.

"That's right. Times are different now. These old towns are about to fold up. It's a lot of old folks here mostly. You got to work for someone else or be on a pension. You kids run off north, and I don't blame you. I don't blame you one bit."

Stucki stopped and looked down at his hands, which he was rubbing together slowly as if washing or warming them. The silence was nerve-wracking. Angie thought he might start crying in that sudden, aggressive way that her father did. But Stucki did not cry; he just shook his head and told her that money was not the root of all evil, simply the soil it grew best in.

"What's the pay?" she asked, smiling sheepishly.

"Pretty much like you'd get anywhere else around here, maybe a little better because of the tips. Six bucks an hour, maybe? I can't put you on a health plan or anything. I got all the taxes on you. You know, the point is to stay in business."

Angie paused and let her chin lower as she weighed the figures in her head. As her mind worked, she squinted and nodded, slightly at first and then two or three times authoritatively and then once with resolve. "Okay," she said. "When do you want me to come in? I can come in today," she said. "Nothing else going on."

"Well . . ." Stucki hedged. He felt around the table for something to distract him. Angie leaned in a little on her elbows. Stucki twisted his mouth around and danced his eyes across the table. One of Angie's hair wraps slipped from behind her ear. She caught it and, without breaking her gaze, replaced it. Stucki began pulling on his fingers one by one, trying to loosen them.

"*You* put out the ad," she said.

"I know."

"I'm going crazy at home, Brother Stucki. You know my father."

Stucki nodded. "And your mother, too, took her to the prom."

Angie laughed loudly, then it dwindled. "Jeez, I forgot about that. But listen, I need to get out of the house, and a little money would help, too." She twisted one of her rings and then another. "Yeah," she continued, raising her eyebrows, "I'm gonna need some money."

"Like I said, it's not going to be city wages," Stucki apologized.

"Better than nothing."

"If you have nothing, you fear nothing," he said.

"Then I'm fearless," Angie said, sitting up and rooting herself in the chair. Stucki reached his long arm around behind his head and scratched his neck. She watched him, unblinking, her eyes slightly narrowed. Occasionally Stucki met her gaze and then went back to his wandering eyes. After a few seconds, they heard the faint jingle of the doorbell. Stucki rose.

"I'll be right back." He left the room. Angie could hear voices and then heavy footsteps. The door opened, and Jens Thorsen's head appeared. "What's he got you locked in the dungeon for? He one of them serial killers?"

"Brother Thorsen," Angie said. She was caught completely off guard.

"Your secret's safe with me," he said, winking.

Angie was alarmed. "What secret? Who told you?"

"I put him up to it," Thorsen said. "He'd of sat here shaking to bits in an empty shop if it weren't for you." Thorsen opened the door a little wider. "Get out here. He's probably saving you the window seat." Angie followed Thorsen out. Stucki was sitting in the barber chair closest to her but farthest from the front door. Thorsen stationed himself in the next chair and gestured to the one beside the window and closest to the door. Stucki turned on the television set and flipped through the channels until he found an episode of *Gunsmoke*. Immediately the room filled with the tinny report of Hollywood gunshots and the rumpled percussion of galloping horse hooves.

The three of them sat there in a row, watching Festus and Matt dismount in front of the Long Branch Saloon. Thorsen and Stucki were silently engrossed.

"Weaver was better," Thorsen said. Stucki nodded in agreement. "That Southern accent is a load of crap."

"How come the sheriff's friends with that hooker?" Angie asked.

Thorsen and Stucki's heads pivoted toward her like faucet handles, their brows furrowed, their mouths agape. "Hooker?" Stucki asked.

"That's Miss Kitty," Thorsen said, shaking his head.

"No hookers in *Gunsmoke*," Stucki said. "That's the first rule of the shop."

"That there's no hookers in *Gunsmoke*?" Angie asked.

"You're darn right," Stucki said.

"The second," Thorsen said, creaking in his chair. "Well, there isn't a second."

"No hookers in *Gunsmoke*." Angie said, half-smiling.

"It's unseemly," Stucki said.

"Ain't Christian," Thorsen said.

"I'll make sure I write that down," Angie said, setting her purse on the floor.

Chapter Seven

Enthroned in his chair, with the late-afternoon light slanting into the room striking the dormant television starkly on the curve of its picture tube, Thorsen enjoyed the calm. Over a week had passed since the backhoe theft, and he was waiting for the other shoe to drop. He held an issue of *National Geographic* in his lap, which lay open to an article on the evolution of dogs. A biologist observed that domestic dogs live in a no-man's-land, neither person nor beast. Thorsen's lips stiffened and he drew a deep breath, read half of the next column, then closed the magazine and leaned forward in his chair until he could see down the hall and into the kitchen, where Lila was kneading bread and talking to their daughter-in-law, Kaylyn, on the telephone.

From what he could hear, they were working out the plans for the food to be served at an open house in honor of his grandson, Brandon, who was waiting on his mission call. From what Thorsen could gather, a letter had come from Salt Lake, but Brandon was still at work. Usually he was home by then. Lila bided her time saying something over and over again about keeping it simple. "People will be there to talk to Brandon and the family. You won't need that much food if you have people start coming around three o'clock."

Then Lila moved, and Thorsen could no longer hear her. His thoughts moved to his grandson and the speech Brandon had asked him to give at the farewell. He found something compelling in the tales of dogs. He might talk about how a dog will serve its master without question. He thought of the stories he'd heard about dogs traveling hundreds of miles, feet torn to shreds, just to sleep next to the refrigerator. That kind of thing had a religious sense to it, something his grandson could mull over on the airplane and consider as he looked for souls to save—there would surely be dogs in that land.

Then three sharp raps sounded on the glass of the mudroom door. Lila told Kaylyn to hold on a minute, flashed across the kitchen, and opened the door. Thorsen set the magazine on the coffee table and hoisted himself out of the chair.

"Well, if it isn't Andy Pearson. Jens will be excited to see you," Lila said. "He's in the living room. Why don't you head on back."

"Thank you," Pearson said.

Thorsen crumbled back into his chair, pawed the remote from the end table, and switched on the television. The heavy clomp of Pearson's shoes filled the hallway. Thorsen gripped his forehead and swore an oath. He could feel Pearson's presence looming behind him, a stomach-churning sensation like learning of a hunting accident.

"*Antiques Roadshow?*" Pearson asked.

"What?"

"My wife loves it," Pearson said, gesturing to the television, where a small man in a bow tie was pointing out the features of a World War II–era lamp whose base was in the form of a hula dancer.

"Yeah, yeah," Thorsen said, making a semi-royal gesture, "they got some good stuff on there—what you want?"

Pearson circled around the chair and coffee table, crossing between Thorsen and the television, then he sunk himself into a corner of the couch. Thorsen muted the television and set the remote in his lap. He heard Lila in the kitchen, though he could not make out what she was saying. Thorsen sucked his teeth and squeezed his cheeks around his jaw. Pearson cracked his knuckles, then the joints of each finger. They lapsed together into silence, each man looking at turns into his lap, at the television, at the collector's plates hanging on the wall.

"It's really pink in here," Pearson observed.

"Wife likes it," Thorsen said.

The bow-tied man on the television had been replaced with a stoutish woman explaining a landscape painting to a plain-looking couple in lightweight nylon jackets. She moved a capped fountain pen from place to place on the surface of the painting: clouds, millrace, waterwheel, peasant girl.

"What do you know about a certain backhoe?" Pearson said.

"Which certain backhoe?"

"The certain backhoe that was left parked behind a certain Lincoln Continental in the parking lot of a certain church building."

"I don't need to justify myself to you, Pearson. That jackass overlooked our town doctor in his time of need."

"Jens."

"That kind of crap dirties our religion, and I'm happy to—"

"Jens, nobody put me up to this. I'm a free agent here."

Thorsen picked up the remote and switched off the television. "We don't have the right to choose who we're going to help and when we're going to do it."

"I agree."

"Bunker turned that man out, not sending anyone."

"It was wrong. I agree with you."

"I'll bet that was hard to say."

"I'm not arguing with you, Jens. I'm here to give you a heads-up and maybe see if you can keep this from going one-hundred percent into the toilet."

Thorsen flashed his eyes up at Pearson, then he made a dismissive gesture with his hands. A quiet moment followed that seemed like a combination of anger and resignation, during which Pearson looked at the various corners of the room, thinking. After a space he sniffed once and then spoke. "He wanted to call a church court."

"He wouldn't dare."

"He was pretty much set on it, but I got him to agree to a public apology."

"I'll take my chances with the council."

"Spencer talked to him too—he was trying to get the law involved. Spencer got him to forget the complaint, considering he's still in possession of the tractor. Don't fight this one, Jens. No one wants it. It's going to do more damage than good."

"It's not like I stole it. If he would have come down to help, he could have brought it himself."

"It was a wrong choice," Pearson said. "He made a wrong choice."

Thorsen nodded.

"So, you think you can pull this stonewall off?" Pearson asked.

"That house should have never been built. Everyone knows that entire canyon drains right into Thompson Wash."

"I know it, but Jens—"

"The person who should be apologizing is Bill Everly. He trades on the strength of his church membership and then ignores the prophets. He's no better than the strip miners. Everly's house isn't anywhere near that wash. He's up on the east side of the valley, turning salad bowls on his lathe like he's the emperor of Sanpete."

Pearson looked like he was trying to add fractions. "Jens," he said finally, "some of us are going to be at the Wizenbergs this afternoon, if you know what I mean. If you happened to be there too, you know, just to help out, you might be able to get this all cleaned up before it starts stinking."

"So that's how to get Bunker interested in decent behavior—shame him into it."

"This isn't about right and wrong, Jens. It's about winning, and I want you to win this one. You eat the tractor thing in public, he loses. He'll have to accept your apology. He'll have to admit something he doesn't want to in front of that doctor and his wife. He'll look like the jerk, and you'll come out on top."

"Fine, if I'm there, I'm there."

"Fair enough."

"I'm not making any promises, you understand."

"I understand."

"You really think he'd try to boot me out of the church?"

"It would never take."

"But you think he'd try."

"He said he would."

"Jerk."

"Well, maybe so. But there's a better way to sock it to him than stealing his equipment."

"Ox was in the mire."

Pearson's eyes sparkled. "You should have seen him trying to get the car out."

A thin smile crept along the right side of Thorsen's mouth. "We could have sold tickets," he said.

"Spencer told me Bunker had somebody videotape the whole thing so he could use it in court, says once he saw it he didn't want to give it back."

Thorsen was nodding, the grin pasted across the whole of his face.

"You can win this one, Brother Thorsen. He's on the mat," Pearson said, then he rose, reminded Thorsen about the work project, and left.

Thorsen sat half-elated and half-enraged in his chair, surrounded by the pinkness of the room. He heard Lila pause in her telephone conversation long enough to say good-bye to Andy and wish his wife well with the new baby.

Thorsen's eyes scanned Lila's collector plates—images of forest glens, German school children, toads on a log, the early and late Elvis, a temple he didn't recognize. As he continued to look around, the walls seemed to push back, and the ceiling seemed to lift. It was as if the room were part of some rising loaf of bread, each part moving away from itself. And Thorsen sat at the middle, fuming over his predicament. He felt slight nausea coupled with a brief thrill, the paratrooper's rush. As he continued to look about the room, the walls faded, became mirages, and Thorsen could see the abrupt edge of the floor change suddenly into open desert, which gave way to juniper chaparral, and as the terrain climbed into the mountains, the space pushed out again into the stately openness of pine forest, and then he was seeing from the mountaintops—east and west—and the whole expanse of land from where he stood to each ocean opened up to him and then retracted. The walls replaced themselves; the plates hung mutely again above the knick-knacks and curios. The television was still, dim, and quiet, dust clinging to the face of the picture tube. Lila's footsteps were growing louder.

"He's been called," she said.

"Who?"

"Brandon. He's going to the Philippines."

"That right?" Thorsen said, but he already knew.

"The Manila South mission. Brandon just got home from work. They opened it while we were talking."

Thorsen nodded.

"What's wrong with you?"

"Nothing," he said. "Gotta eat some crow."

"So that's what Andy came over to tell you?"

Thorsen nodded.

"You've eaten it before. Just plug your nose and swallow."

"Pearson says if I do, then I win."

"Oh, Jens, do it because it's right," she said. "Do it because your grandson is going on a mission, but don't do it to get back at Darrell. Don't dirty up a good thing."

"Yeah, that's what Pearson was saying."

"That's good advice. And Brandon wants you to call him back."

"What for?"

"He didn't say." Lila looked at Thorsen suspiciously.

"What's that evil eye for?"

"You're *not* going to embarrass us," she said.

"What do you mean?"

"That's not a question, it's a command. Brandon had to drive the missionaries to an appointment, but Kaylyn says you can call him later tonight."

"What do I need to call him for?"

"To talk about this farewell business."

"What's there to talk about?"

"You are not going to embarrass us," she repeated. "I won't have it."

As Thorsen pulled into a spot in front of Stucki's, he saw Angie Bunker getting out of her car. She was wearing denim overalls that ended in a skirt, a white T-shirt underneath, and a gray and yellow work shirt over that. She carried two white bags from the Frost Stop Drive-In in one hand and a forty-four-ounce fountain drink in the other. The straw had been chewed into a paddle.

"H'lo, Angie."

"Hi, Brother Thorsen."

"Enough of the Brother Thorsen—Jens works just fine."

Angie averted her gaze for a moment, a girlish gesture that made Thorsen smile. "What?" he said.

"I've never been able to get my dad as pissed off as you did," she said, nudging the car door shut with her hip. "And I've pretty much mastered it."

Thorsen closed his truck door and stepped up to the curb.

"You're all they've been talking about in there this week," Angie said, gesturing with her drink. "You're like some kind of outlaw hero."

"Well."

"Not like I mind it. I've been off my dad's radar for almost a week now, and that's a relief."

"Nice to be of service."

"You're going to have to ease up, Brother Thorsen. You've bailed me out two times already. I'm going to be in hock to you until I'm sixty-five." She took a drink from her soda.

"Just give me your firstborn, and we'll call it good," Thorsen said, pulling a ball cap from the back pocket of his work pants.

Angie coughed violently, the straw pulling out of her mouth.

"You all right?" Thorsen asked. She set the soda on the ground and nodded and pounded the thumb side of her fist against her chest.

"Wrong pipe," she gasped.

"What's that?" Thorsen asked. "Stucki got you to fetch his lunch?"

"When I'm not sweeping up hair—I'm going crazy in there."

"Stucki's geezers probably aren't used to someone like you touching their heads."

"Someone like me?"

"Pretty, young, not their wife."

Angie coughed a last time and smiled. "So we're back to the standard church line—everything between men and women is sexual. Why don't you just put us in burkas?"

"A donut in a bag is still a donut. Look, I don't imagine it's the church so much as geriatrics in general."

"The church *is* geriatrics. Joseph Smith was the last young man to run things."

Thorsen nodded a touché and then thought about Sanpete and the slow drying up of its youth. The outside world was too attractive, and it took more money to get through a year than it used to. *Can't pay an HMO with a bushel of onions—can't get things fixed when they break—got to throw them out and get new ones—should put the Wal-Marts next to landfills so you only have to make one trip—only new blood in town anymore is artists looking for some barn to paint their pictures in and rock climbers looking for a place to park their Volkswagons. It's boom, bust, and fizzle out here,* he thought. *Hell of a way to go.*

"I got to get back to the shop," Angie said.

"Sure," Thorsen said, "I'll go in with you."

Angie walked past Thorsen, opened the door with her bag hand, and went into the shop. Thorsen followed, and as Angie crossed the room to give Stucki his lunch, Thorsen hung his cap on a hook and crawled into Angie's chair. Passey was parked on the far side of the shop reading *Popular Mechanics,* and Leroyce Leavitt waited next to him with his knobbled hands piled up in the lap of his overalls. Another customer, Merrill Templin, was packed into Stucki's chair, about halfway through his haircut. Gray, black, and silver tufts of hair littered the floor like discarded steel wool.

"Howdy, Jens," Stucki said, making an almost imperceptible bow with his scissors hand in front and his comb hand in back. Passey winked once and went back to his magazine. Leroyce gave Thorsen a crooked thumbs up, shook his head, then resumed his blank stare.

The television was off.

"You know," Passey said, touching his cap, "I'd like to say I didn't approve."

Thorsen flattened his lips and flicked his eyes across the shop.

"But that would be lying, and I'm not interested in bearing false witness," Passey said.

"I'm not one for taking sides," said Leroyce, "but we're behind you on this one, my friend."

"You're a regular Robin Hood," Passey said.

Thorsen waved them off and got settled in his chair.

"See what I mean?" Angie said. "They'd be carrying you through the streets if they were up to it."

"Bishop's a bishop," Templin said. "Got to respect that."

"Oh, Merrill, blow it out your ass," Leroyce said.

"I don't need your foul language," Templin said. "If everyone started following their own conscience we'd be no better'n a bunch of savages. We got to have some respect."

"How about for our town doctor. I didn't see the bishop blessing away your hernia, Merrill," Leroyce said. "Or praying away my arthritis. Bill Everly took Wizenberg for a ride, and I wouldn't be surprised if Bunker wasn't in on it somehow. There isn't an Everly project that doesn't have Bunker Excavation equipment all over it. Put the law on this one, and it'd be a whole lot worse than a car wash. It's easy to throw Indians and Mexicans in jail around here, but pretty hard to lock up a bishop. It's kind of like that—what do you call 'em, those embassy fellas?"

"Diplomatic immunity," said Passey.

"That's right, diplomatic immunity."

"I'm through with it," Templin said. "You see what you started, Thorsen."

Thorsen nodded, took out a pocketknife, and began to clean his nails. *You get five of us in a room, and you'll get seven points of view,* he thought.

"You here to bask in your glory, or did you come as a paying customer?" Stucki asked.

"I'm here for the services. I've got to get cleaned up. I'm speaking at a mission farewell down in Cedar City."

"You're speaking *again?*" Stucki asked.

"I guess the folks down there haven't heard the tale of the turkeys," Passey said.

Leroyce slapped his thigh.

"Well, there's at least one of us glad for the turkeys, ain't that right, Angie?" Thorsen said.

"I've got mixed feelings," she said, washing her hands.

The shop erupted into laughter. Even Merrill Templin was doubled over.

"You done a good job with this one," Leroyce said.

Angie reached for a towel, and when she turned back, her face was red and a smile curled up, revealing her large incisors.

"I know when I'm licked," Thorsen said.

"Well, you got a line here, Thorsen. Early bird gets the worm," Stucki said.

"Oh, I'm here for the girl," Thorsen said, and Angie's face went blank. "That's right. The way that old man cuts hair, I'll be here all afternoon, and I got people to see."

Angie was in a frenzy, shuffling combs and scissors around on the countertop. "You'll have to give me a minute to kind of get things organized," she said. She turned in circles a few times, then stopped suddenly. "Stucki, where are those little tissues—"

"The collars," Stucki said. "In the drawer right up there . . . at the top."

Angie fussed around for a little while longer, then stopped suddenly. "Okay," she said. "Let's get started."

"How about we put one of those aprons on?" Thorsen asked.

"Oh crap," she said. "Hold on." She unfurled the cloth and swung it around Thorsen like a matador. Then she darted out from behind the chair, grabbed one of the regular sitting chairs from where Leroyce and Passey were watching in amazement, and shoved it up against the sink in the corner. Passey raised his eyebrows, and Thorsen shrugged. Stucki looked like he was about to ask Angie what she was up to, but he didn't, thought better of it. Angie pulled a towel from her shoulder and laid it gently and carefully across the lip of the sink. She crossed back to Thorsen's chair and ducked behind, returning with a bottle of shampoo.

"All right, Brother Thorsen."

"That's the strangest haircut I ever had. You were so gentle, it was like you never even touched me."

"I've got to wash your hair," Angie said, deadpan. "I can't cut it when it's dry like that." Laughter from the gallery, and she ignored it. Thorsen was slightly distracted, but he shrugged.

"We've got a spray bottle," Stucki said. "I'm not using it."

"I can't cut it when it's dirty either."

"Hear that, Thorsen?" Passey said. "You've got to wash."

Thorsen waved him off and hauled himself out of the barber chair. "You're in charge, Angie. Do what it takes." Thorsen crossed the room and came around past Templin and Stucki and lowered himself into the chair. Angie followed and squeezed past him.

"You've got to lay your head back," she said.

Thorsen jockeyed himself into position, which involved a series of failed attempts and practice runs. When he finally had himself lowered into place, he said, "I'm not sure I'm going to be able to get back up."

"Well, this sink's not really made for this kind of treatment."

"Neither is my neck."

"You'll live."

"Stucki," Thorsen called out.

"It was your idea," Stucki answered.

"You hired her."

"Just calm down," Angie said, running the water. "You're going to like it."

"I've washed my hair before," Thorsen said.

"Some people wonder," Leroyce said, slapping the armrest of his chair with his knurled, arthritic hand.

"Maybe so, but *I've* never washed your hair before," Angie said.

Silence. "Well, okay then," Thorsen said, staring at the ceiling. "Stucki, you got them pressed tin panels up there."

"Sure do."

"With all that paint you can barely tell it—say, that feels nice."

"I told you," she said, then after she finished wetting Thorsen's head, she squeezed a dollop of shampoo into her palms and lathered up her hands.

"They were like that when I moved in here," Stucki said.

"What?"

"The panels—the painted ones—oh, for crying out loud."

Angie ran her hands around Jens' skull and lifted his head from the towel.

"Feels like I'm a-floating," Thorsen yodeled. "You boys really ought to get a piece of this. It's cheaper than a trip to the chicken ranch."

"Quiet," she said. "I might get soap in your mouth."

"Lila's been trying to do that for forty years," Passey said, chuckling.

"Shut your pie hole, Passey. I'm in heaven. The world is a place of beauty," Thorsen said. Angie cupped her hand and ladled the water over Thorsen's head and then used the flat of her other hand to squeegee the rinse water into the sink.

"All right. Up," she said and wrapped the towel around Jens' head. He sat up, crossed the room with his head swaddled like a prizefighter's, and plopped limply in the chair.

"Man," he said. "I feel like I'm forty-five again."

"That's enough out of you," Stucki said. "I got decent folks in here."

"I'm happy to sit here and watch," Leroyce said. "My wife won't let me get the premium channels." Passey chuckled and turned the page. Stucki finished Templin's haircut and vacuumed him off. He paid with a ten he peeled off a roll of ones and fives and then headed out.

"Everyone in town is locking their doors, Thorsen," Templin said as he left. "You can revel in that for a while if you're done with your pornography." The door closed behind him.

"What's eating him?"

"Forget it, Jens," Stucki said. "He's trying to get your goat."

Angie came around and snapped on her clippers. "What am I doing for you, Brother Thorsen?"

"You could wash it again, if you want to."

"I don't have all day," she said.

"Just cut it like it is, but shorter."

Angie didn't say anything, just went to work. Passey climbed into Stucki's chair and Stucki aproned him. Passey's eyes went immediately to the sink. "Don't even ask," Stucki said.

"All right," Passey said. "Just lower the ears like you're used to."

Conversation dropped away while the two barbers set to work, clippers buzzing and combs guarding the liver-spotted skin of the old men in their chairs. Leroyce looked up from time to time to see if there would be any conversation. He'd look to Passey and then to Thorsen, who kept their heads tucked down, their boots poking out from under the front hems of the aprons. Angie kept half an eye on Stucki as he moved the clippers around, spinning the old chair one way and then the other. Angie was constantly touching Thorsen's head, turning and lifting it while she dabbed gingerly at the back of Thorsen's skull. Stucki never touched Passey except with the clipper guard. The two moved like they were riding double on a motorcycle, anticipating the turns.

Thorsen spread his apron from underneath and exhaled. Angie leaned over. "How are you, Brother Thorsen?"

Thorsen grinned. "That hair washing should be illegal."

"You never wanted me to wash your hair before, Thorsen," Stucki said.

"There's a lot of things I never wanted you to do, Stucki," Thorsen said, exhaling again.

"Brother Thorsen, you're sinking," Angie said.

Thorsen pushed himself up and apologized. In the next chair, Passey and Stucki were whispering.

"What kind of secret combination are you two fellas cooking up?" Thorsen asked. They stopped, a little alarmed, and went back to the haircut. Leroyce shook his head and gestured to Angie with a couple of gnarled fingers. Thorsen looked at the girl in the opposing mirror, saw her thin lips and lowered eyelids. She was reciting something to herself like a ball player running over a coach's instructions. *More of this Bunker garbage,* Thorsen thought. *'Least they're kind enough to talk around her.*

Angie came around the chair and squinted at Thorsen.

"What?"

"You want me to take care of the strays?" she said, gesturing above his eyes with the comb.

"Sure," Thorsen said, "if you can do it without blinding me."

Next door, Stucki started dabbing some lather onto Passey's neck, and he opened his razor. "On second thought, Stucki, I got to get out to that Doctor Wizenberg's place here pretty quick. We can just call it good."

"Suit yourself," Stucki said, and he toweled off Passey's neck and behind the ears. He brought out the vibrating massage unit, strapped it to his hand, switched it on, and began running it across Passey's pate like a gravel compactor. Passey's eyes rolled back in his head, and he gripped the armrests vigorously. "We all got our tricks," Stucki said to Angie, winking.

When Stucki switched the unit off, Passey gasped, "I need to teach Adele to use one of those things."

Angie and Stucki finished at the same time, and they brushed off Thorsen and Passey and vacuumed up the hair and cut them loose. Passey paid Stucki with a ten, and Thorsen paid Angie with a twenty. She got change from the cash drawer and handed a ten back to Jens, who was already plucking his cap from the coat rack. "Here's your change," she said.

"Easy come, easy go," Jens told her.

Angie folded the bill and slipped it into the breast pocket of her overalls skirt. Passey donned his cap and announced that he was leaving for the Wizenbergs' place.

"My dad's down there," Angie said. "He took down some equipment this morning. Some big service project."

"You coming, Jens?" Passey asked. "Might could use you on account of you knowing the terrain."

Leroyce burst out laughing and then fell silent. Everyone's eyes drifted toward Angie.

"I don't care," she said. "Do I look like a person who'd be on his side?"

The mirrors of the barbershop faced each other and threw complementary reflections, the motley collection of old men duplicated infinitely, along with the red-haired girl they had all known since she was scab-kneed and in braids. The picture of the silent group rose as it repeated, and they all seemed to be climbing as they moved on in succession, like a line of pilgrims on a straight path skyward.

"Okay, then," Thorsen said. "Stucki, why don't you ride with me?"

"I'm not going anywhere. Leroyce has been sitting here twenty-five minutes," Stucki said. Leroyce nodded.

"That's what you've got the girl for," Thorsen said.

"The girl has a name," Angie added.

"Leroyce, you mind if Angie here cuts your hair?" Thorsen asked.

Leroyce's eyes lit up. "Don't believe I do. Except I *will* need a wash, I think. It's been a couple days." Angie shook her head and sighed.

"Does the girl know how to run the compactor?" Leroyce asked.

"I have a name."

"I never showed her," Stucki said.

"You just strap it on," Passey said, "and it kind of drives itself."

"You all are a bunch of filthy old men," Angie said, glaring at each of them in turn.

. . .

When they pulled up, the work party was in full swing. Bunker was behind the levers of a D-8 Caterpillar, the engine clacking, the treads squeaking horribly as he shoved a berm of nearly liquid dirt across a low spot on the property and dumped it onto a bed of drain tile. Some other men were lowering another length of drain tile into a second ditch, while others shoveled gravel out of a flatbed truck into small boxy trailers hitched to four-wheel all-terrain vehicles. Passey was there already, sawing a length of blue PVC pipe in half.

Above the tumult, Wizenberg and his wife stood watch, she with her arms folded, a steaming mug in her hands, he with his hands on the rail of the upper deck. When he saw Thorsen and Stucki, he motioned for them to come up and pointed them to a set of stairs.

"Better late than . . . never," Stucki said, and he started out across the field.

Thorsen followed after him, shaking his head. They crossed the open ground slowly, Thorsen noticing how stiff Stucki's movements had become. He had always been tall, and in his younger days, he could walk forever, like some heron moving through shallow water, never quite graceful, but never ungainly either. Now his movements were robotic, hinged. He seemed like more of a contraption than a person. Thorsen himself had become heavy in his gait, his feet chronically stiff but his back and arms strong. The two of them out there among those other men made Thorsen think suddenly of Methuselah. *If I clear eighty,* Thorsen thought, *I'll call that a game.*

Once cleared of the yard, they mounted the stairs and saw the whole industrious swarm, thick across the property.

"They just showed up," Wizenberg said.

"Kind of like the cops," Thorsen answered, breathing heavy. "Never around when you need one, always there when you don't."

Sondra Wizenberg leaned toward Thorsen and shook his hand quickly before refolding her arms. "Is this kind of thing common around here?"

"You mean guerilla . . . excavation?" Stucki said. "Yep, we're a peculiar people. Like using power tools . . . heavy equipment."

"This is my good friend, Lewis Stucki," Thorsen said, "Stook, this is Dr. Wizenberg and his wife."

"Sondra," she said, unsheathing her hand.

"Seth," the doctor said. They all shook hands and exchanged nods.

"By the way, I went by to see that friend of yours—tried to, anyway."

"Phyllis get after you?" Thorsen asked.

"Something like that," Wizenberg said. "Pointed a shotgun at me and told me to get lost."

"It was a lot worse than that," Sondra added.

"Well, that doesn't matter really. What was it you wanted me to say to him, anyway?"

Thorsen glanced over at Stucki, thought for a moment, and then cleared his throat. "Round these parts, most any counsel you'll get is of a religious nature. Doesn't matter what's wrong with you—legal, political, medical—you get the same type of answer off people. It's pretty straightforward. If you pray and read your scriptures and go to church, then you'll know that whatever's wrong with you, you brought on yourself."

Stucki rolled his eyes, and Wizenberg looked on with fascination.

"Old Karl just needs someone to tell him there's nothing shameful in dying. I'm not sure he thinks so. What do you say, Stook?"

"Don't know. Seems like he's thinking about it," Stucki said, looking down at his shoes like a young boy caught horsing around. "Still, there's Phyllis, and she scares me."

"You keep showing up, and she'll quit being so skittish," Thorsen said.

"Skittish?"

Thorsen and Stucki laughed. "You got one thing going for you, Doc—you aren't from the church," Thorsen said. "You weren't wearing a white shirt, were you?"

"No."

"Good, don't," Thorsen advised.

They lined up against the rail and watched the effort. "You think they know what they're doing?" Wizenberg asked.

"It'll be hard to tell if they don't," Thorsen said. "You know you got dealt a crooked hand here, Doc." Wizenberg looked intrigued. "We got a no-account land baron around here that sells Florida swampland at Park City prices. I wish we would have seen you looking at this place before you settled. Brigham Young himself came to Sanpete in the 1860s and told folks not to build here on the north side of Thompson Wash. A couple places have sunk— you remember them, Stucki?"

"Jeb Nichols and that other fella, the newspaper man—foundations set on gypsum and they cracked right in half," Stucki said. Wizenberg looked at his wife, who shrugged but leaned slightly toward Thorsen with interest.

"Everyone who's been around for a while knows to stay clear, but that jack realtor Bill Everly looks to sell to gentiles—"

Wizenberg burst out laughing. Thorsen turned to Stucki.

"I'm sorry, fellas, it's just that I've never been called a gentile before."

Thorsen's face went blank. Stucki whispered the doctor's last name into Thorsen's ear. and Thorsen cracked a smile.

"Sorry, Doc, Mrs. Wizenberg," Thorsen said, bowing his head. During the pause, the pounding of heavy boots boomed up the stairs. It was Pearson.

"Jens," he said, cheerfully, taking time to also nod to the Wizenbergs. "Good to see you here."

"Thanks, Andy. Now quit beating around the bush," Thorsen said.

Pearson looked nervous and unsettled. Glances knocked around the group like pool balls, while Pearson tried to compose himself. "As you can see, the bishop's here."

"Is that the guy you tried to get down here before?" Wizenberg asked.

"Doc, excuse me," Thorsen said, holding up his hand like he was stopping traffic.

"What's going on, Thorsen?" Stucki asked.

Thorsen boiled. Pearson tried to touch his shoulder, but Thorsen stared him down. "All right," he said finally. "Let's get this over with." Thorsen made a ring of his thumb and forefinger and whistled. The men in the yard looked up at the deck, and Thorsen pointed to Bunker, who was dozing another load of mud toward one of the trenches. Passey waved Bunker down and pointed up to the deck like a man directing aircraft. Bunker let the D-8 settle to a rough idle, then he stood up and turned towards Thorsen. "You got something to say to me?" he shouted.

"Jackass," Thorsen said under his breath, then he took a lungful of air and hollered back. "I'm sorry I stole your backhoe to save these people's home and property!"

"What?"

Thorsen looked at Stucki incredulously. Stucki shrugged.

"You heard me," Thorsen hollered. "I said . . . I'm sorry . . . I stole . . . your backhoe . . . to save . . . these people's . . . home . . . and . . . property!"

Down in the yard, Passey pulled off his cap and covered his mouth with it.

"Apology accepted," Bunker said, and then he reengaged the D-8 and continued leveling the ground.

"There you have it," Thorsen said.

"Men are the most absurd creatures on this entire planet," Sondra Wizenberg said, shaking her head. "What was that about?"

"Don't ask," Wizenberg said, taking hold of his wife's arm. "I think it's church-related."

Chapter Eight

THORSEN'S PICKUP SNAKED along the interstate through the narrow slots thrust between Richfield and Beaver. Traffic was light, and the truck sailed westward on the open road. Before they left, Thorsen had put a lead fuel additive into the gas tank and taken the carburetor apart, spraying it with solvent until it drooled. Lila had watched him from the kitchen, her fingers against the glass. When Thorsen turned around to fetch a tool, she dropped back into the shadows.

Thorsen tapped the wheel and turned to his wife in the passenger seat. "She's been a good girl," he announced, too loud for the cab.

Lila knit a stitch and nodded. "It does what a car ought to."

"Truck," Thorsen said. "Don't hurt her feelings."

Lila nodded again and then looked at Thorsen, whose face twitched once in the cheek. He drove for a bit, then swung his eyes to meet Lila's, and they held the gaze until the tires barked on the shoulder grooves. Thorsen corrected the swerve.

"I hear Angie Bunker is working for Lewis down at the barber shop," Lila said. "He's been by himself a long time. Wonder why he'd hire someone all the sudden."

"He's been wanting to fish a little more."

"Mmmm," Lila said, pulling some slack from the bag at her feet.

"The rest of the fellas are retired. He's been feeling like he can't get free when he wants to."

"So I guess it'll be nice for him to have a girl there. What do those old birds think of her?"

"Dunno. I think old Leroyce Leavitt is kind of sweet on her."

"I think it's interesting to have her back home."

"Like how?"

"Just popping up out of nowhere. Kids leave Sanpete on a one-way road. Only ones that ever come back are either pregnant or divorced."

"What about Pearson?"

"Okay, pregnant, divorced, or Pearson," Lila said, "but you know what I'm talking about."

"Maybe she ran herself out of money."

"Maybe."

They drove on, cresting the mountains just past Joseph and then coasting down to the interstate. On the outskirts of Beaver, Thorsen gassed up and returned with two pecan clusters and a bottle of vegetable juice.

"It's Sunday, Jens," Lila said.

Thorsen stared at her like an old dog, then he tossed the candy and juice onto the seat and climbed in. He pulled the wrapper off one of the pecan clusters and gnawed at the corner. Then he wiped his mouth on the sleeve of his jacket, uncapped the juice, and took a swallow. "Just about there," he said, gasping. Lila was eyeing the candy and juice.

"It's pretty good," Thorsen said, tearing off another bite. "You better hurry up before I get into the other one."

They pulled into the parking lot of the church building five minutes before eleven o'clock. Thorsen turned off the truck and dropped the key in the ashtray, then finished off the V-8. Lila took the key out of the ashtray and handed it to Thorsen. "Not around here you don't," she said. "The last thing we need is someone stealing our transportation." Thorsen was about to take issue, but someone knocked on the side window and waved. Thorsen rolled the window down, and a hand sprung through the gap. It was Tyree Bulloch, a man Thorsen had worked with at the Highway Department. "I hear your grandson is heading off on a mission," Tyree said.

"That's right. Good to see you, Tyree," Thorsen said.

Lila took the key herself and leaned over. "Hello, Tyree, how's your wife?" she asked.

"Well, Lila, she passed back in April," Tyree said.

"Oh, Tyree." Lila covered her mouth with one hand.

"I'm sorry to hear it," Thorsen said.

"Well, it's okay now. She's better off—took sick about this time last year."

"What was it?" Thorsen asked.

"Cancer—pancreatic."

Thorsen nodded. "That's not an easy one."

"No way out except through it," Tyree said and stepped aside to let Thorsen out of the truck. Lila got out as well, and they slammed the doors at the same time. Thorsen patted himself for the key, but Lila held it up and then dropped it in her bag. The three of them walked into the church together.

They met their children, Jens Junior and Kaylyn, inside the foyer, no grandkids in sight. Lila hugged Jens Jr. and Kaylyn, while Thorsen dug his hands into his pockets and nodded to both of them.

"Dad," Jens Junior whispered, sidling up alongside him. Thorsen grimaced. "Listen, I know Brandon is set on having you talk, but . . ." He looked around. His wife and mother were talking. "Can you maybe steer clear of the turkeys, this time?" Thorsen coughed, which made Jens Junior a little nervous. "It's just that I've been asked, you know . . . we've got a bishop down here that used to live in Gunnison, and he's . . . well, he knows all about you and Bunker and the whole deal."

"I see," Thorsen said. "You're out to censor your old man."

"We sort of made a deal."

"On my behalf? That's mighty white of you, Junior." By this time Thorsen was talking at normal volume, and his son was trying to hush him. "Maybe I wasn't planning on talking turkey today at all, sport. In fact, I was thinking I might talk Holsteins this morning, or maybe hogs—you know, I could go on for hours about bird dogs or trout or ravens or mules or chickens or ticks or deer mice or jackalopes or pretty much anything else you want, son. You name it, and I'll talk on it. How about I just talk on Noah and hit them all at once?"

The foyer had gone silent, and everyone's eyes were on Thorsen, except Lila's. Jens Junior looked around and chuckled nervously and clapped his hands together once, ushering his parents into the chapel. "Remember, Dad, we live here," Jens Junior said, placing a hand squarely on his father's back and the other lightly on his mother's shoulders.

They all took their seats, Lila with Kaylyn and the rest of the family. The two Jenses went to the front of the chapel and sat on the stand with the rest of the speakers and the bishop. Jens greeted his grandson with a warm handshake. After a hymn and a prayer and a litany of announcements and items of church business, they partook of the bread and water.

When that was over, Thorsen was introduced and he reached down and took hold of each arm of his chair and lifted himself. He turned slowly and crept toward the podium as if in compound gear. Jens Junior and his son sat as if pushed apart by Thorsen's empty chair. The strange, electric rustle of paper vibrated through the chapel as the congregation opened their programs. A baby started screaming, making its mother rise and inch toward the aisle. Behind the podium, Thorsen pulled a white handkerchief from his back pocket and snorted into it vigorously. Then, taking each finger up in a bight of the cloth, he dug into his nostrils.

He wore a dark-blue blazer and a plaid shirt unbuttoned at the top. A jawbreaker-sized turquoise bolo tie hung down from underneath the stainless-steel-tipped ends of his collar. The silver tips of the tie strings ticked against the plastic and steel shirt snaps.

"I left my scriptures out on the workbench," he began, "so I'm just going to guess at things here. I haven't been too many places nor seen too many things," Thorsen continued, "but I've got some notion of what makes people tick.

"Genealogy aside, I have to say that grandson of mine is going to make a great missionary, and it isn't from anything I taught him. I suppose it's a good thing I'm not dead yet, but I ain't putting off the day of my repentance. In fact, I'm repenting right now, right from this stand. But I suppose something as serious as that don't take hold until you buy the farm and can't sin anymore.

"What's good about old Brandon here," Thorsen continued, "is what's best in a horse, and that isn't something a man can just add to the batter—it's what he brought with him from heaven. I know I don't have much say in how that works—don't hear him asking anyways." Thorsen hitched up his pants. "I don't go in for quoting the prophets, mostly since I haven't seen eye to eye with any of them since Brigham Young, or maybe you could count Spencer W. Kimball in there too. He's a good, hard-working Arizona boy, and that's good enough for me. But I can't respect a man that thinks enough of the federal government to draw a paycheck from the dang tyrants. After that—well, what I mean to say is that old J. Golden once preached that if God needed men to keep the church afloat, she'd have sunk somewhere out in Iowa."

Thorsen stopped and drew in a deep breath and let it out slowly, then he looked over at his grandson and smiled. Brandon gave him a thumbs-up. Thorsen then looked out into the congregation and searched for his wife. When he found her, he saw that she was smiling in a strange, half-confused way.

"I didn't baptize anybody on my mission," he continued, "and I tell you, preaching to the Dutch is like trying to trailer a mule. I didn't have luck when I was trying. But when I was in this little town of Maastricht I had this companion with two years at the Colorado School of Mines who was all set to go back and finish up and get a job at the Berkley Pit outside of Butte, Montana. He thought he knew more than enough about dang near everything in God's creation. I thought he had a leaky mouth. Every now and then I told him to plug it, but he'd wave me off and drip on about the tides and concrete retaining walls and windmills and whatever else we happened to be walking by, so I learned to sing a hymn to shut him off. If you can hie to Kolob, there's enough verses to make it through just about anything your companion throws at you.

"Anyways, one night we were trying to get home, and we were on our way through the town square, and we come up on this statue of the Virgin Mary. Wasn't much taller than a crow—cast bronze, if I remember right. A little bit pitted, but overall it was in pretty good shape. Them Maastrichters had it in this glass case right upside this fountain with a statue of a little kid or something holding a bucket of fruit.

"So this companion of mine said he could get that statue out of the box. I told him that there was no way in hell he could, and he said he's studied it out and then opened up his overcoat and took out this huge screwdriver and showed me. I told him he ought not to smash up the glass or he'll get thrown out of the mission. He didn't answer me or anything, he just bent up a plate on the top, and the lid sprung right off. I got over and looked down and the head of the statue is down in there like the top of a bowling pin, and my companion hauls it out and displays it with the kind of grin on his face reserved for imbeciles and politicians.

"So, I looked around the place," Thorsen continued. "I was looking for those crazy-looking Dutch cops, and I told my companion to put the dang thing back. He said, 'Come on, let's go to town,' and then he ran across the street with the Virgin and carried her up the steps of the town hall and set it right up under this archway in front of the doors. And then he ran down and closed up the case. Then he said come on, and we went home.

"That whole night, he kept asking what I thought was going to happen, and I kept telling him to shut up. Next day, we went down to get some bread from the bakery, and we went past this newsstand. All the papers said, 'Virgin Mary Visits' and 'Blessed Mother Calls Town Fathers to Task.'

"Well, them Dutch jugheads built a shrine on the steps of the city hall and put up some kind of perpetual gas flame. And that was the only thing anyone talked about until I got transferred up to Amsterdam. You pretty much couldn't go door to door after that." Thorsen dragged a finger under his nose and then stopped and stared out into the space of the cultural hall. He started to speak again, but couldn't. He leaned into the microphone and said, "I'm sorry." Then gathered his composure. He stood there for a long time with one hand on the pulpit to brace himself, his other arm hanging to one side. Thorsen looked down at Lila, who was clutching the top of the pew in front of her. Thorsen nodded and then swiped at his cheek with the back of his wrist.

"So I spent the whole rest of my mission thinking I helped

convert a whole town of Dutch to Catholicism. I never told the mission president or anyone else over there. I just figured that I'd have to baptize some whole other town to pay the Lord back for me being such a smart mouth kid. Now that hasn't happened yet, but maybe my grandson here can put a few on my list."

Jens Junior lifted his head as Thorsen returned to his seat and sat slowly. His son stared blankly out across the ward at the opposite end of the room. Brandon sat still and waited while two of his mother's sisters came forward, one bouncing across the organ bench, and the other climbing up to the stand. She bumped the microphone around until it satisfied her and then began to howl from the hymnbook.

Thorsen leaned over to his grandson and whispered, "We ought to get her out on opening day of elk season," then he jabbed the boy with his elbow. Brandon laughed so hard and so suddenly that twin cords of snot rocketed from his nostrils. Embarrassed, he covered up his face. Thorsen told him to calm down and pulled out his handkerchief. The boy took it gingerly and wiped down his face and the papers that lay in his lap.

"Keep it," Thorsen said. "It's no good to me anymore."

Jens Junior looked over and scowled. "What's wrong with him?" he asked.

"Don't know," Thorsen said. "I think he's just caught up in the Spirit."

"I wish you wouldn't tell that Maastricht story, Dad. It's light-minded."

"The hell it is," he said loud enough to be heard over the ailing hymn. "You didn't even go on a mission, so what do you know?"

"Okay. Not now," he said, shushing his father.

The bishop leaned over and stared at Thorsen and gestured to Thorsen's grandson. The boy's aunt shattered a few more notes of "God Be with You Till We Meet Again" and continued to sing the song in an alien harmony. The dissonance made people nervous, but they smiled. When she was done, the boy rose and took his place at the stand.

"Well," he said, "to quote another hymn, 'I stand all amazed.'"

The ward laughed, and the rest of the meeting went as planned.

"Jens Thorsen," Lila said once the truck door was shut. "I don't want to hear that Maastricht story come out of your mouth ever again." Thorsen held out his hand, and Lila handed him the key, which he slipped into the ignition and turned. "Brandon was crazy to ask you to talk. I'm not sure whether to be more worried about you or all those foolish kids you inspired to break their mission rules."

"I didn't inspire anyone. I just told a sober tale, Mamma."

"Sober? I'd have sworn you were drunk."

"It jerked my tears," Thorsen said, growling the throttle. "But I thought Brandon needed to hear that his old grandpa has some regrets for fooling around on the Lord's time."

Lila finished with her seat belt, set her purse and scripture bag across her knees, and stared straight out the windshield. "I'm not talking about it. Take us over to Junior's. I need to help Kaylyn with the refreshments." The car directly in front of them backed out, and a woman squinted and then waved at her. Lila smiled and waved back and turned to Thorsen. "Come on, let's go before I get too mad to sit in here with you."

Thorsen gunned the motor, gripping the steering wheel. "I'm letting it warm up, dear," he said through his teeth. "I'm letting it warm up."

Junior's driveway was already full of cars, so Thorsen parked in the street and took the key out of the ignition. As he was about to drop the key into the ashtray, Lila slammed it shut. "Take the key with you," she growled.

"What in Sam Hill?"

"Take the key with you," she said.

"Who's going to steal this truck, woman? That doesn't make any sense. Haven't we been over this already?"

"Take the key. That's all I'm saying about it. You hear me? I'm short-tempered as it is, and I need to be sweet for the next couple of hours. And that won't be possible if you keep at me."

Thorsen opened the door, hopped down, and hobbled up to the front of the truck and hurled the key into Jens Junior's lawn. "There's your key," he said, and then stuffed his hands down into his pockets and scowled. He waited for an answer, but Lila just leaned over and pulled the driver's door shut and popped her hand down on the lock, and when she leaned back up, she hit her own lock with her elbow.

Up in the bay window of Junior's living room, someone ap-peared in silhouette and stared down at the Thorsens, one inside the truck, one outside. Thorsen pounded on the hood and commanded Lila to get out. Lila sat inside and stared forward as if Thorsen were invisible. Thorsen kicked the tires and crabbed around the front of the truck to Lila's side. More people appeared in the bay window, and Junior opened the front door and stood there with a dishtowel in his hand. Down the street another car turned onto the cul-de-sac and drove slowly toward the house.

"Woman!" Thorsen cried out, with one hand clutching his hair. "I don't know whether I'm coming or going."

Lila stared out into the sky and began to sing to herself.

"Dad," Junior called out. "Hurry up. We're about to start setting out the food."

Thorsen stared at his wife, watching her lips move silently through the glass. He stood there and watched as she closed her eyes and began to rock back and forth. A rapture fell across her face as if she were tracing the path of angels across her mind. Her cheeks became flushed, and Thorsen saw her draw deeper and deeper breaths until finally he could hear her muffled voice through the window. He stepped up to the truck and knocked lightly on the window, but Lila did not hear him. He looked down; her hands were folded lightly in her lap, her wedding ring snug against the knuckle of her hand, the skin spotted and loose.

"Dad," Jens Junior called out again, "is Mom okay?"

Thorsen ignored his son and dropped his head against the window. Lila kept rocking and singing, though her eyes flickered over at Thorsen when she heard his head thump. When she finished her first song and began with "I Am a Child of God," Thorsen drew himself up, then quietly he turned and hobbled up onto the lawn, dropped to his knees, and began patting around in the grass with everyone in Jens Junior's house looking on.

After about five minutes, one of the neighbors appeared in gray coveralls, a metal detector in one hand and a set of headphones cowling his neck. "Your son gave me a jingle. Said you might need some help in the detection department," the man said. He was in his mid-sixties, bald as a mole rat and doughy complexioned. Thorsen stopped patting around and wrenched himself back to a standing position. He looked down at the truck, and Lila was staring straight ahead. Some women had come through the garage and down the driveway with a plate of refreshments. Lila cracked the window and received the plate but refused the punch. "No telling how long I'll be in here," she said. The women nodded and headed back toward the house.

When Thorsen turned around, the man was scything the detector back and forth in a nine-to-six pattern on the lawn. He stopped, knelt down, and dug into the lawn with the blade of an old hunting knife. He held up a small washer, scrubbed it on his coveralls, and pocketed it.

After the man had dug up three quarters and a dime, a handful of old nails, and a medical bracelet belonging to one of the neighbor kids, Thorsen hollered. The man pulled his headphones off one ear and said, "It's not like I can set the dial to car keys," then he replaced the headphones and continued on.

When he eventually found the key, he handed it to Thorsen and said, "Good luck, brother."

"Thanks," Thorsen said and then walked slowly down the lawn to the passenger's side of the truck. Lila sat inside, her eyes resolute. Thorsen produced the key, unlocked the door, and opened it. She stepped down and walked up the driveway. Thorsen watched her wave at the window and turn up toward the house. She did not stop to see if he would put the key in the ashtray.

He locked the door, pocketed the key, and followed her into the house.

The inside of the house was swarming. Thorsen and Lila were relieved of their coats, given more food, and ushered around the room. As Lila sat down on the couch with another plate of food in her lap, their daughter Lilly pushed through the wall of people with a clipboard in her hand. "Mom," she said, making an end run around the coffee table before she plopped down. Thorsen sniffed, smiled, and took a bite of potato salad. Lilly threw her arm around Lila. "I'm working on that family history project, Mom. I need you to talk into the tape recorder again. The last time something went crazy, and all I got was static."

"Lilly, this will make it three times. There must be something more interesting going on in this family than how your father and I met."

"Unfortunately not," she said. "It'll be different this time, Mom. You'll have an audience."

Lila looked bushed. "I've already had all the audience I can take," she said, tossing her head toward her husband, who raised his fork and continued to clean his plate. Lilly put her hand on Lila's knee and looked at her plaintively. Lila turned her plate slightly and unfolded her napkin. "Let me eat first. Then I'll talk."

• • •

"Go ahead," Lilly said, "The tape is running."

Lila cleared her throat and started her tale slowly. "Jens had just come home from the Netherlands—you've heard about his service over there. He was just about twenty-two or twenty-three years old then. Skinny. And he had a full head of hair, if you can believe that. But it seems to me that he was already starting to shine in his own way. I was out of school—it was summer—and I was working for my father at the pharmacy in Richfield. They called us soda jerks back then, and we made sundaes, malts, brown cows—you name it. It was a good place for a girl to be back then. Lots of attention and plenty of boys to come through. Well, Jens strolled into that pharmacy dirty as a wheel rut. His hair was a mess, his old dungarees were covered in oil with dirt stuck to it. His T-shirt was smeared in grease and dirt and tufts of animal hair, but at least he had the decency to wear a work shirt over it, which wasn't much cleaner, but it was better than nothing.

"He came into the store with that clomping, lordly boot walk you don't see anywhere but out here. He certainly didn't pick it up in Amsterdam. By the look of him, you'd think he wouldn't have had any idea that Europe even existed, much less that he'd just been over there for two years. I watched him mill around the store. He was careful and slow, and once or twice he caught me watching him."

Thorsen adjusted himself in his chair. "Seemed like she thought I was gonna steal something," he interjected.

"Well, the thought did cross my mind. He ended up coming to the counter with a box of tooth powder, a pocket comb, and a tin of pomade. 'Can I pay for this here and get something from the counter at the same time?' he asked. I told him, 'Yes, if you don't lean on anything.'"

"And I didn't."

"He surely did. I had to wipe down the whole counter. He ordered an egg cream, which I made for him, and he tipped the glass back and let it pour straight down his throat. He clacked the glass back down on the counter and wiped off his mouth with his sleeve and gasped. One by one he set his things on the counter, and then he ordered another and drank it the same way. 'They taste better,' I told him, 'if you let it pause somewhere before you swallow it.'

" 'Do it that way, and you only get to taste it with your mouth,' he said, grinning. Then he winked, he actually winked. He sure thought he was something else."

"This room would be empty if you wouldn't have agreed with me on at least a couple of matters." Thorsen found a grandchild and winked.

"I can't explain that," she said, falling quiet to allow her audience some time to laugh.

"So he paid, left me a fifty-cent tip, then started out the door. But he stopped, stuffed his bag of things under his arm, and said, 'There's going to be a dance for the twenty-fourth. You like to maybe go to that, just for kicks? I'm not trying to marry you. I'm just working here for the summer.'

"Well, I just stared at the boldness of it all until he said, 'Never mind,' and eased the door off his shoulder and headed for his truck. 'Wait,' I said—stupid girl that I was. 'I have to work until eight.' That's what I told him.

"He caught the door and peeked back inside. 'Until late?' he asked, half-deaf even then.

" 'Until *eight*,' I said. 'The fountain's open until eight. You can come pick me up then, if you get clean first.' He just smiled and lifted up his little bag and went on his way.

"Pioneer Day was a week away, and I didn't see hide nor hair of him. I thought I saw him riding with a bunch of hooligans in the back of a truck, but I couldn't be sure. But my whole insides were in spasms. I spent the week feeling like I was going to be sick. I didn't tell anyone about him. It would have been unbearable to have had to explain myself. I would have had to lie to maintain even an ounce of respectability. Better to be completely mum about this boy and see what happened. Maybe he'd forget. Maybe he'd find some prettier girl, and then I wouldn't even have to worry about what he may or may not have been up to.

"But he came anyway," she said.

"Yes, I did," Thorsen said, grinning like a butcher's dog.

"And he cleaned up pretty nice—a white shirt, clean pressed pants, and his boots were clean and polished, too. He had this little string necktie with an Indian on it, and he had a single black-eyed susan in his hand, the most perfect one I'd ever seen, like it had come out of a photograph. He passed it over and said he'd gone through a whole field of them, looking for the right one. I took the flower and followed him out of the store. We walked down to the square, talking about the summer and Richfield and his mission. I told him how I was going to go to college that fall to study botany. He said he was going to work a while and get back some money since his mission broke the bank. He thought maybe he'd come down here to Cedar City for some school or maybe go on up to Logan. He wasn't too sure, he said. We danced a little, but mostly we just strolled around listening to the music.

"A bunch of kids went running past us. They were headed for a big hay wagon. We followed them and climbed on board and rode around the square, laughing and looking up at the stars.

"Well, we were coming back for the fireworks and my purse slipped out of the wagon somehow. I felt it go and heard it hit the street. Jens went right after it, over the side, and I heard him hit the street as well. I crawled over to the edge and saw him in the street hobbling around making all kinds of noise, my purse in his hand, the strap flailing around. He had obviously hurt himself, and when he heard me calling after him, he said, 'Keep going, I'll meet you at the pavilion.'

"When we got back together, he handed me my purse and said he was sorry he missed the rest of the ride. He walked me home, limping the whole way. I tried to help him, but he didn't take it. He left me right at my house. I thought he might try to kiss me. He'd been bold on all fronts that night, but he just nodded his head a little and limped off toward Main Street. I stood on the porch and watched him until he disappeared."

"Isn't that how Grandpa broke his ankle?" a granddaughter asked.

"That's right," Lila said.

"And isn't that how come we're all here?" a second grandchild chimed in.

"Well, there's a lot to that part of the story, but your grandfather didn't go into the infantry. They put him in the headquarters, which kept him safe for the whole war." Lila glanced briefly at her husband, who had lowered his head. He sat with his legs planted widely on the carpet of the room, with his hands on his knees and his arms bent. He nodded a few times slightly.

"If he wouldn't have broken that ankle, things might have turned out differently. I might have had to marry someone else."

The tape machine squealed and clicked off, and Lilly turned the tape over and set it to record again, but Lila said the time for old stories had passed. Lila motioned to Brandon. "Tell us your thoughts on the Philippines," she directed. "What have you learned about these people you'll be serving?"

Thorsen watched Lila move the spotlight away from herself gently, quietly. The thought of marrying someone else caused him to feel flushed and strange. It was something he had never really considered. There was always too much going on with kids and work and trials of one kind or another. He wondered what would be going on at this address if he had not jumped after the purse. If he'd died in the war, Lila would have heard through the grapevine, though she would have been concerned for months because the letters would have stopped. Eventually someone would have sought her out when the packet of her letters made it back to Sanpete with his other effects. His mother, perhaps, would have written the girl to tell her that Jens had been killed, that she was sorry. Lila would have wept, but time would have passed, and she would have met someone else and married. Perhaps some of their kids would have come to her anyway, but they'd have been different, changed slightly by the other man and his history and his ways.

Thorsen squinted at his wife and the family that surrounded her. The thought that he might not have been part of it at all made his heart feel like a piece of wood.

Chapter Nine

The sun was low over the mountains as Thorsen pulled up the drive of his house and parked. Light from the front room shone through the blinds, yellow and clear. A light snow sifted through the twilight, the flakes like dust motes. Enoch was away from the barn and down the rise. He leapt once or twice as if fighting with another horse, but he was alone in the pasture. Otherwise the air was still and cold, and occasional leaves clung to the trees, though it was only a week into October.

Thorsen climbed out of the truck with a pair of work gloves and an oblong carpenter's pencil in one hand. He called to his horse, but the animal ran along the fence, skirted the barn, and returned to the tree, the sound of his hooves rich and wet against the ground. Thorsen headed toward the house, ambivalent about the turn in the weather. He half-wanted it to blizzard and half-hoped they'd hold on to the mild days.

Passing through the mudroom, he set the gloves on the near edge of the dryer and pocketed the pencil. "Mamma?" Thorsen called. "I'm done with Karl and Phyllis. Nobody called, did they?" He continued into the kitchen and saw a phone number and Andy Pearson's name on the blackboard next to the phone. "Mamma?" The range-hood light was illuminated, and a pot sizzled on the stove, the burner glowing orange. The pot itself was empty, a thin, white film peeling away from the sides. A dozen eggs sat on the countertop. Thorsen turned off the burner and headed down the hallway.

When he came into the back room, he saw Lila lying prostrate on the floor, the coffee table turned over on its side. Thorsen felt the air rush out of his lungs. The room split into planes, the walls fading. He saw across the yard, through the juniper hedges that ringed the upper half of the property, across the road and the fields of the valley and up the foothills. Then suddenly everything receded, and Thorsen heard the furnace kick on. He knelt by his wife and touched her gently on the back.

"Oh, for God's sake, Lila," he said, then his head dropped.

The chairs in the funeral home were lined up in ten rows of ten with an aisle in the middle. Lila lay in her coffin at the front of the hall, the lid open, the scalloped brocade of white silk framing her chest and arms and face. When the last of the guests had filed past, the funeral director dismissed everyone but the immediate family, who gathered in the front of the room. Jens Junior and Kaylyn were there with their children. Lilly and Hunter had come without their youngest. After a short prayer, Thorsen veiled his wife, and the funeral director closed the coffin.

• • •

Bud Miner conducted the church service, excusing the bishop's absence. "Darrell asked me to preside," he said, tugging on one ear. A short eulogy was given by Lila's sister, and Lilly played a hymn on her viola, one string of the bow going haywire. At the end, Bud announced that a meal would be served in the church hall for friends and for those who had traveled.

"People are welcome to it," he said.

The church hall was a simple gymnasium flanked by a long accordion door on one side, a stage on the other, and basketball standards on each end. Two long banquet tables had been arrayed in food and silverware. There were a number of foil-wrapped hams set on serving plates, some of them scored and glazed and covered in pineapple rings. A pair of large salad bowls came next: green squares of iceberg lettuce, grated carrots, and purple cabbage. After that came the coleslaw and potato salads, macaroni, and gelatin. Some of the bowls were half-gone, some completely empty, and those were being steadily replaced by women in checkered aprons. One such woman came in with a green-bean casserole in one hand and a potato casserole in the other. There were plates of dinner rolls and a pan of biscuits, and at the far end were sheet cakes and pitchers of ice water.

People moved along the table, serving themselves. Children played in their suits and dresses and stocking feet, and there was noise and the occasional flutter of children running around on the stage. The room was full of whispers, hands on shoulders. Jean

Seiler, the Relief Society president, came into the hall with a tub of ice cream and set it next to the cakes. She was looking for Thorsen but spent time moving about the room talking to people. Someone pointed to one of the many round tables where people were sitting. There was a plate of food sitting there and a suit jacket hung over the back of the chair. Someone else pointed Jean out of the hall.

She found Thorsen in the kitchen with his shirtsleeves rolled up to the elbow and his hands down in a sink full of suds.

"Jens, you don't have to do that," she said.

"There's nothing else I can do," he said, and he took another glass from beside the sink and dipped it carefully into the water.

Part Three: Alone

Chapter Ten

Snow had left the valley, but the mountains kept their whiteness. The frosted shingles of the Thorsen house lay in precise rows, and the fogged windows surrounding the back door seemed like old, unread books. Steam poured from the dryer vent. The back door opened, and Thorsen stepped across the threshold, coming down the steps deliberately. The sound of the door slamming caught Enoch's attention, and he turned, steam chugging from his nose, to watch Thorsen as he made for the henhouse. The ground crunched beneath Thorsen's boots, leaves frozen together with hoary crystals. Occasional wrens swooped from one tree to another, leaving no trail in the stillness.

Thorsen unfastened the gate and ducked into the coop, returning with a hatful of eggs. He closed the gate and drew a deep breath and looked down at the eggs, dung-smeared but otherwise perfect. Enoch's tail flickered, and he dipped his head and tore a thin mouthful of grass from the pasture. Thorsen watched him lift his head again and took note of the slow, ungulate sideslipping of his jaws. Thorsen snorted and spat onto the ground and went back into the house.

A pan had been set out on the stove, butter next to it, a slice of ham, a spatula. Thorsen carefully set the eggs into an empty bowl, hung the hat on a back stile of the closest chair, then stripped off his coat, crossed the room, and hung it on a wire hook in the entryway. All of his movements were heavy but smooth, the curve of his hands tool-like and balanced, his cuticles and fingertips dry and split. He crossed back to the stove, switched on a burner, cut a quarter-inch slab of butter, and watched it melt in the belly of the pan. Thorsen cracked four eggs into the heat and tossed the shells in the sink. Immediately the eggs began to take form and go white. He arranged them a little with his spatula, but he was interrupted by the buzzing of the clothes dryer, which he crossed the room to empty.

When he came back, the eggs had become cellophane-like at the edges. Thorsen pulled the pan from the stove, cut the heat, and worked the eggs loose onto a plate. After setting the pan down and peppering the eggs, he sat at the table, said a prayer to himself, and then cut into the eggs with the edge of his fork.

Stucki's was quiet, only a couple of vehicles out front besides Stucki's truck and Angie's car. Thorsen turned sharply in the road and parked across the street. As he did, Spencer pulled through the intersection in his squad car and flipped on his lights. When he saw that it was Thorsen, he switched them off but kept turning, eventually pulling slowly behind the truck. Thorsen lowered his head to the steering wheel and appeared to fall asleep with his forehead against the back of his knuckles. Spencer watched for a few minutes and then drove on.

When Thorsen woke up, he climbed out of the truck and crossed the street and went to the door of Stucki's shop, but he didn't go in. He just stood outside and watched Angie washing somebody's hair in the low sink at the far end of the shop. Stucki sat in his own chair, enthroned—his feet on the rest, the remote cradled in his hand like a scepter. Thorsen watched until he thought one of them might turn toward the window, then he slipped away, crossed the street, and climbed back into his truck.

Later that day, he returned with three pumpkins, which he unloaded by the door.

The sky was gray, with a faint texture in the clouds to the west. A few of the mountaintops were cloaked in weather, gathering snow but remaining dark at lower elevations. The wind gusted occasionally, causing a strange buffeting around the truck's wing mirrors. The gusts weren't quite strong enough to make the truck swerve.

Thorsen looked in the rearview mirror and checked his load: a half-dozen pumpkins that weebled in the truck bed as he cornered. The starkness of the orange against the white truck bed made Thorsen think of fire. He pulled up to the Wizenbergs' and sat in the cab, surveying the property. The house was still standing, and very little of the ground seemed to have washed away in subsequent rains. The squat levee of sandbags appeared to be holding, hunkering down in the easternmost corner of the yard.

There were no lights on in the Wizenberg house. The garage door was open, but there were no cars inside. Thorsen zipped up his jacket and chose two pumpkins from the back of the truck and hauled them up to the front door and left them there.

When he got home, the bed of his truck was empty, and as he came around the hedgerow, he saw his daughter Lilly's car parked alongside the house. Lights were on in the kitchen. Thorsen threw the truck into reverse and backed out onto the road. He looked at his watch as he drove off, wondering if he might not just park somewhere in the sagebrush on the back forty and wait for her to get tired of waiting.

Late-afternoon light crested the trees on the eastern perimeter of Thorsen's property as he stooped in his wife's garden forking mulch from a cart onto the soil of the raised beds. He cut the remnants of old beanstalks down from their stringers and made sure the rabbit wire was fastened down and firmly buried. In the flower garden, he dug up bulbs and packed them in sand and newspaper, then tied them in old burlap sacks and carried them into the barn. Three ingots of light broke through the south wall of the barn just under the gable, and they hung there in the dust, like daggers marking the seasons. Thorsen watched the bars fill with shadow on the north wall of the barn. In a matter of minutes they had darkened and disappeared, and a single bird flew into the barn and swooped up to its nest in the rafters.

Outside a raven croaked. Thorsen watched its shadow sail across the ground outside the barn door. Then a cloud passed across the sun and took everything back to gray. A pair of Lila's gloves lay on a beam by the door. Thorsen picked them up and held them in his hand. She had torn out the palm of the left one; the right was fine. He touched the empty fingers of the gloves and thought for a moment about how it's possible for a pair of garden gloves to outlast a person.

The sun crested the roof of the barn, and light spilled through the uncurtained portion of the kitchen window and over the carcass of an IBM Selectric typewriter. Thorsen was hunched over it, a small can of compressed air in one hand, a rag and a can of WD-40 in the other. He poked the thin straw of the compressed-air nozzle down into the body of the machine. A hiss filled the room, and dust danced into the beam of light. Thorsen wiggled one of the spring-loaded mechanisms and then tested a key. The ball spun suddenly and struck the paper, leaving behind another "k." Thorsen wiped down a few smaller parts of the machine and then hit the "k" key over and over until he was satisfied. He turned the power off, then on again, listened to the hum of the machine, then typed the name *Enoch* four or five times. He slipped the case back over the guts of the machine, took it into his lap, and began securing the screws into the bottom.

After he washed his hands, Thorsen rubbed the typewriter down with a dust cloth and set it in a cardboard box lined with newspaper, then he took the box out to the truck and set it in back. He paused at the truck, his forearms resting on the lip of the bed, the front of his thighs pressed against the cold metal.

. . .

Upstairs, in the spare bedroom on the north end of the house, Thorsen positioned himself with his legs spread, and he jammed a pry bar underneath one edge of the window molding and yanked it, nails shrieking, from the wall. He worked around the window that way until it had been completely stripped and the window hung obscenely in the scarred wall, tufts of old yellow insulation feeding on the light. Thorsen wrote precise measurements of the window dimensions on a piece of a cereal box with a stubby, knife-sharpened pencil and then carefully drew the profile of the molding that ran around the rest of the room. After he checked his figures, Thorsen opened the window and tossed the molding out onto the ground below. Then he closed the window again and twisted the lock.

He left for Provo in the morning with the typewriter and more of the pumpkins in back, everything covered in a plastic tarp that was weighed down at intervals by a variety of rocks and small, seemingly defunct metal parts, such as pipe couplings and transaxle bushings. Highways 89 and 6 were more or less empty, and he saw traffic only as he came into Spanish Fork Canyon and joined up with the interstate.

He drove straight to Lilly's, but no one was there, so he left the typewriter and the pumpkins in the garage with a note that said, *I thought this might help with your family history project.* He signed it from *Dad.*

From there he went to the lumberyard and sat in the parking

lot reworking the rough sketch of the spare bedroom window on the piece of cereal box. He dozed a little as he was working, the sun warming the space inside the cab. Thorsen's face was drawn, the skin pale, his whiskers thick and white along his chin. They didn't have a match for the millwork he requested, so he drove to two more places before he could find something that would pass.

On the way home, he stopped at the Dairy Queen in Mount Pleasant for a cheeseburger. Although he bought his food inside, he ate it in the truck with the radio off. When he had finished, he fell asleep against a balled-up jacket stuffed between his head and the window. One of the girls from the restaurant knocked on the window, waking him. She said something, asked if he was all right, but Thorsen just started the truck and drove home.

Although outside the barn, Enoch hung his head across the small gate and watched. As Thorsen mucked out the stall, he took note of the straining muscles in his back, the toughness in his skin. He turned with a loaded shovel and dumped it into the wheelbarrow and stared at the horse, its black eye slick and reflecting the clean square of light from the open window above the hayloft. Enoch adjusted his weight and exhaled sharply.

Thorsen rested against the shaft of the shovel. It was still early and cold, but the weather hadn't turned completely. He'd be able to work in shirtsleeves in the afternoon, but once the sun crossed behind the mountains, the whole valley would turn cold. Such a change marked out the day into clear zones: a beginning, middle, and end—each one only leaning against the next, not blending. The change was always sudden, like coming out of a tunnel, or going in. It always caught Thorsen off guard, and in a way, he liked the surprise. It took the edge off the monotony, made it seem like something was actually shifting gears. Heading into winter was more decisive than coming out. Thorsen didn't know why. It just was.

Enoch lifted his head and turned slowly toward the pasture and walked down the hill until he was gone. Thorsen shook his head, as if to clear it, and went back to work.

He hauled himself out of bed. It was five-thirty and pitch black—the clocks had fallen back a week before. He stood in the window and watched Orion and his hounds set behind the mountains, then he showered and dressed himself and sat in a rocking chair reading, his heavy finger following the type and turning the thin pages, one after the other, until the small alarm clock on the wall read six o'clock and the sky began to halo the mountains, at which point he shut the book and set it on the floor next to the rocker and rose.

He crossed the room and took hold of the bedclothes and tore them off, wadding them into a ball, which he carried down the stairs to the mudroom and separated into piles. He started with the sheets, and while they were in the washing machine, he folded the blankets and then went to the kitchen and made himself some breakfast. As he ate, the sheets went through their cycle. Thorsen listened to each phase, making a mental list of things he would do that day. During the second rinse, he remembered Noreen Hafen's car and how she had said she needed an oil change.

Her husband used to take care of those things, but since his death, she hadn't bothered, hadn't really known that such things needed looking after. They were always just done.

She'd been seeing more of her husband in dreams lately. He'd come to her while she was in the temple or in the kitchen, and Noreen said he would ravish her. It embarrassed Thorsen to hear her talk like that, but he knew there was no one else she could tell. She tried her bishop, but he thought she should see a doctor. His wife, the bishop said, had been a little "nervous" when their son passed away, and a doctor in Mount Pleasant had given her some pills, which took the edge off. Noreen politely told the man that she didn't want to stop meeting her husband. She wanted him to come more often, and she wouldn't mind dying at all if it meant she could be with him. The bishop told her that plenty of people made fine use of their twilight years and asked if she had considered some kind of church service.

Thorsen knew that Noreen just needed to be listened to, so he did. He also made sure that the gas to her furnace was turned on, that her pipes didn't freeze, and that she had enough cut wood and kindling.

Later, Thorsen pulled up in front of Noreen Hafen's house and switched off the ignition. As he sat there, gathering himself together, the curtains in Noreen's front window parted slightly and then fell back into place. A few seconds later the front door opened, and Noreen beckoned Thorsen with her small and withered hand. Thorsen got out of the truck and smiled at her. She told Thorsen that she was sorry for not thinking about the oil and radiator earlier. Thorsen said not to worry about it, he was just going to take it down to his friend Ernest Passey, who knew it was coming.

Noreen said, "Bless your heart," and Thorsen just nodded.

"Getting old's not so bad, Jens," she said, not really noticing that Thorsen himself was only a dozen or so years younger. "I don't think you'll mind it at all."

Thorsen nodded again and asked for the key. Noreen looked down and turned over her hand; a single key lay there in the folds. Thorsen held out his hand, and Noreen tipped hers so that the key slid into it. "How's Lila, Jens? She was going to bring me some snap peas, but I haven't seen her."

Thorsen let his breath rise and fall. "She's passed on, Noreen."

"Nonsense," she said. "You tell her to come by and bring those peas."

"Noreen," Thorsen said, but he thought better of arguing with her. "I'll bring the car by when Passey's finished with it."

"You're very kind to an old woman, Jens."

Thorsen dropped Noreen's Buick off at Passey's shop. Passey was out testing a car, and the Leavitt kid was holding down the fort. "Tell Passey I've got Sister Hafen's car here—she needs a flush and an oil change."

"He'll be right back," the kid said.

"I'll be down at the IGA. It's okay. He'll know what to do. It's a regular deal."

Thorsen walked down Main Street to the corner and went in the front doors of the store. He yanked a grocery cart loose and headed inside. The light was pale and flickering, casting strange shadows on the produce. He unspooled a half-dozen plastic bags and loaded them with apples and carrots. He lowered a bag of Idaho russets onto the bottom shelf of the cart and set a bag of yellow onions in the basket. He bought sugar and flour and navy beans. Not much else he'd need. He chose some sports drink and saltines and threw in some tins of sardines and a few cans of tuna fish. On the way to the front, he paused in the candy aisle and bought two one-pound Hershey bars.

The kid manning the till was thin and acne-encrusted. His hair was orange like an Irish setter's, and it looked to Thorsen like he had caused it to be that way. He slouched as he slid the items across the glass plate of the price scanner, each pass seeming more of a burden than the last. "What kind of apples are these?" the kid asked.

"It's on the sticker," Thorsen said, and the kid flashed him a dirty look. "I don't know," Thorsen said. "They might be road apples." The kid grimaced and then entered a code, which turned up pomegranates. Thorsen didn't correct him. The mistake cost him a dollar-fifty.

As the kid bagged the groceries, Thorsen peeled a twenty-dollar bill off his roll and set it on the counter. The kid made change and then slumped against the back wall of his register area. "Have a nice day," he said.

"Right," Thorsen said, and he wheeled the cart outside. He took the cart back down to Passey's, the wheels skittering along the pavement. He knew that he looked like a homeless person, and he did not care. When he came round the corner and into the open space at the front of Passey's garage, Thorsen saw that Noreen's car was on the lift. The Leavitt kid was draining the oil, and Passey was on the phone, chewing out some parts distributor.

Thorsen waved and Passey waved back, putting the receiver against his chest. "Chip's on the oil change. We put the Quaker State in there. Thirty weight." Thorsen nodded, and Passey put the phone back to his ear. "No, I didn't order the joints, I ordered the boots," he said. "And even if I did, you send me joints and no boots, I still got zip."

Thorsen took Noreen her car, transferred the groceries to his truck, and knocked on the door. There was no answer, so he let himself in. Noreen was asleep in her recliner, her mouth open, a thin rasping snore filling the room. He left a note and the key on the dining-room table and drove home.

After unloading the groceries, Thorsen took a casserole out of the refrigerator and ate what was left directly from the dish with a fork. When he was finished, he carefully washed out the dish with soap and a sponge, being careful not to scrub off the masking tape with the name *Roland* written on it in black marker. Once the dish was clean, Thorsen rinsed it and dried it and took it to the mudroom and set it in a cardboard box full of similar dishes and plates. There must have been twenty-five in all, each one clean with a name on it somewhere in black marker.

Chapter Eleven

Thorsen shut off his truck and sat behind the wheel, listening to the engine tick. A sparse snow fell vertically through the morning light, coating the cars and trucks clustered together in the merchant's lot behind Nickerson's Vacuum Repair. The sky above the snow and the roofs of the Main Street shops was iron gray, snipping the distance, causing the whole valley to feel spaceless. Fall had slipped away, and Thanksgiving was not far off. Thorsen made the observation that time had never simply slipped before. This lost time was a slow, percussive revelation that knotted his stomach.

Sudden movement in the rearview mirror interrupted his thoughts, but when he glanced up, he saw nothing but the door to Stucki's shop slowly swinging closed. *Maybe I'll try this in another week*, he thought. He wanted folks in town to forget a little. Their consolations were exhausting him. Surely there must be some other charity case in this county. It had come to a point where he wanted people to just nod and get off the eggshells.

After a stretch, Thorsen got out of the truck and crossed the street. He paused briefly at the door, committed but still considering his move. Then Stucki saw him through the glass and waved at him with the remote. Thorsen pulled open the door. "Thorsen," Stucki called, his voice cracking a little as he spoke. "Been a while."

"Well ..." Thorsen started to say, but he stopped to hitch up his pants. "Yeah, it has," he said, then he noticed Passey and Angie sitting together at a small table in the nook just past the television. She was massaging his left hand, and his right hand was soaking in a small dish. His wedding ring sat on the near edge of the table. When Passey heard Thorsen's voice, he snatched up both his hands.

"Morning, ladies," Thorsen said.

Passey groped around for a towel and draped it across the tight array of scissors, files, and cuticle tools. "How's it going?" Passey asked, his face pinched.

Thorsen glanced villainously at Stucki, who shook his head and shrugged. Angie pulled the towel off her tools and told Passey to put his hands back where they were. "Go ahead, Ernest. Show him what you've got."

"Stucki, you gonna do makeovers now?" Thorsen asked.

"Wasn't my idea. As a matter of fact, wasn't Angie's either," Stucki said. "Dick Lovell came in here last week, said his hands had toughened up some since he stopped working in the temple."

"He said his wife wouldn't let him touch her," Angie interjected. "Ernest's daughter is getting married, isn't that right?" Passey nodded. "I think it's sweet," she said as Passey hung his head. Angie went back to working the cuticles with a slender steel tool. "All that working with cars has really taken its toll. That hand cleaner really dries out your skin. That's why they're cracking all the time," she said while she worked. "A father should have soft hands."

Thorsen took the empty chair next to Stucki and watched along with him. "What's on?" Thorsen asked.

"A thing on the Hope Diamond," Stucki said.

"Never heard of it," Thorsen said.

"It's cursed. Some feller stole it out of a statue in India."

"Pissed the Hindus off?"

"Looks like," Stucki said.

"Got Marie Antoinette killed, then some actress got hold of it. She went off the deep end. They have it in some museum now," Angie said.

"Marie who?" Thorsen asked.

"That French woman. The one that got her head chopped off," Angie said.

"Which one?"

"The queen—husband lost his too," Passey said.

"Usually it's one *or* the other," Angie said.

"Not this time," Stucki said.

"Hope Diamond, huh?" Thorsen said.

"Yep."

"Why don't you just switch over to the shopping channel, Sister Stucki?"

Stucki waved Thorsen off. "It's pretty interesting how that thing got around."

"Anything else on?"

"Don't know."

"*She Wore a Yellow Ribbon* is supposed to be on thirty-five," Passey interjected, Angie now working on his other hand.

"*Yellow Ribbon?* That's John Wayne, right?" Angie asked.

"It's that one where he's supposed to retire and he rescues the rear guard before midnight so they can't court-martial him," Passey said.

"Let's change it, Stook," Thorsen asked.

Stucki slipped the remote down behind his leg and folded his arms.

"Yeah, Stucki," Passey said. "Switch it over."

"You guys sound like you're fourteen years old," Angie said. "It's Stucki's TV."

Passey and Thorsen burst into laughter, Passey throwing his arm up over his face and Thorsen gripping both armrests. Stucki shook his head and said, "Here we go on this one again."

"What's so funny," Angie asked.

"You going to tell her, Stook," Thorsen said, "or is it up to one of us?"

"You're going to ruin my reputation."

"Now you *have* to tell me," Angie said, "or I'm going to take pictures of Ernest getting his cuticles softened, and I'll put them on the Internet."

Stucki started scowling, and Passey was beginning to choke.

"Ernest," Angie said, jamming her tool into the quick of Passey's index finger.

"So, back in the day, Stucki was barbering with Bill Chamberlain in a shop over on Main Street next to the Dairy Maid," Passey said.

"Bill Chamberlain the polygamist?"

"The very same, except he was running at only twenty-five percent capacity," Thorsen interjected.

"Stucki had his shop down there, and Bill rode shotgun. That must have been ten, fifteen years back, wasn't it, Stucki?"

Stucki waved them away.

"It was a slow day. I dropped by with my lunch and sat with them two, watching some old *Rockford Files* episode or something. It was about some murder at a beauty pageant. The whole screen was full of bathing suits and not much else. Old Bill was up on the edge of his seat like a kid at Christmas. We were all kind of caught up in it. Bill had brought in that set maybe a couple of weeks before, brand new and straight out of the box. He set it up and paid for the cable. Before that we pretty much just listened to the radio. Stucki had an old short wave, or sometimes he had a CB scanner, but old Bill had designs, and it was his treat.

"So there we were watching these women, and Stucki here cracks wise about being polygamist himself if they all were gonna look like that. Old Bill, he just shook his head and told us there was no joy in it. Just then one of old Bill's wives shows up with a stroller for twins, a red-haired curly-headed baby in the one seat and a black-haired one the same age in the other. Neither one of them looked a whit like Bill. She took one look at the screen full of bathing suits, and she almost knocked Bill's ear off with a clipboard she was carrying.

"Her mouth filled up with all kinds of severe talk. She told him he's a lying no-good so and so and then laid into him again with those two little half-brothers squeezing some kind of chocolate paste between their fingers.

"Turns out a couple weeks before old Bill had come into one of their houses with a pistol just like Elvis Presley, and he shot out the TV. The room was full of kids and they were watching *Snow White* or some such thing, and old Bill said there's no way seven men, dwarfs or not, would cow down to one woman. Anyways Bill forbade any TV at all and said he had more than enough ammo to see to the problem.

"Well, Bill's old lady asks him whose TV it was anyway, and wasn't it new? Bill said it was Stucki's and he was just watching it until a customer came in. Couldn't really ask Stucki to turn it off, seeing it was his shop. She just stared him down and asked for some money. Once he gave it to her, she asked Stucki how he liked the TV. He said he liked it just fine. It was a good picture, and the remote had big buttons. She grilled him so long over that TV a blind man could have seen what was going down.

"When Bill struck out on his own, he had to leave the set where it was."

"So you stole this TV set off a polygamist?" Angie asked.

"Stole is a harsh word," Stucki answered.

"Well, it's not yours, is it?"

"He hasn't picked it up . . . yet."

"But if Bill does come get it, he's going to have to put it out of its misery," Thorsen said.

"I'm worried that fella will end up with a bullet in the pan," Stucki said. "I don't think those women cotton to being swindled."

"At this point, *you* might end up shot—you go out there," Passey pointed out.

"True," Stucki said. "They aren't afraid of lawlessness."

"You people are ridiculous," Angie said.

"Hey, you've got to respect your elders," Thorsen told her. Angie swung a look at Thorsen like the boom of a crane, staring from under her brow until Thorsen smiled. "We don't deserve respect, we just demand it," Thorsen said, looking around the shop. "Do whatever you want."

"Now, can we switch it over to the Duke?" Passey asked.

"Yeah, your Hope Diamond thing is just about over," Thorsen pointed out.

Stucki handed the remote to Thorsen across the gap between chairs. "I just don't care anymore," Stucki said. Thorsen asked what channel and switched it over. John Wayne had just mounted up and was leading a party through Monument Valley, the Mittens in the background, clear as the American flag.

Stucki sighed, his head trembling slightly, his hands motionless where they were perched on the arms of the barber's chair. Thorsen watched with enough pity to have upset Stucki if he had been aware of it, but Stucki's eyes were fixed on the television, oblivious to everything else in the shop. Angie and Passey had resumed the manicure, her voice softly asking where their reception was going to be and if he liked the boy. The reception would be in the church hall, and Passey didn't think all that much of the boy. He was too thin and his hands were soft. He kept everything in a leather-bound planner that he was constantly zipping and unzipping. Angie asked Passey if there was anything he liked about the guy, and he told her that he seemed to be able to come up with money. "I don't suppose that'll do her any harm," he said.

"Oh, jeez," Angie said suddenly. "Can you hang on a minute, Ernest?" she asked and then pushed away from the table and made a beeline for the bathroom. The men all looked at one another bewildered, then faintly, they heard Angie retching. After a few seconds filled with the TV's sound of Henry rifles and horses, the toilet flushed and the sink ran. Thorsen looked at his wristwatch and noted the time: ten-thirteen. Angie came back out and returned to the manicure. Her face was drawn and her lips thin and compressed. She apologized to Passey, who told her not to worry. "Hey, when nature calls," he said, shrugging. "I had a house full of girls. It's nothing new to me."

Angie stared at him hard, taking his hand carefully. She trimmed and filed his nails in silence, the sound of the Western filling the room: hooves, gunfire, a speech to the troops. When she was done, Passey looked at his nails proudly. "You aren't going back to work with those hands," she chided.

"No, I'm off to get some extra chairs from the church building," he said. "Then we have to get the cake."

"An hour under the hood and this'll be ruined. You know that, right?" Angie scolded. Passey nodded and handed her a twenty. "I'll get your change," she said.

"Aw, keep it," he said, sticking his wallet back into the bib pocket of his overalls. "I got to go. You take care of things, fellas," he said as he lumbered past them. "See you at the wedding."

"We'll be there," Stucki said.

"Might even dress up for it," Thorsen said.

"Don't go to any trouble."

"It's just church clothes," Thorsen said, grinning. Once Passey was gone, Thorsen shifted his weight and told Angie that he was impressed. "Looks like good business," he said, cocking his head toward Angie. Stucki ignored him. "You might could start giving permanents," Thorsen said, stroking his pate. "I'd pay fifty dollars to get my curls back."

Stucki lifted the remote and switched back to the Hope Diamond. Some curator at the Smithsonian was talking about having it there in Washington D.C. He said that he and the other curators wondered if the curse was still on it. "Sure," the man said, "if someone's car won't start or if we get a bomb threat, someone always blames the curse. But, I mean, if you believed in curses, the whole world would turn upside-down."

"You believe in curses, Stook?" Thorsen asked.

Stucki shrugged.

"I do," Angie said, cleaning up the nail table. She let her eyes drift up toward the ceiling for a moment, then she nodded silently. "If there are blessings in this world, there have to be curses, too." Stucki's eyes shot toward Angie, then ricocheted back to the television. "I have no trouble with curses, Brother Thorsen. No trouble at all."

"Stook?"

Stucki lifted his eyebrows and exhaled. "I suppose there's at least something like a curse out there. Maybe it's the way dark means having no lights or dry means not being wet. I'm not all that objective about the subject, what with these." Stucki lifted his hands like Charleton Heston, and they began to tremble.

"You want me to get behind you and hold them things up?" Thorsen asked.

Stucki chuckled. "I must look like some old Joshua tree blowing in the wind."

"What about you, Brother Thorsen?" Angie asked. She looked at him askance, her eyes narrowing and her head drifting slightly from side to side.

"Me?"

"Yeah, you think people can get cursed?"

"I think the ground can get that way pretty quick—water dries up or some bug gets into the trees. That gets to feeling like a curse. I might be with old Stook on this one. I don't think God takes after people. It seems like most people just fall asleep at the wheel and expect the old guy to wake them up, and when he doesn't, they call it being cursed."

"Not me. I think God's got a mean streak," she said.

Despite the droning of the television narrator, silence filled the room like concrete. Stucki worked his lips and blinked. Thorsen scratched the back of his head three or four times and then scrubbed a finger under his nose. The narrator spoke on, and then he was interrupted by a commercial for some disposable dust mop. Stucki reached out with the remote and switched off the set. Angie heaped her tools and lotions into a small plastic basket and then swabbed off the table with a towel. Thorsen said something to Stucki about the snow pack, and Stucki said something about another year like last one.

"You know it's not as simple as you guys think," she said, her head lowered.

"No, young lady, it's not," Stucki said flatly. "Nothing in this world is simple, not even the breeze."

Angie stopped and looked at her hands. "I know," she said, "but people around here have this kind of algebra for getting to heaven. Tithing plus no R-rated movies over endure-to-the-end equals going to live with Heavenly Father. I get sick of it, really sick of it . . ." Her eyes started welling up, and she wiped the tears with the sleeves of her shirt. "I'm sorry. I don't know why I'm doing this. I mean, I don't do this kind of thing normally. Crap."

Thorsen and Stucki shrugged in unison and then looked at one another, astonished.

"I'm an idiot. Ignore me," Angie said.

"Sure," Thorsen said.

"Okay," said Stucki.

"I'm starving. I'm going to get something to eat. Is that okay, Stucki?"

"I guess," he said. "We're not really doing land-office business in here this morning."

Angie sniffed. "Thanks. I'll be right back. Just ignore me. I'm an idiot."

"We've spent most of our lives around women, Angie," Thorsen said. "We're used to being confused by them."

"And ignoring them," Stucki added, chuckling.

As soon as the door had closed completely, Thorsen turned to Stucki and said, "That girl is pregnant, isn't she."

"I kinda sensed she was," Stucki said.

"It's going to hit the fan around here, isn't it?"

"I guess so," Stucki said, switching on the television.

"We got to have that thing playing?"

"*Gunsmoke*'s on at ten-thirty," Stucki said, but he still hit the mute button.

"So do you think her parents know?"

Stucki shook his head. "Depends on if they want to or not."

Thorsen glowered.

"Well, I suppose they don't know, then. You sound like you're almost sorry for Bunker."

"It serves him right," Thorsen said, and Stucki raised one eyebrow. "I mean, it's always the bishop's daughter, isn't it?"

"You gotta walk a line."

"You try to lord over them, and they just run off," Thorsen said.

"Worse than wild horses," Stucki said.

"What do you know about wild horses, Stook?"

"I know they're likely to run off just as quick as anything else."

"What are you going to do?" Thorsen asked.

"I'll have to run the ad again, I guess."

"Not that, you ignoramus. What are you going to do to help that kid? This town's going to run her down and tear her to pieces. Bunker's going to say you were in on it."

"He can say what he wants. I can't really fire her for being pregnant, even if I don't like it."

"You think that's going to stop that S.O.B. that calls himself her father?"

"Can't say."

"But what do you guess?"

"I figure I don't want to be around when that bomb hits."

Chapter Twelve

Thanksgiving came and went without much fanfare. Thorsen
went to Lilly's house for the meal. Everyone was careful around
him, like they'd been coached, and Thorsen despised it. The
grandkids showed him their toys and told him about school, but
they didn't climb on him. They said "yes, sir" and "no, sir." When
Thorsen asked Lilly's husband, Hunter, about his zombie children,
Hunter said they'd all been drinking cough syrup. Thorsen said,
"Just so long as they're not coddling me."

Thorsen headed home the next morning and spent the day
making rounds. He chatted with Noreen Hafen, whose family
had come up from Arizona. As Thorsen and Noreen stood talking in the entryway, the Hafen kids tried to supervise a sand-
wich-making project. Noreen was oblivious to the chaos. She
kept touching Thorsen on the shoulder of his jacket, telling him
that she was glad he came by, that he was the only one who didn't
treat her like a charity case, her eyes darting into the kitchen and
then back at Thorsen.

"Your bishop still trying to drug the joy out of you, Noreen?" Thorsen asked, touching her lightly on the arm.

She smiled gracefully and blushed a little. "No, Jens. He's given up on that."

"So, your husband's still coming by?"

"Not so much lately. Owen says the Lord has work for him." Then she leaned in closer and whispered, "He mostly comes on Sunday afternoons when his meetings are over."

"You tell him hello for me, will you."

"Not much time for chitchat anymore," she said, winking, "but I'll try to remember."

"Owen's a good man, Noreen."

"Yes, he is. You tell that Lila hello. It's been ages since I've seen her."

"I'll tell her. She'll be glad you asked," Thorsen said, raising his voice back up to a normal conversational level. One of Noreen's sons poked his head out of the kitchen and told them there was plenty of chow left. Noreen ignored him. Thorsen nodded and waved. "Is there anything you need, or are these sons of yours making sure you're okay?"

"No, Jens. They've been very kind to me."

"Be sure to call, okay?"

"I will."

From there Thorsen drove over to the Ramkes and took out a bunch of trash and fed the animals. Karl was asleep. Phyllis had one cigarette in an ashtray and another in her left hand.

"Your man from out of town came by," she said. "Thought he was a bill collector."

"Don't know what you're talking about," Thorsen said.

"Dr. Kevorkian."

"It's Wizenberg."

"Don't matter to me. Quit sending him by."

"He drinks coffee on Sunday. Thought you'd enjoy the company," Thorsen said.

"I know what you're trying to do. I just ain't ready for that."

Thorsen tried to change the subject by asking about Thanksgiving.

"Thanksgiving," she sighed, immediately dragging deeply, the smoke circling her head in a white haze as she exhaled, "is a joke—worse than Christmas. Built on a bald-faced lie. God didn't bail those pilgrims out. It was the Indians taught them about planting fish with the corn, not some angel. Without those Indians, the whole Mayflower business would have been mass suicide—all those Puritans starving in the cold, surrounded by witches. Whole thing would have been over before it started. And how did those English sons-a-bitches thank them? Small pox. Hell of a thing to be thankful for, don't you think? Those Indians would be well within their rights to scalp every last one of us."

"Sounds like you've studied up on it," Thorsen said.

"As long as I got to pay for public television, I might as well watch it."

"You got a point."

Phyllis turned to stub out her cigarette and pick up the other one. "Karl's bird's nest is coming back. You think you might be able to drag that skinny fella back out here and do a number on him again?"

"Stucki? Sure. I can get him or the Bunker girl. She's been working for Stucki lately."

"Perfect! Go on ahead and bring her out. The sight of her'll get Karl pole-vaulting around the room. Well, at least it'll keep him off the Internet."

"Call me when he's up to it. I'll get somebody out here."

When Thorsen got into his truck, Phyllis was still watching him from the porch, stubbing her cigarette against the siding.

From the Ramkes' place, Thorsen drove to Roy and Leora Meeks' house. They lived on the opposite side of town, just past the body shop. An old Toyota pickup truck rested on four old rusty rims that had been flipped on their sides and set under the springs. The hood was missing, but the engine was still there, mostly in one piece. A sign in the windshield read: *100 bucks cash, as is. You tow it.*

Thorsen knocked at the door, and a tired woman answered. "Leora," Thorsen said. "Just came by to chat. Roy around?"

"He's out back. Come on in." She eased open the screen door, and Thorsen slipped in. "Watch the cats," Leora said. Thorsen moved into the living room, and Leora switched off the television as she passed it, calling for the kids to come down as she headed toward the back door. "Honey, Jens Thorsen's here. Why don't you take a break and come inside." On the way back into the living room, she stopped again to yell at the kids, then she apologized. "You want something to drink?" she asked.

"No, thank you. I don't want to be any trouble."

"It's no trouble. We got water, grape juice, some of that orange punch the kids like."

"Well, just some water, I guess. And I don't need any ice."

"Suit yourself."

Thorsen took a seat on the rocking chair facing the window. He could hear doors slam and the sound of feet and Leora calling again to the children. The screen door slapped shut, and then the regular door closed behind it. "Honey, could you take this in to Jens," she said. Then the heavy clomping of Roy's boots filled the space. "Here's your water," he said in a deep voice. Thorsen tried to get up, but the water was already in his hand.

"Keep your seat. The Meeks family isn't fancy." Roy sat down deeply in a corduroy recliner, his hands like a pair of greasy tools perched on the armrests. "Those girls are half-naked. Leora's up there making them presentable. Shouldn't be too long."

"How you like working for yourself?" Thorsen asked.

Roy nodded. "It's more work, but I like the boss." Roy sucked his teeth and looked at his watch. Thorsen drank some of his water and noticed a number of small black flecks in it. He set the glass on the side table.

"How's Deloy?" Thorsen asked.

"Not great. He got in some kind of fight. We haven't been to see him in a couple of weeks."

"He in solitary?"

"Looks like."

"He didn't kill anyone, did he?"

"No," Roy said, exhaling. "I don't think it got that bad."

"They've got to stake out their territory in there," Thorsen said, and Roy nodded. "But I don't know anything about it, really, just what I've seen on the TV."

"I think we'll be lucky to get him back in any kind of good shape."

"Any breaks on the case?"

Roy shook his head. "Far as we can tell, they've got him fair and square on the weapons charge."

"So, even though he didn't actually pull the trigger—"

"Afraid so. He knew what those kids were planning, and he gave the pistol to them anyway. Don't suppose it's right to try and help him worm out of his responsibilities."

"Hell, Roy. You want me to go down there? Talk to him?"

Roy turned and looked out the window, pondering the offer. Thorsen reached for the glass of water while he was waiting, then he remembered the flecks. "Sure," Roy said. "Might do him some good. He comes out of solitary right before Christmas."

Just then Leora came into the room, ushering her daughters Holly and Jamie, both with their hair up in towels. Their fingernails and toenails were painted bright blue, and Holly, the older of the two, was wearing bright red lipstick. "Have a seat, girls," their father said.

"I don't have any kind of message or anything," Thorsen said. "Just came by to see how you all were doing." The girls looked sullen and depressed. Leora glanced at Roy and then back at the girls. Thorsen watched the exchange, and adjusted himself slightly in his chair. It hadn't occurred to him that they wanted a pep talk. He would have shot anyone who came out to visit him with designs on lifting his spirits.

"Oh," said Roy. "Normally when church folks come over, they've got one of the magazines and some kind of message. We've been kind of hoping someone might come by and get our mind off some things."

Thorsen thought about that for a minute and said, "You know, when Lila passed on, I pretty much slipped out of myself." He rubbed his thumb and forefinger together and went on. "A man can live his whole life knowing that one day, unless he's lucky, he's going to end up cooking dinner, cleaning the bathroom, sitting in church, driving to town all by himself. He can know it's going to happen, but one day out of the blue, it does. It catches him completely off guard."

Thorsen's voice quickened slightly, and he leaned forward, his eyes flickering around the room. "You think about all this enduring-to-the-end garbage they throw at you at church—even the kids talk about how you've got to be like the pioneers and endure. That's fine, I guess, but nobody talks about what it *takes* to endure like that. Everyone who gets behind a pulpit thinks they can just talk about the handcart companies for fifteen minutes and feed the flock. Well, I don't know anything about the handcart companies. What I'm trying to say is that the church is full of jackasses with good hearts, but they won't know your pain because they never went through it, and they don't want to. That's why they turn to the past—because it's over with. It's the future that scares the hell out of them." Thorsen paused to catch his breath. The Meekses looked around at each other, dumbfounded.

"You folks love your religion and try to do right by it," Thorsen continued. "And still you end up in the kind of fix nobody can really talk about. There's no bishop out there who knows what you people have to deal with every day, what you girls have to deal with when you go to school. Every day you've got to make it up as you go along. Probably doesn't seem like there's any good answers anywhere, and it's easy to lose your way. I understand that." Thorsen stopped and drew a deep breath, then cleared his throat. "When my wife passed, I looked to the scriptures and found zip, nothing. When someone dies in the scriptures, people tear their clothes and then the chapter ends and a hundred and fifty years have passed.

"So what do you do with it all? Hell, I don't know. You keep going. You just keep going."

When Thorsen finished, he sat up straight again, squinted apologetically, then noticed that Leora was crying and Roy was gripping his mouth and chin. The girls were mute, their eyes downcast. One of the cats crossed under the blades of the rocking chair and slithered dryly around Thorsen's right leg and crossed to the couch.

"When you go down to Gunnison," Roy said, pausing for a second to make sure Leora wasn't going to stop him; she nodded. "When you see Deloy, I want you to tell him what you just told us. Would you do that?"

Thorsen shrugged.

"He needs to hear that, from you." Roy's eyes stayed briefly with his wife before settling back with Thorsen. "Promise me you'll tell him."

"I got carried away," Thorsen said, embarrassed. "I'm sorry."

"Promise me," Roy said, leaning forward. His voice was tense. "He won't listen to us. We've been over that ground too much. We need somebody else who will go down there."

Thorsen nodded. "I can do that. Tell me when I need to go."

• • •

He sat in his truck with the engine on and the heater running for five full minutes before he drove off. He felt like a crazy old man, ranting in there, and they were just making polite with him. The streets were clear, and Thorsen was unsure of where he would go. He kept turning and stopping and driving until he found himself near the Wizenbergs' house. The garage door was down, and a few newspapers in their yellow plastic sacks littered the front porch and driveway. He took stock of the yard and saw that everything seemed fine, though nothing had really had the chance to grow back in. But the storm channels had held. The real test would be with the spring runoff and next summer's monsoons.

Thorsen backed out of the driveway and headed home. A quarter mile down the road, he saw two trucks parked along the side of the road. One of them was Bunker's, a magnetic sign on the door panel saying ZION SURVEYING AND EXCAVATION, the other, a new Dodge, belonged to Bill Everly. Bill stood a dozen yards away from the trucks with a small planner in a zippered case in one hand. He was chatting into a cellular phone and gesturing to the property with the planner. Bunker was nowhere to be found.

Thorsen stopped and got out of the truck. He stood around on the side of the road, looking at the property. It was the same setup as the Wizenbergs' land. The bulk of the space was low-lying. A steep rise leapt up at the back of the property, with a wash breaching it in the middle. The wash itself was full of gray debris that had been carried down and flattened against the rocks. Garbage had plastered itself against some of the larger tree branches.

Bunker came down out of the wash with a framing hammer and a bundle of eighteen-inch wooden stakes. He didn't notice Thorsen as he barged across the sage-covered ground. Bill Everly continued his pitch on the cell phone, unaware of Thorsen until he was right on him.

"What do you think you're doing?" Thorsen howled. Everly jumped a little, nearly dropping the phone. He tried to carry on his conversation, but Thorsen came at him again. "Is that another sucker on the line—don't buy it!" he hollered at Everly's phone. "It's right in a wash."

Everly glared at Thorsen and pressed the phone against his jacket. "Thorsen, get out of here." Then he spoke back into the phone. "Hold on just a minute, okay? Thorsen, I'd appreciate you getting the hell off this property."

"They ought to lock you up and throw out the key. It's highway robbery selling this land to anybody for any price. Charles Manson's the only guy deserves land like this."

"What are you talking about?"

"Anybody who's lived one year around here knows what happens in this wash come September. You can just about set your watch on it, Everly. Is that why you sell this property to people from Connecticut? Can't dupe folks who know better?"

Everly lifted the phone. "Can I call you back? Okay." Then he folded up the phone and held it in his palm. "I don't know what you're talking about, and I think you better get out of here."

Thorsen burst into laughter. Bunker looked back to see what the noise was. Thorsen pointed toward him and said, "You should watch out for that one, Billy. There's no honor among thieves."

"Why don't you get out of here before I call the cops."

"You don't have to call anybody. You two make me sick."

"Fine."

"Don't think I won't go to the county."

"Go ahead."

"I'd like to find out who you bribed."

"Get out of here, Thorsen."

"You can kiss those building permits good-bye."

Everly ignored Thorsen, opened his phone, and started dialing. Bunker appeared suddenly from behind a juniper; in one hand he carried the hammer by its head. "What are you doing here, Thorsen?" he asked.

"This land is on loan, bishop," Thorsen said, thrusting a finger skyward.

"I think you better leave," Bunker said.

"I'm fixing to. And by the way, I wouldn't stand around with your knees locked. Your life's about to take a U-turn."

"Is that a threat?"

"Nope, it's just information." Thorsen strolled back to his truck, got in, and stared at Bunker and Everly for half a minute, then he cranked on the ignition and drove off, running a roster through his head, people who would either owe Thorsen a favor or be willing to go after these two on principle. By the time the two trucks were out of sight, Thorsen had drawn up a long list.

Thorsen puttered around the house, fed the animals, cleaned Enoch's hooves, and primered the molding for the window he'd torn apart earlier in the month. Lilly called to talk, but she ended up saying over and over again that they were thinking of him, and if he ever wanted to, he could come live with them. Thorsen told her that living with him wasn't the kind of torment he'd wish on anybody, but if he were tempted to move in with any of his children, he'd spring himself on Jens Junior, if only to make him pay for his childhood.

In the evening, Thorsen read another issue of *National Geographic*. First an article on food safety—one in four people suffered a food-borne illness each year; *Listeria monocytogenes* could survive refrigeration. Then one on people trying to put vaccines into fruit. Photos of moths. A map of the Inca kingdoms. Thorsen took the map out of the magazine and spread it on the kitchen table: a painting of Machu Piccu and a time line, the Spanish coming around 1532. Thorsen read on, not really letting any of the information seep too deeply into his head. It washed over him, making him feel full and drowsy. He slept two hours with his face on the map, then he rose, drank a glass of water, and went to bed.

Church came and went, normal except for a strangely contrite look on Bunker's face. Thorsen watched him for the whole of the service. He spoke softly, and while sitting, he lowered his head into one hand, like he was thinking. Second thoughts about Everly, Thorsen wondered. On the way home, Thorsen drove past Stucki's shop. The street was empty except for Angie's car. Thorsen got out and saw that the car was full of blankets and boxes. He stooped and stared into the windows; every inch of space was stuffed full of something. He turned and saw that the shades had been drawn on the shop, something Stucki never did.

Thorsen walked up to the door and, placing his hand on the glass, peered inside. Television light flickered across the inside of the shop, but he couldn't see anything else. "I'll be hog-tied," Thorsen said. He knocked on the door, and suddenly the television went out. He paced back and forth in front of the door, alternately jamming his hands into his coat pockets and rubbing them together. After a few seconds, he knocked again. Still nothing. Thorsen knew that Stucki kept a key in a magnetic box stuck on the side of the dumpster out back. He went directly to it and got the key and came back to the front door, opened it, and saw that the shop was empty except for a soft-drink cup sitting on the floor next to the far chair. The picture tube was also glowing faintly, and as he waved his knuckles past the screen they crackled with static electricity. The cup was still cold.

Instead of digging Angie out of the back room directly, Thorsen took the remote from the top of the set, climbed into the chair, and switched on the television. He flipped through the channels until he found a nature documentary about the arctic fox. The mother and her kits were just emerging from their den. The world around them was spellbindingly white, though their coats had not yet changed. Thorsen watched that for a while, and then he switched the channels again, stopping on a bass-fishing show. Two men in a deluxe motorboat were fishing a reservoir in Texas. The fish were getting the best of them. So, he switched the channels again, this time to MTV. Some black kids were driving around in a convertible with two women in bathing suits sitting up on the trunk of the car, their high heels stabbing into the leather of the back seats. The words of the song were unintelligible. Thorsen left the television where it was. After the black kids came a band of four white kids with their faces pierced. The song was fast, and people were running around in their jockey shorts. Next came another carload of black kids being chased by a helicopter. This song was indistinguishable from the earlier one.

Thorsen eased back in Stucki's chair and waited. In a few minutes a light came on in the storeroom, and then Thorsen heard some shuffling. The song changed again, and the door opened. Angie stepped into the room in sweatpants, slippers, and a long-sleeved T-shirt. A plaid flannel sleeping bag was heaped in her arms.

"Angie, what are you doing here?" Thorsen asked, with mock surprise.

"Really, I should be asking you that question," Angie said.

"Stucki lets me come down and check up on my…my…" Thorsen gestured to the set.

"Your MTV," Angie asked. "Don't tell me you want your MTV?"

"That's right. We don't get it out at the house. So I just … you know. What about you? You getting things ready for Monday?" He winked.

Angie's lips thinned as she stared at Thorsen, who feigned interest in the television. After a moment, she crossed the room and switched on the lights. "Are you really watching that?"

"Is it bugging you?"

"Not really. It's just kind of strange, that's all."

"There's lots of pretty girls."

"Right."

"I've got to keep up."

"Keeping it real with your peeps."

"What?" Thorsen asked.

"I thought so. You're not down—you're a poseur."

"What's down, and why am I not there?"

"You said you were trying to keep up."

"Listen. You should respect your elders."

"Respect my elders' right to get busy in the hood? I'll make sure I remember. I hate to say it, but you sound like my dad."

"He likes this jungle music? I thought we had nothing in common."

"You guys were, like, separated at birth." Thorsen winced, and Angie ignored it. "You're both stubborn. You're both convinced that everyone in the world is either with you or against you. You're both anti-government, unwilling to see anything but your own way of doing things, and you both hide behind the church."

"Hey, now," Thorsen said, switching off the set. "I don't like how you're talking."

"It's true," she said. "You all are interested in the truth, unless it's bad news or criticism."

"How'd you get so you're pointing the finger at us? I seem to recall being there at your baptism, Sister Bunker. So, how do you fit into this world of lies?"

"I'm done with churches—none of my wishes ever came true."

Thorsen was about to really let her have it, but he stopped. He was caught between understanding her completely and wanting to knock her block off. She was right, but he hated how close this cut to the bone. His people often blended truth with hope, a mixture as dangerous as nitroglycerin. There was no grace in endurance. Thorsen thought of horses standing out in the weather with their backs to the wind. Not much nobility in that. *Those horses are a long way from Eden,* he mused. *Who would have thought we'd all be thrown out of the garden? They didn't do anything, and they're in the same fix as we are.*

"Nobody ever gets what they want," Thorsen said quietly. "They tell people fairy tales so folks won't go out of their skulls. But anyone who's been around knows that there's no happy endings. Best you get is a little satisfaction." When he was done talking, he noticed that Angie was starting to cry. "Here, sit down," he said.

Angie shook her head.

"Then go sit in that one," he said, gesturing to the second chair. "There's a room full of chairs, and you're in no condition to—"

"In no condition to what?" she asked.

"Never mind. Just take a seat. You're making me nervous."

Angie drifted slowly to the chair and slipped into it like a book on a shelf. She folded her arms tightly and rocked the footrest with her slippers in quick, annoying clicks. She kept at it until Thorsen looked down at her feet. "What did you mean by 'in no condition to'?" she asked. "In no condition how?"

Thorsen slipped the remote into his breast pocket and hoisted himself higher into the chair. "It's like this. Me and Stucki have been around women most of our natural lives. We've lived with them, raised them, married them off—the whole nine yards. And when one of them turns up in the family way . . . well, we're just in the habit of seeing the signs. You can tell me I'm wrong if you want—I'd love it—or you can tell me to go to hell—I'm no stranger to those words either—but I bet you a dollar I'm right."

Angie pursed her lips and stared straight ahead, her chest rising and falling with her breath. She lined her slippers up side by side on the footrest and sniffed. "So," she said.

Thorsen scratched the back of his neck with one hand and then checked his watch.

"You must think I'm an idiot for coming back here," she said.

"Well, I've got no love for your old man, so that would make the decision for me right there."

Angie laughed a little. "You guys are nuts."

"Home has a strong pull," Thorsen said. "Some kids can't get out of the house quick enough, but there's others you pretty much have to kick out. In my day, a man would strike out to seek his fortune. That's what the military is for—you got to try yourself out. But these days, the little vampires just put a trailer in your driveway and hook up to your power and water." Thorsen looked over at Angie; she was crying and doing her best not to show it. "A girl like you gets pregnant, it's got to be like the whole world is out to get you. I think the only reason men don't get pregnant is they couldn't handle it."

"I don't know if *I* can handle it."

"If it doesn't kill you, you can handle it," he said, and Angie flashed him a glare. "What I mean is, women less capable than you have been through it."

Angie chuckled.

"You've got a situation," Thorsen said, "but you're taking charge of it."

"Sort of."

"Look, you came home. You got a job. There's all kinds of people around here who can help. There's probably two tons of baby clothes for every square mile of this county. And when things get hot, you can slip down here to old Stucki's shop and let things cool off."

"No," she said, "that's not it." Her face convulsed.

"Oh, jeez," Thorsen said. "He didn't, did he? He found out, huh?"

Angie nodded.

"He threw you out."

Angie's eyes flickered.

"When?"

She looked rapidly around the shop and then drew a shallow breath. "Last night . . . he said if I wasn't going to church, I couldn't live in his house."

Thorsen exhaled sharply through his nose, a word caught in his mouth.

"That's when I told him I was pregnant. It was over at that point. He wanted to know who the father was. I told him it was some guy from California. He asked if I was going to marry him. I told him I didn't even have his phone number. He asked if he was a church member. I told him I didn't know but he probably wasn't. He asked me if the guy was a drug addict. I told him I didn't know. Then he tried to get me to confess to him. He said he was still my bishop, that he had my church records held here until I would send for them, but I never did. He got on his knees in my room and wanted me to pray with him, but I wouldn't do it. I told him it made me lightheaded to get on my knees. He said, 'How would you know it didn't sound like I had much practice.' I told him there was more than one reason for getting on your knees. He slapped my face, and I told him that begging was one of them. And then I told him I wasn't going to beg from him anymore. I threw all my stuff in the car and drove around until my tank got low. So, I came here. It's the only other key I still had."

Thorsen shook his head. "I'm surprised he didn't have you stoned."

Angie shrugged. "I don't think about it, really. It's not like he's exhibiting any new behavior. The thing that kills me is that he wouldn't let me tell my mother I was leaving. He said she was sleeping. If I wanted to go I could go, but he wouldn't let me wake her up. God knows what he told her—that I'd run off again."

"What's he thinking? You're going to run into her in town. And what's he going to do, set up a perimeter and stake out his own house? Just go back, when he's not around."

"I couldn't tell her. It's better that she thinks I just ran off. Then at least it's not her fault."

Thorsen felt a kink somewhere in his chest that he never felt with his own children. He felt as if she were sitting on the floor and he were looking down at her. Her face had gone red, and her gaze dropped to the floor. She fingered the rough edge of the zipper with her fingertips, and Thorsen noticed her torn red cuticles and the irregular bite patterns in the nails themselves. Her knuckles were large and whorled, her fingers thick like a man's but smooth. She sniffed once, sharply, and threw her head back, her red hair still veiling her face.

"You're not leaving Sanpete, are you?" he asked.

"I don't know."

"What would you do for a job?"

Angie shrugged.

"But you've got one here, of course. Stucki won't throw you out."

"But I don't have anywhere to stay."

"There's places to rent. We'll get the paper."

"There's not many. I looked. Anyway, I was trying to save money for the baby." Angie lifted her head and glanced at Thorsen. Her eyes narrowed slightly, apologetically, as if to remind Thorsen that she wasn't asking for anything. "This isn't how it's supposed to go. I know that." She bunched up the sleeping bag in her lap. "Nobody has to tell me that. Maybe I should just get in the car and go somewhere. I've got five months." She exhaled and slumped in the chair. "I don't know what I thought, coming back here."

Thorsen stood and walked the remote over to the television and set it on top.

"I'm sorry I even brought this up," she said.

"No," Thorsen said. "Don't be."

"I just don't know what I'm going to do next. I've been in worse situations than this."

"No, you haven't," Thorsen snapped, and his shortness surprised him. Angie looked offended. "This kid's going to need you stable, not living out of your car." Thorsen walked back and forth along the aisle between the barber chairs and the front wall, stroking one hand along the bald curve of the back of his head. "All right," he said once, and then went back to walking. A few seconds later, he stopped and squared himself with Angie. "You can come out and stay with me. I've got a whole house out there and just me in it. It's clean and safe and free."

Angie's face sprung wide. "I can't do that, Brother Thorsen."

"Why not? I won't make you go to church."

"Are you doing this to piss off my dad?"

"I don't know yet. I'd like to think my heart wasn't that dark."

Angie laughed. "You are the weirdest person I ever met," she said.

"Get your stuff, Sister Bunker. We got to clean this place up, or Stucki'll go straight through the roof."

Part Four: Calamity

Chapter Thirteen

Snow was light on the trees and rooftops, new coverage over the remnants of old. The sky was gray, only a thin strip of pale illumination toward the south and east. The San Pitch and Wasatch ranges were enrobed in whiteness, which sank into darker pine and junipers. Snow wasn't plentiful enough to drift, but it was cold enough to stay. A great stillness pooled in the valley, then stirred slightly, spilling without shadow across the western slope. The back of Thorsen's barn glowed slightly as thin remnants of larger clouds flushed in the eastern sky. A pair of wrens shot through the air, alighting in a tree at the far end of the pasture. As the hue of the clouds richened, a single owl disappeared through the cottonwoods.

Thorsen's hogs began to stir, nosing out of their shelter and into the open area of the pen, pissing on the hard ground in the far corner, then nosing at the trough, steam billowing from their dappled snouts. When they saw there was nothing to eat, they went back inside. Enoch peered from the barn and twitched his rump. He took some stray bits of hay into his mouth, chewed them, lifted a hoof from the ground, snorted, and looked over his shoulder. All the lights in Thorsen's house were out, and a thin coat of snow covered his truck and Angie's car. The roof was snowclad as well, along with the cottonwood on the south side of the house populated with a dozen crows. In the gathering dawn, they began squabbling like the institutionalized. As the light grew more complete and the clouds lost their color, the crows became louder and louder, some flying from the tree a ways before circling back. Those that didn't call out croaking instead mimicked the barks of dogs and babbled in frail voices that were silenced by three sharp shotgun blasts. The crows scattered, black and rustling. In the chaos, two crows fell, bouncing back and forth against the naked branches, thudding on the snow at the base of the tree. Some of the crows paused on the roof of the barn, others burrowed into the thick, dry branches of the junipers surrounding the property. Most flew on in quick dodging arcs until they could be neither seen nor heard.

Jens Thorsen stood just outside the doorway in a felt-lined canvas jacket and snowmobile boots. His bare legs rose from the boots only to disappear at the knee into his thin white undergarments. He held the shotgun in one hand, and with the other he fished a garbage bag from his jacket.

Above, the curtains in one of the dormers flew to one side, and Angie stared out at the empty tree and then down at Thorsen. Her face was a mix of sleep and confusion. Thorsen did not see her as he juggled the shotgun into the crook of his arm and opened the garbage bag awkwardly with the other hand. He kicked the birds around with the toe of his boot until their tightly curled feet turned up, then stooping, he snatched up each one by the gnarl of its toes, slid them both into the bag, and carried them over to his truck and dropped them in the bed. Angie rapped on the window, and Thorsen looked up. When he saw her, he lifted the shotgun in a genteel salute and headed into the house.

Thorsen laid the shotgun crosswise on the kitchen table. Upstairs he heard the clomping of Angie's feet heading toward the stairs. As he unzipped his coat, he realized he was not at all dressed, so he slipped into the mudroom where the washer and dryer were and found a pair of overalls.

"Brother Thorsen?" said Angie, her voice and footsteps growing louder. Thorsen leaned against the lip of the dryer and lifted his skinny legs out of the snowmobile boots and stabbed them into the legs of the overalls. "Brother Thorsen," she said again, "what was going on out there?" Thorsen was just getting to the point of fastening the bib and suspenders together when he realized his coat was still on. Angie then appeared in the kitchen, and when he could see her through the door of the mudroom, he took both suspenders in one hand and hoisted. "Is everything all right?" she asked.

"Not for the crows," he said.

"What were they doing?"

"Roosting. It was just a few at first, but then word got out and they kept coming. It can really get on your nerves."

"So you shot 'em?"

"Just a couple. Got three before Thanksgiving. Thought it might run off the rest. They must figure it's the cost of being a crow around here."

"You scared the hell out of me."

"I just figured you could use the quiet," Thorsen said. Angie's eyes drifted incredulously to the shotgun on the table. "I guess I should've thought that one through."

Angie ran one hand through her hair and yawned. She turned out one of the kitchen chairs and sat it in it. "Quoth the raven: nevermore," she said to herself.

"Say again," Thorsen said.

"Nothing, it's this poem they made us memorize in high school. Some guy sees a raven that creeps him out."

"Never read it," Thorsen said, rehoisting his overalls. He reached down and lifted the shotgun and headed down the hall. "I'll be back in a couple of minutes and whip up some breakfast. You like eggs?"

"Protein's good for the baby's brain," Angie said, stretching.

"I guess so. Protein's the one thing we got plenty of around here," Thorsen said from the hall as he climbed the stairs.

After breakfast Thorsen asked Angie if there was anything in particular she wanted for dinner. She pushed her plate away and said she was too full to think about that.

Thorsen rose, his plate in one hand and a bundle of silverware in the other. "Used to be when Lila was pregnant, she could eat like a linebacker. Never got sick. She'd just pile it on—pork chops, mashed potatoes, hamburger, zucchini, blackberry pie."

"Not me," Angie said, looking at her half-empty plate. The eggs were gone, but the hash browns and toast were still there, explored but uneaten. "Nothing sounds good to me really, except meat and milk and oatmeal."

"No blackberry pie, huh?"

"Well, I wouldn't say no if it was on the table, but it's December. Where are you going to get blackberries now?"

Thorsen set down the dishes and disappeared into the basement. He came back with a one-gallon freezer bag of blackberries and set it on the table in front of her. "What good are grandkids if you can't put them to work?"

"You're a rotten grandpa."

"The trick is to let them eat till they're sick of berries. Then the rest are yours."

"You've got it all worked out."

"Yes, ma'am." Thorsen put the bag in the freezer and cleared the plates. Angie tried to get up and help, but he wouldn't let her. "The first week you're a guest. After that you can fend for yourself. So, you think any more about dinner?"

Angie shrugged and picked a piece of food off the table with her fingernails and dropped it into her napkin.

"How about spaghetti? Hard to mess that up," Thorsen said.

"That's fine, if it's not too spicy."

"Well, that's how the geezers eat it—stave off the heartburn. It's the real penalty for eating that forbidden fruit. They always make it out to be an apple, but I'll tell you, and I've got a buddy down in the state of Tabasco, Mexico, who'll tell you the same thing—it was no fruit that got those two kicked out of Eden."

"What was it?"

"A habanero."

Angie laughed but looked like she didn't want to.

"Ate that thing seeds and all. No need to punish them for it either—natural consequences for the natural man."

"So what kind of fruit was on that other tree?"

"What's that?"

"The other tree, the one God had to protect? What kind of fruit was in that tree?"

"Bananas."

Angie's eyes opened wide and she started laughing. "Bananas?"

"That's right."

"Bananas?"

Thorsen nodded.

"Why bananas and not . . . limes or something?"

Thorsen turned from the sink with a dishtowel in his hands, which he flung over his shoulder as he began to speak. "Well, you know that Darwin fella said we all come from monkeys and us Christians say not so, we come from God. So, those old monkeys sure like a banana when they can get one, and God didn't want us eating that particular fruit so we wouldn't get ourselves all tangled up with the wrong ancestors."

"So what are you doing with a bunch of bananas sitting right there," she said, pointing to the counter, "if God doesn't want us getting into them?"

"Well, they take care of the leg cramps."

"Why did I agree to this?" Angie said, bringing the rest of the dishes to the sink. "You're crazy."

Thorsen shrugged and went about his work in the kitchen, shooing Angie away. When everything was tidy, he called up to

Angie and told her he had some chores to do and she should hol-ler if she needed anything. Thorsen took the slop tub and the rest of a gallon of two-percent milk from under the sink and hauled it down to the hog barn. The creatures barreled through the low door, grunting, their noses filthy and pulsing. They plunged their snouts immediately into the bare trough and swarmed over each other until they realized it was dry. Thorsen slapped one on the back of the neck and drove him off. "Shadrach, you'll get nothing if you don't let me get a bucket in there." The hog grunted and leaned against the next one and began edging it out of the way, which cleared a spot. Thorsen lifted the tub and slopped them, saying, "Watch out, hogs, there's some bacon floating around in there somewhere." Once the slop hit the trough, the hole closed up, and the pigs writhed in foul ecstasy. Thorsen took the milk and unscrewed the cap. "Date came up a week ago," he said, then he dumped the contents across their heads, which didn't even faze them.

Enoch was skittish when Thorsen got to him. "You looking at that car, buddy?" Thorsen said, stroking the horse along the back-side of its jaw. "That's Angie. She's Bunker's kid. Fixing to foal." Enoch tossed his head. "Hungry? I like your priorities." Thorsen pulled a flake of hay from a bale sitting outside the stall. Enoch started into the hay before Thorsen could even get it situated. "You better get used to the girl. I'm going to get her out here eventually. She'll send you to the glue factory if you don't watch yourself."

Thorsen grabbed a coffee can and dug it into a sack of feed and held it as he picked up another small can of ground oyster shells that sat next to an old red cast-iron grinder. He took both cans out to the chickens and spread the shells and feed around the coop then flushed the hens out and collected the eggs. He paused outside the coop, staring at the seven eggs lying there in his hands, one pale green, the rest brown.

The seven eggs made him think of scripture, and scripture made him think of serving others. Service made him think of Angie. He knew how it all looked from the outside, and he understood what a town like Sanpete could do to an act of charity that wasn't properly correlated. As he was loading the eggs into his pocket, the green one dropped to the ground. He scooped it up with a shovel and quit thinking about the girl. He carried the remaining eggs back into the house and put them into the refrigerator.

Angie came down the stairs with a slip of paper. "Brother Thorsen," she said, "Sister Hafen called."

"What are you calling me Brother Thorsen for? You trying to make me feel religious?"

"Listen, is she okay?"

"She's fine."

"Everyone in town says she's bats. I didn't know you people went crazy. I mean, I knew you *could be* crazy, but I didn't know you *went* crazy."

"Some people in town would probably say she's nuts, but I'm not a hundred-percent sure nuts doesn't help some folks endure to the end."

"My dad thinks people like that are just weak."

"'Course he does. That's why the crazies don't trust him," Thorsen said. Angie pinched her lips and looked around. "What did she say? She's usually looking for some help around the house."

"She made me write it down. She said, 'Tell Lila, I need Brother Thorsen to come down today and help me get this trash out of my compactor. Owen has a meeting and can't come until later.'" Angie lowered the note. "Isn't her husband dead?"

Thorsen nodded.

"And your wife . . ."

"She's gone, too. Noreen doesn't draw all that much of a line between the living and the dead. She's been getting visits from her husband for about a year now. Says at first he came by to catch her up on some family matters, since he could talk to folks directly. After a while of that, they started . . ." Thorsen paused and gestured vaguely with his hand. "Getting romantic. Noreen said it made her feel like she was twenty years old again, without kids underfoot and full of energy. Owen told her they'd be together as soon as she passed over, but they both had work yet, so they'd have to settle on once a week, after church."

"Oh, my God," Angie said.

"It's pretty interesting," Thorsen said. "People wanted to put her in a home and drug her up to stop the delusions. That's when she started calling me, asking me to talk to her kids and the bishop. 'Keep their noses out of my marriage' is what she told me to say. They got her some drugs, but she just spit the things out once they were gone. I mean, if it was you and you were that far gone and not looking forward to much—if that was you, and your husband was coming and sweeping you off your feet every Sunday afternoon—even if you were just crazy, would you want to be cured of that? No, sir. Let me stay nuts. Let me go out like that. Some kinds of nuts is a gift."

Angie took it all in, nodding her head, then she said, "Well, she called. I think she's hoping you'll come down before lunch."

"I was planning to drop in on her anyway. Listen, I've got to load up a bunch of stuff from the barn and take it to the dump, then I'll pick up some groceries. We're still on for spaghetti, right?"

"You don't have to feed me."

"I don't know how to cook for one, and if I don't eat it, the hogs do."

Thorsen snugged the cap around his ears and went back to the barn without waiting for Angie to answer. He dragged out two busted forklift pallets and eased them into the bottom of the truck bed, then dragged out a rusted quarter-roll of old fence wire and threw it in. Next came two torn and three new lengths of rain gutter and half a workbench vise with most of its paint chipped off. He followed that with a parade of cardboard boxes: one closed, another with a damp spot in the bottom, three filled with old chipped and broken glass bottles and jars, and the last with three brake rotors for two different vehicles. When Thorsen brought this box out, he set it on the tailgate and inspected the rotors with the edge of his thumb, then pushed the box further into the bed. Finally he brought out a half-dozen milk jugs full of spent motor oil, positioned them carefully, and, with some effort, shut the tailgate. As he tested the latch, a thought came to him, something his mother used to say: *Stoop and let it pass. The storm will have its way.*

• • •

Thorsen drove through town, turning north of Sno-Cap Lanes, where he headed for the dump. There was a great stillness in town and on the outskirts, not a gentle one but a kind of exasperation, something hard to notice. Thorsen drove on, following the road along a hill before he came abruptly to the gates of the county dump. Bob Ashton sat bundled up in a narrow green shack. When Thorsen stopped, Ashton reached out with a fingerless glove and slid open the window. In the other hand, he held a thick science-fiction novel. "Thorsen," he said, "what's new, you old pirate?"

"Just cleaning out the barn, Bob. How's the grandkids?"

"Oh, I stopped counting. Listen, I'm sorry about Lila. It's hell on a man when they go first."

Thorsen nodded. "I appreciate the thought."

Bob nodded back. "Say, I heard you really gave it to old Bill Everly the other day over at that property he's trying to get together with Bunker."

"Cowards," Thorsen spat. "Both of them lily-livered."

"We're all lily-livered, Thorsen. Ain't a one of us can hold our liquor."

Thorsen laughed.

"Well, that no-account deserves every word of it and more," Ashton said, setting the book down. Thorsen noticed a picture of a half-naked woman and a tiger-headed man in a glass helmet on the cover.

"I know it," Thorsen said.

"I suspect you told him so."

"What good is religion if a man can't use it to shame his brothers?" Thorsen said.

"My point exactly. Say, what you doing out here anyway? It's cold as the devil."

"Frost keeps the flies down."

Bob Ashton stretched a little in his chair, sizing up the load in Thorsen's truck. "Looks like half a load to me."

"Don't you go cheating the county on my behalf," Thorsen said.

"If you can see out the back window, it's half a load."

"Okay, then."

"I also got some oil here and some glass for the recycling."

"Ain't you just a regular hippy, Thorsen. You're an embarrassment to your NRA membership."

"I'm an embarrassment to everything I'm a member of."

"You know anything about those women in your ward? I've heard some strange stories about them getting together, having some kind of secret meetings."

"Bunko?"

"Could be. Might be something else going on. Sounds like they're hatching some kind of scheme."

"Don't know anything about it," Thorsen said.

"Hmm," Ashton said, scratching his head. "Okay, just set it over by the bins. I'll get to them after lunch. It's a buck for the oil. The glass is on the house."

Thorsen scraped some quarters off the dash and turned them into Ashton's gloved hand.

"One more thing I was meaning to ask you," Ashton said. "Is it true the Bunker girl is living at your house?"

Thorsen's eyes went huge.

"The Russians say gossip needs no carriage," Ashton said.

"You need to quit reading."

"Knowledge is power," Ashton quipped, picking up his book, his thumb across the half-naked woman's buttocks.

"How in the world did a hermit like you happen to come by such prized information?"

"Bill Chamberlain was driving by your place this morning—"

"Chamberlain?"

"He's not so bad, far as pligs go. 'Course, it depends on which wife you ask."

"What's it to Chamberlain?"

"Dunno. Kind of sounded like he thought you'd joined up with the cause."

Thorsen spat out the window. "What did he say, exactly?"

"Just asked if I knew why that Bunker girl was staying out at your place."

"She's not a girl."

"Got a girl's name."

"She's twenty years old, Bob."

"I know it."

"And she's pregnant, for crying out loud."

"Pregnant?" Ashton said, setting down his book. "Now that's pretty darn interesting."

"Don't you go running off half-cocked."

"Wouldn't dream of it," he said, taking a small notebook and ballpoint pen out of his pocket. "I'm fully cocked, Thorsen. I'm semi-automatic."

"What are you doing?"

"Got to get my facts straight."

"I'm done talking," Thorsen said, yanking down on the shifter.

"I won't say nothing." Ashton covered his heart and gave all three fingers of the Scout salute. "I swear, but you know as well as I do, it won't be more than a week before this burns through the Relief Society women like range fire."

Thorsen gripped the wheel and hung his head. "Maybe Bunker planned it this way."

"Thorsen, you know better than that."

"He knew it would all come to this. The pig."

"Thorsen, you know as well as I do that you can't help yourself when there's damsels afoot. You're a regular Sir Walter Raleigh."

"You gotta lay off the books, Bob."

"The Chinese say if your books are unread, your descendants will be ignorant."

"Lemme get going. I got a bomb to defuse."

Chapter Fourteen

As soon as he was in the house, Thorsen shouted for Angie. He stopped in the kitchen and looked around. The place was immaculate: the table clear, dishes clean and put away, the sink empty, towels threaded through the handle of the refrigerator door. "Angie," he called again, heading down the hall. "Angie, it's Thorsen." A muffled voice came from the front room. Thorsen followed it. He found Angie still mostly asleep on the couch, one pillow between her knees and another folded in half and propped under her head. His eyes shot to the coffee table and then to the carpet next to it. He took a breath to calm himself.

"Brother Thorsen," she mumbled. "Sorry. I fell asleep. I was just gonna lie down for a minute." As she sat up, carefully and with more than a little grogginess, Thorsen felt the panic begin to drain out of his body. "Something wrong?" she asked. Thorsen continued to look around the room at the curtains and the overly ornate wallpaper, both in pink. Dust coated the television, and the ivy plants unfurled their tendrils in all directions.

Thorsen shook his head once as if to clear it. "You didn't have to clean my kitchen."

"I wasn't doing anything anyway."

"I'm just saying."

"I appreciate it, but it makes me feel like I'm not freeloading so bad," she said, swinging her legs to the ground. "Won't be too long before I can't do anything."

"Good point," Thorsen conceded, then he considered his next move. Angie hauled herself out of the couch and stretched. Thorsen went to the window. "Listen," he said. "I need you to move your car."

"Sure."

"How about you pull it into the barn."

"Okay." Angie was perplexed.

"Permanently," Thorsen said, letting the curtain drop.

A small shiver of alarm moved across Angie's face. "Is it in the way?"

"We got people snooping around. There's going to be trouble once somebody finds out what we've got cooked up."

"Who's snooping? My dad?"

"Worse. Bill Chamberlain's been trying to sniff out the dirty laundry."

"Crap."

"He's been shooting off his mouth. So the fuse is lit," he said. Angie's face slumped. "Only thing for us to do is run for cover."

"I shouldn't have come out here," she said.

"I've been through worse, but you know as well as I do that this town has got a taste for gossip." Thorsen started pacing. "Only way to fight it is to get to the high ground before it comes a-washing through the valley. So, let's move that car."

Angie got her keys and nosed the car into the barn, and once she was out, Thorsen closed the doors. The operation fell under the watchful eye of Enoch, who tossed his head in protest. "Listen, you bug-eyed devil," Thorsen hissed. "This ain't any business of yours." Angie went up to the horse and spoke softly to him, holding her hand out. Enoch stepped up to the fence and lowered his head and breathed out heavily. Steam rose from the space between his nostrils and Angie's palm.

"You're a good boy, aren't you?" she said.

Thorsen scratched behind his ear and mumbled something.

"Yes, a good horse. A pretty horse too," Angie said. Enoch swung his head around and looked at her. "You going to watch out for my car—make sure the creeps don't bug us?" Enoch uncurled his lips and nibbled around Angie's palm. "That's right," she said. "Good horse." Enoch kept nibbling right up her arm.

"He can probably smell the baby," Thorsen said.

"Really?" Angie said, turning back.

Thorsen shrugged. "They're just as sharp in the nose as a dog."

Angie stroked the side of Enoch's face and told him she was going back inside. "I'm freezing," she told Thorsen. "Let's get inside. I've got an hour's worth of phone messages to give you."

"Oh, hell," Thorsen said. "Noreen."

"Not just her. Mrs. Ramke called and Brother Meeks. You're a regular celebrity."

Thorsen grumbled.

They went back inside. The furnace was running, so Angie

crossed the kitchen and stood over the heating register and shivered. Thorsen dropped his coat on the dryer in the mudroom and went right for the refrigerator. "Sorry, I don't have all that much to eat around here," he said.

"Whatever," Angie said. "It's not like I'm crippled. If I get real hungry I can just go down to the Frost Stop or the store."

"It's bad manners not to have enough food."

Thorsen reached into the egg container and felt around until his fingers closed on an egg. He backed up and walked over to the kitchen sink. "So, why don't you run those phone messages down again. What did Phyllis want?" He swung the egg against the lip of the sink. The egg immediately collapsed, the white and yolk oozing through Thorsen's fingers in long clear strands. Angie watched him in amazement. "Thought it was boiled," he said, dropping the egg and shaking his fingers. "Listen, I've got to find out what's going on with these people."

"Oh, right," Angie said. "Mrs. Ramke said Karl's breathing was getting pretty bad and he's been asking for you to bring Stucki by as soon as you could."

"When did she call?"

"About forty-five minutes ago."

"You said Roy Meeks called?"

"Yeah, he said he got word from Deloy that they let him out of solitary early. Had some kind of inspection, and he passed. He wants you to see Deloy as soon as you can."

"Okay, good."

Angie refolded her arms. "Deloy's in prison?"

"It's pretty sad."

"I knew him in high school. He was younger, but he was a pretty good artist. We had a couple of classes together. I went out with him once. He was nice. What happened?"

"Nobody really knows but him."

"I hadn't heard anything. I mean, I didn't really keep up, but still . . ."

"Once he lost the trial, people kind of gave up saying much," Thorsen said. "What I put together was Deloy used to have this buddy, Nick Viola. He was older, from somewhere out to Kane County. Nobody really knew who he was, just that he was trouble. Didn't seem to have a job. Rented a place south of town by the lumberyard. Had this beat-up old Ford pickup with a bullet hole in the back window. People figured he was selling drugs, but no one could ever catch him. Viola would shack up with the wife of that guy who was the foreman out at the gravel pit. Everlast was his name, I think. Everlast used to knock his wife around, and Viola didn't like that—strange moment of virtue, I guess. Viola told Deloy he needed a gun to take care of Everlast, said he just wanted to scare him, or so says Deloy, and I pretty much believe him. So Deloy gave him this .357 he'd use for target shooting. According to Deloy, he didn't even have any bullets in it, but no one could track down any proof that Viola bought any .357 shells within six months of the whole thing. So that's how they got into the whole idea that Deloy knew what Viola was up to, which got him the accessory-to-murder charge."

"But what happened?" Angie asked, turning out a chair from the table and lowering herself into it. "Did that Viola guy kill the husband?"

"Well, Viola said he and Deloy went out to Everlast's place in Sterling. Deloy said Viola went by himself. All the cops know is they found Everlast's body tied up with boat rope to a couple of old tractor rims and dumped in the reservoir with five .357 slugs, one in each leg and three in the back."

Angie dropped her head slightly and put her hands on the table.

"I don't think Deloy had any part in it, and if Everlast was beating his wife like Deloy said he was, it gets kind of hard to feel sorry for him. But it was a mess from start to finish, and Deloy's going to have a long crawl back," Thorsen said.

"Kind of makes me feel like a whiner," Angie said.

Thorsen shrugged.

"Plenty of people have babies," Angie said.

"I suppose so."

"It's so weird," Angie said, her voice thin. "It's not like I was best friends with him, but we went out once. You know, just for burgers and stuff. I think we even went bowling or something. He was a nice kid, wanted to draw comic books. He was better than that, but he wanted to go to art school. I told him he should. He said his parents thought art school was crazy. Plus they wanted him to go on a mission. He didn't want to. It's just so weird."

Thorsen nodded. "So, I'm going to talk to him. Been tough in there, and he doesn't really want his family around. He writes, but he doesn't want to see them."

"He'll see you?"

"Don't know. It's worth a trip to find out."

Angie sat at the table thinking. She picked at the fringe of the placemat with her thumb and forefinger. Thorsen got a piece of paper to set about writing a grocery list. As he sat down at the opposite end of the table, Angie cleared her throat and asked, "What if I went to see Deloy . . . with you?"

Thorsen stopped the pencil and let it hover over the list.

"I mean," she said, "what if I went down and talked to him. I mean, I know him and everything. Maybe he'd even like it, and I don't really *look* pregnant."

Thorsen nodded. "That could be a good idea."

"I can't talk church, if that's your mission. I could at least try to tell him something. What are you supposed to say to people like that? It can't be that hard just to talk, let him talk. Whatever, you know."

"I don't see why not," Thorsen said.

"I'm off next Monday, and it's not that far."

"Gunnison's a tough place. You ever been?"

"Been by it."

"Inside is different."

"I figured, but it's not like I've never seen the inside of a jail."

Thorsen chuckled. "This is prison. It's different."

"What do you know about prison?"

"Well, I've been *in* there."

"Not to stay."

"Not to stay," Thorsen confirmed.

Angie nodded.

Thorsen tore the list off the pad and set it on the table. "I'm going to run down to Noreen's, then I'll stop by everywhere else on my way back. If I catch you doing any more work around here, I'll tie you to the couch, you hear?"

Angie said nothing but gestured in an indistinct way.

Thorsen headed out, stopping only to grab his coat from the top of the dryer.

Noreen didn't answer the door, so Thorsen let himself in. There was a faint series of percussive noises coming from the kitchen, which he followed. It was Noreen kicking the drawn-out and crooked drawer of the trash compactor with her small canvas shoes. She was muttering. Thorsen drew off his gloves and hat and unzipped his coat.

"Noreen," he said, softly.

She kicked the compactor drawer two more times.

"Noreen," he said again, stepping into her field of vision. "It's Jens." He waved. She turned. "I'm sorry I wasn't here earlier, Noreen. Had a kind of emergency."

Noreen turned around and swept her hair out of her face. "Well, I broke it. Now they can say whatever they want to."

"Who can?"

"When you didn't come, I figured I didn't really need you, so I went to pull the drawer out, but the garbage was stuck in it. So I pulled some more." Her voice became tight and high. "I never thought I'd be able to do anything to it. I'm just an old bird, Jens."

"You're a whole lot tougher than you think you are."

Noreen looked around sheepishly and then went over to the kitchen table and picked up a small sledgehammer and brought it to Thorsen. It wasn't gigantic, but it was heavy enough. "Owen used this when things needed a little coaxing," she said.

Thorsen lifted the sledge and let the head smack the palm of his hand, then he shifted himself a little and spotted a dent on the far left side of the compactor drawer. He laughed. "Sure looks like you coaxed it," he said. "It's probably not ruined. I'll try to bend it back." Thorsen stepped toward the compactor and noticed that Noreen was beginning to cry.

"I'll just get down here," he said.

Noreen stepped back and sobbed. "I just gave it a little rap. I didn't mean to. I just don't have any experience with these things. Owen used to—"

"It's okay," Thorsen said, going down on one knee. "There's a lot of things Lila used to do—canning, baking. I'm all thumbs with that stuff."

Noreen looked up at Thorsen suddenly, her mouth hanging open. "Jens," she said. "Lila's gone?"

Thorsen nodded.

"Gone," she said.

"Since just before Halloween."

"Has she come back to see you yet?"

"No, Noreen. She hasn't."

"She's probably busy over there."

Thorsen nodded.

"They do get busy over there. That's what Owen says, tells me it's work, work, work all day long. People over there need teaching. They need the word. Says it's just like here except he doesn't have to eat and his back never hurts."

Thorsen laughed, then went back to examining the appliance.

"But Lila hasn't come . . . to you?"

Thorsen shook his head.

"It's okay. They're not supposed to anyway. Owen said he just couldn't help himself."

Thorsen took the sledge and rose up on one knee and laid the tool on a placemat and stripped off his coat. He knelt down by the compactor and took hold of the slide and yanked it back into place, then tested it. The drawer moved, but it was difficult to manage. So he pulled it out and continued to work on it.

"He's stopped coming, Jens."

"Who?" Thorsen asked.

"Owen."

Thorsen looked up at Noreen, who was shaking slightly. "It's been two weeks."

"Didn't we just talk about him?"

"I was fibbing."

Thorsen blinked and shook his head.

"I didn't want you to think I was crazy."

"I don't think you're crazy."

"He didn't even tell me. He just stopped coming." She snapped her fingers once to punctuate herself.

"Maybe it's like you say. Maybe he's busy."

"I don't know, but I don't like it."

"Maybe they caught him sneaking back."

"Maybe. I'd still like to know."

"You could pray about it."

"No, sir, Jens Thorsen. I'll not pray about that. I am too upset with the Lord right now to use a civil tone. He broke my heart. He should have told me Owen wouldn't be able to come. They should let him come back and tell me that much. Makes me want to just quit."

"Don't say that."

"Well, I want to."

"You aren't sick."

"No."

"But you're . . ." Thorsen didn't want to say the word.

"I'm lonely," she finished, folding her arms. "I have a right to feel this way."

Thorsen nodded and fiddled a little with the drawer and slid it closed. It worked better, but it was still far from perfect. He opened the drawer and pulled out the compacted garbage and then shut the machine. He took out the garbage and came back. Noreen was sitting at the kitchen table with her hands on the sledgehammer. "I married Owen to be with him, not apart."

"I understand that."

"I know you do," she said calmly. "I don't look like a crazy person, do I?"

"No," Thorsen said.

"No, I don't. But it's the ones that don't look crazy that generally are. Haven't you seen that before?"

"I haven't seen anyone who's been crazy like that," Thorsen said. "Mostly I see people I don't like. Doesn't make them crazy."

Noreen nodded, then she stared at the hammer for a long time. Thorsen took up his gloves and hat from the counter and zipped up his jacket. "You want me to call someone?" She shook her head. "Your kids, maybe." She shook it again. "Call if you need anything."

She nodded. "You should know, that Bunker girl doesn't take good messages."

Thorsen gripped his forehead and leaned against the jamb. "I'll talk to her about it," he said.

When Thorsen pulled up to the Ramkes' place, Phyllis was already outside. She wore a cheap ski jacket, and steam huffed from her mouth as she stamped her feet against the cold. Thorsen put the truck in park and was about to undo his seat belt just as Phyllis appeared in his window, knocking with one hand and holding an unlit cigarette and disposable lighter in the other.

Thorsen cranked down the window. "What's the uproar?" he asked.

"What's with the Jew, Thorsen?"

"Got me scratching."

"This Weizenheimer, or whatever he's called. What's the deal? He's been out here twice, trying to talk to Karl. What's he selling?"

"He's a doctor, probably an atheist like yourself, Phyllis. Thought you might appreciate a little secularizing of Karl's medical options at this point."

"Well, he's been run off."

Thorsen shook his head.

"I gave him a little rock salt in the ass," she said, starting to shiver.

"Phyllis."

"How am I supposed to know him from a bill collector?"

"You *ask* him."

She gave Thorsen a raspberry. He grabbed the wheel and stared into his lap and started chuckling softly and shaking his head.

"I sent him," Thorsen said.

"What?"

"I told him to come out here. Karl's been wondering about some options—you know, what's his next move, things like that. Listen, are you going to let me out?" Phyllis stayed put, and Thorsen slumped back in his seat.

"What does Karl need extra medical advice for? Don't you think these quacks have done him enough damage?"

"Well, it's not strictly medical," Thorsen said, "but it's got a lot to do with doctoring, or at least it used to."

Phyllis was trying to light her cigarette, but the wind kept snapping the flame off the top end of the lighter. She tried twice more and then resigned and dropped her arms. In the pause, Phyllis looked up at the house and then back at Thorsen. "You don't get to decide when he goes."

"I just told the doctor to give him some options."

"So you're trying to get Karl to kill himself?"

"Not really."

"That's exactly what you're doing." She tried the cigarette one last time, and then in a fit she threw the cigarette to one side and stuffed the lighter in her pocket.

"You shot at him?" Thorsen asked.

"Just once."

"Did you hit him?"

"He's the doctor—*ask* him."

Thorsen stared at Phyllis until she slumped slightly, her wind-reddened cheeks both cold and embarrassed. "One of these days you're going to point your gun at the wrong person, and they'll pull one back on you—shoot you where you stand."

"Let them. It's their right."

"Now you're talking like a crazy woman."

"Am I?"

"Listen, if I bring him out here myself, will you not try to shoot him?"

She shrugged.

"I'm coming back, and I'm bringing him."

"Today?"

"Not today."

"When?"

"I don't know. Maybe the end of the week. I'll call first."

"What's that gonna do?"

"It'll let you know we're coming. That way if you kill us dead it'll be premeditated, and they'll give you the chair."

Phyllis stepped back from the truck. Her teeth were chattering. She tossed her head toward the house. "Maybe you should go in and see him. He's not doing so good."

Thorsen followed Phyllis back to the room where Karl's bed and oxygen were set up. As he came into the room, Thorsen heard the strange cadence of Karl's breathing, an almost silent inhale and the slow rattle as he tried to clear his lungs. Karl was no longer sleeping on the couch but was fixed up on a twin bed that had been jammed into the far corner of the room, away from the windows but still in clear sight of the television. His skin was pale and blue; his chest was still inflated. He was unshaven, and his head was attached to his body with a thin tangle of cords that disappeared under his chin. Thorsen looked for a place to sit, but a stack of towels occupied most of the recliner, and a pile of old bed linens lay sprawled across the far end of the couch. Then he noticed a chair that had been moved next to the television in order to make room for the bed. Karl raised his hand as Thorsen turned to face him, his fingers curled and limp like blades of grass. He tried to speak, but Thorsen told him not to worry about it.

"I'm just here to sit watch," he said.

Karl nodded and took another breath. With the air he hissed, "I'm a mess." He drew another breath through his cannula. "Worm's turned."

"Looks like it has," Thorsen said, nodding. "Bright side is . . . no taxes."

Karl laughed and began coughing and seizing up.

"I'm going to have to put on my church hat," Thorsen said.

Karl shook his head and gestured weakly. When he got his breath, he said, "Tell me a joke. I want to go out laughing."

Thorsen sat and placed both feet on the floor with his legs spread. As Karl continued to breathe, Thorsen noticed the oxygen tubes collapsing slightly as he exhaled. "Phyllis ain't doing so good," Karl said.

"I didn't think she was. She was almost nice to me."

"Been yelling at God." Karl drew another quick breath. "Sounds awful."

Thorsen nodded. "Not sure what to make of it?" he asked.

Karl shrugged. "She likes yelling." As he drew his next breath, he smiled. "And he doesn't yell back."

Thorsen chuckled and shook his head, then started nodding. "You don't either, anymore."

"I ain't scared," Karl said.

"I was wondering."

Karl shook his head slowly, the cannula tight behind his ears. "Thought I would be . . . I'm just bushed . . . that's all." Thorsen leaned forward, his forearms braced crosswise against his knees. "I'm ready to hang it up . . . but . . . ain't no dead man's . . . switch." Karl leaned over and spit into a small garbage can at the base of his bed. "Just gotta run myself out of gas."

"I got a guy," Thorsen said, "a doctor."

"Jewish fella?"

Thorsen nodded.

"He's been by."

"I know it."

"She shot him."

"I heard."

"Maybe she just . . .shot *at* him."

Thorsen shrugged. "Probably."

"She's got no aim . . . couldn't hit the ground . . . with a horse-shoe."

"I think he's okay. You want me to bring him back? He might be able to coach you a little—"

"Bring me across the plate?"

"Something like that."

"Don't need him." Karl held up his hand and drew hard through his nose. "Don't need him . . . trying to clean up on my own. I need the time."

Thorsen nodded. "I didn't want you getting your medical and spiritual advice mixed up."

"Ain't no difference anymore." He drew a breath. "Pansies . . . buncha pansies. Say, bring Stucki over, will ya?"

"When you want him to come?

"I don't know."

"I'll go talk to him."

"Tell him I need a shave."

"Anything else?"

"Just the shave, when he can. And the joke. I need the joke."

"We'll come."

Karl held up his hand again and pulled heavily on his oxygen. Thorsen lifted his hand and nodded. "Don't worry, I'll come up with a good one," he said. Karl pulled again and waved Thorsen on.

Thorsen met Phyllis in the kitchen. She was nearly asleep in her chair, her head bowed and her arms folded. Thorsen knocked lightly on the threshold. Phyllis started and looked around the room, disoriented.

"Says he wants a shave."

"He needs one."

"I'm going to bring that other fella back."

"The doctor?"

"No, the barber."

"Okay."

"Maybe tomorrow"

"Okay."

"If I can."

"That'll be fine."

On the way home he stopped at the store and got groceries and then went to tell Roy and Leora Meeks that he was going down to the prison in a week. They said to stop by first. They had some things to send along. As he left the Meekses' house, it began to snow again. The ground was cold and dry and began almost immediately to whiten. By the time he was home, there was close to an inch on everything, and the wind was beginning to stir the darkening sky. The lights were on, and a thin coil of smoke rose from the chimney. Thorsen took the groceries from the passenger seat and went inside.

The kitchen was bright and humid. The table had been set and Angie, in one of Lila's aprons, was busy at the stove. "It's just about done," she said, "but there's salad if you want to get started."

Thorsen set the groceries on the counter. "You didn't have to do this."

"Of course I didn't. That's what makes it fun."

Thorsen took a seat. "Well, we got extra groceries. That won't hurt us."

"I guess not. Dig in. Anyways, you left the list. I just thought . . ."

"Probably need to say a few words over it," Thorsen said, taking off his hat.

"Oh, okay," she said. "Sorry, I'm not in the habit."

Thorsen nodded and scooted his chair forward. As Angie carried the steaming pot over to the sink, Thorsen unfolded his napkin and pushed it down into his lap, surveying the table. There was a green salad of iceberg lettuce and pale tomato quarters with a small jelly jar of dark salad dressing to the side. There was a bowl of spaghetti sauce with meat and chunks of green pepper in it and a foil cradle of French bread, and in front of either plate was a twelve-ounce can of Coca-Cola and a glass of ice.

"There we are," Angie said, sliding into her seat awkwardly with the colander of noodles. "It's all here, I think." They looked at each other.

Thorsen said a short blessing over the food and then reached for the Coke. Angie's eyes were on him the whole time. He dug his finger under the tab and popped it.

"Didn't know if you drank that stuff."

"Not in a long time," he said.

"I figured you might need a little boost."

"Well, it's been a rough day." Thorsen lifted the can right to his lips and drank.

"Amen," she said.

"Amen."

Chapter Fifteen

Jens was parked in front of Stucki's shop, the motor running but the wipers off. Snow tapped the windshield and melted into droplets. Thorsen stared through the mess and began to wonder if he should have brought Angie out to the house. He watched the tachometer of the truck and listened to its steady idle, thinking about how bad it could really get. He was unsure if he even cared. He liked having her around. He even liked being able to do something Bunker couldn't. It was superiority, maybe even pride, but he didn't care. It felt right under the circumstances, but the rightness of it wouldn't stop Bob Ashton from spreading the word.

Stucki honked and pulled into the parking space along the driver's side of Thorsen's truck. Thorsen leaned over and rolled the window down about halfway. Stucki got out of the truck rigidly and poked his face in through Thorsen's open window. "Got to get my gear," Stucki said.

"Well, go get it."

"Then we've got to wait for Angie."

"What for?"

"I still need to make a deposit. She doesn't even know I'll be gone. I tried to call her, but her mother says she doesn't live there anymore."

"It's a miracle," Thorsen said.

Stucki squinted in confusion. "Sort of sounded like she'd run off again." Stucki extended his arms and rested them on the roof of the truck. "Kids around here run off all the time." Thorsen nodded in agreement. "Small town doesn't hold much interest. Jobs are boring. Stores are boring. Church is boring, and so are the people. Got to be, if you're young. Can't blame them if they feel like leaving."

"Nope," Thorsen said.

"There's no opportunity for a girl like Angie if she keeps leaning on the generosity of old geezers."

Thorsen turned his head slightly and lifted his eyes, "Sure," he said, "I guess it's too bad."

"Holy smokes," Stucki said. "There she is." Angie's car drifted into the space on Stucki's driver's side, and she got out.

Thorsen nodded and watched Stucki walk around the truck and meet Angie in front of the barbershop door. Nothing seemed out of the ordinary. The lights switched on, yellow against the dimness of the morning. They spoke for a second, then Stucki went to the back room. A few minutes later, he returned with a small bundle under his arm and got into Thorsen's truck. Thorsen drove to Main Street and headed north.

After a minute or so, Stucki said, "I gave Bob Ashton a call."

"How's the dump? Your girlfriend live out there?"

"Don't try to turn me around," Stucki said.

Thorsen adjusted his grip on the steering wheel and shrugged. Two blocks went by.

"I was asking Bob if he'd heard anything about Angie Bunker moving. You know, since he's known to keep his finger on things."

"He rigged his police scanner to pick up cell phones."

"I don't think that's strictly legal," Stucki said.

"The law's an interesting beast," Thorsen said.

"Bob told me a pretty interesting story about this guy who's feuding with a bishop."

Thorsen shrugged. "Probably a lot of that going on around here." Then he added, "People hate a snoop."

"True, true, but he told me that Bill Chamberlain thought he saw Angie's car at your house night before last and all day yesterday."

Thorsen gripped the wheel and sped up. He came to an Oldsmobile with Nevada plates, and he gunned his engine and passed it even though he had a double line. "What's wrong with these people?" Thorsen muttered under his breath, making it sound like he was upset with the other driver.

"What did you say?" Stucki asked.

"Nothing."

"Okay," Stucki said, nodding slightly.

"Okay." Thorsen changed his position in the seat and then looked at Stucki. "I'm not trying to explain myself."

"I know."

"Don't figure I should have to."

"You don't."

"Okay, then."

"Okay."

Thorsen rolled slowly into the Ramkes' place and parked. Phyllis stopped them at the door. She looked as if she hadn't slept at all, and she kneaded her fingertips with the pads of her thumbs and her feet shuffled a little from side to side. "He's got a pretty bad infection. Had him to the hospital. They say if it's not this one it'll be another." Her empty hands looked hyperactive.

"How's he feeling about it?" Thorsen asked.

"He told them not to do anything. He asked them to send him home."

Thorsen glanced at Stucki, whose mouth tightened a little, then relaxed.

"When was this?"

"About a week ago."

"So, he knew," Thorsen said.

Phyllis nodded. "So, here we are . . . at home." She backed up and let them into the house so they could close the door. The kitchen was a mess of dirty glasses and plates and frozen-food boxes. One side of the sink was full of onionskins and carrot peelings, and the other was full of cans and bottles. "You'll have to forgive me," she said. "I've been trying to get it together." Phyllis placed the back of her hand against her forehead and took a deep breath. "I know they said his crop dusting is what probably made

Karl sick, but I've been reading." She stifled a sob. "Do you think it was my fault?" She flipped her thumb against her forefinger and then did it again.

Thorsen shook his head. "Don't know."

"Because Karl never really smoked. You all really pounded that into his head. But, I mean . . . Jesus, I hate it when you people are right."

"It was probably the chemicals," Thorsen said.

"I just don't know how it's supposed to work. What if I killed him?"

"Come on," Thorsen said. "If you'd wanted him dead, you'd have done it quicker than this."

"I'm serious. Now nobody can do nothing but sit around here and wait. Why don't you just go back and see him. He's been talking about going home nonstop since you left. I don't even know what that means."

Thorsen headed down the hall and stopped half way. Stucki nodded and motioned forward with his bundle. When they came into the room, Stucki said, "I need to get some water," and then he turned and went into the bathroom he'd used before. Thorsen stepped into the room and found Karl asleep, with a book on Rocky Mountain elk open on his chest. Thorsen sat down on a chair that had been pushed randomly against the near wall, and he waited for Stucki to come in. His bundle was jammed under his arm, and he was carrying the shaving brush and mug in each hand. He shuffled into the room, his disease more apparent. "Is he asleep?" Stucki asked, and Thorsen nodded. Stucki set his gear down on the coffee table and told Thorsen he'd need a chair.

Thorsen pulled the chair closer to the bed and positioned it so Karl could slip into it without too much trouble, then he stepped back and unzipped his coat and shoved his hands down into his pockets and watched for a few seconds.

"Karl?" Thorsen said, clearing his throat. "Wake up, brother." Karl's eyes opened slightly, then closed. He drew a deep breath through his nose and exhaled, then opened his eyes again.

"You're the ugliest angels I ever saw," Karl said, stopping to breathe again.

Thorsen backed away and cleared a spot on the recliner next to the television. A small archipelago of child-resistant pharmacy lids lay scattered on the floor between Thorsen and Karl.

"We're no angels," Stucki said, now beginning to work the brush into the soap at the bottom of the mug. "And you ain't dead."

"You never get what you want."

"I heard you could use a shave," Stucki said.

"Couldn't hurt."

"I guess not."

"It's you"—he drew breath and exhaled—"or the undertakers."

"Never thought about that, but I guess you'd have to," Stucki said.

"Hair keeps growing," Karl said.

"You all have been brighter company," Thorsen said from the chair. He wasn't smiling.

Karl nodded and exhaled, pushing the air. "Fight ain't worth it." He looked around and smoothed out the covers. "I'm calling it . . . quits." He pushed himself up with his hands and sat up on the bed. This small exertion brought on a bout of coughing that nearly consumed him. Karl gathered a mouthful of sputum and spat it into the small garbage can next to his bed. He arranged his oxygen tubes and inched over to the edge of the bed and dropped his legs to the floor. Stucki leaned over to help him, but Karl pushed away his hand. "It's my workout for today," he said. "It's all I got . . . except for the toilet."

Karl used his legs only for a brief moment as he shuttled from the bed to the chair. It took thirty seconds of coughing to recover. When he did, he looked up at Stucki and said, "Make it clean. I want to feel . . . like I was just born."

Stucki unrolled his bundle and draped the towel around Karl's neck. He undid the razor and set it on the coffee table and took out the mug and brush. After waggling the brush a few times in the lather, he held out the brush and saw that his hand was trembling slightly. He steadied himself, then lathered Karl's face. Once the brush made contact with Karl's skin, the tremors disappeared. Thorsen noticed and looked away.

"Stucki, last time Phyllis cut you off," Karl said.

"Did she?" he said, touching up the lather.

"You were talking about the other side."

Stucki glanced at Thorsen, who was twisting his wedding ring and staring at the floor. Thorsen saw Stucki watching and said, "I'm watching the hallway."

Karl looked Stucki in the eye and said, "Don't give me the official line."

"Well, that's my line, too, Karl." Stucki picked up the razor and stropped it lightly on his sleeve. He watched his hand tremble in the air and then turned the blade flat and pressed it against Karl's face. As soon as he did, the trembling ceased, and Stucki began taking off the lather in direct, masterful strokes.

"Don't lie to me," Karl said, lifting his eyes.

Stucki exhaled and looked about the room. He took another stroke with the razor and wiped it clean on the smaller towel he had draped over his arm. "Once you kick, it all starts. Way I see it is you have to be somewhere. If there's any of you left, then that stuff has to be somewhere. I like thinking that he gives you a minute or two to see yourself dead so you know what happened."

Karl seemed like he agreed. Thorsen looked more sullen.

"It all gets pretty foggy for me at that point." Stucki kept shaving. "I guess you go somewhere, but I don't know where that where is. Haven't studied it much. Bet it's like stepping off an airplane in Mongolia. You don't know the lingo. Can't read the signs. Everyone's busy, and you're full of questions. I'd like to think my old man would show up in the middle of all that and answer them."

Karl shook his head and moved each of his hands to different parts of his thighs and braced himself again.

"Far as I can tell," Stucki continued, "they don't give us bodies. Not sure when we get solid again."

"Fine by me," Karl said.

"Then I guess we go to work, least I hope so. Don't know how it works without a body, but I'd just as soon do something as sit around playing the harp all day. Some people think it's like going to church, all day long. God help us if it is."

"I wouldn't like it unless I was busy, and I don't like singing," Karl said.

"Tell the truth," Stucki said, "seems like it'll be a surprise once we get across. I don't spend a bunch of time on it. Maybe I ought to, but I don't." Stucki took the last of the lather off with the razor and whisked off some stray spots with his thumb. Then he wiped Karl's face and neck with the towel and stepped back. "You use any lotion?"

"Got some in the bathroom. A dab'll do me. I don't want Phyllis getting all romantic. She'll get caught in my tubes."

"Well, that's a whole other way to go," Thorsen said.

"Beats this one," Karl said, patting his oxygen tank.

Thorsen hoisted himself out of the chair. "I'll get the lotion. You two keep figuring things out."

As Thorsen left, Stucki began picking up his things and setting them in the center of the towel. He checked to see that Thorsen was all the way gone and then he said, "I'm pretty sure dying is harder on the people who get left behind."

"True," Karl said. "We got our test. They got theirs."

Stucki nodded. "We do have ours," he said, "I've got a comb and scissors, Karl. I can get you a cut if you want it."

"Thanks," he said, "but I like it this way. Drives Phyllis nuts. Keeps her from thinking about the future."

Sitting down, Stucki looked around the room and then down at his hands, the wrinkles deep and the skin dry. He curled and uncurled them, feeling the tension. Before too long, they began to swim in the air—not wildly, just a little at first. "Karl," Stucki said, turning his hand over and over again.

"Yeah?" Karl asked.

"I said . . ." Stucki paused, looking up for a second before continuing, "I don't know anything about what's over there."

"Me neither."

"I just know there's a *there* there."

"I suspect I do too."

"I don't imagine that's the end of it either. I think it's just another leg in a pretty long trip."

Karl smiled weakly. "Phyllis said Thorsen's wife is gone."

"She is, Karl. Heart attack."

"He talking about it?"

"Thorsen? No. He will when he's ready," Stucki said. "For now he's using us to keep going."

"Fine with me," Karl said.

Thorsen returned with two bottles of aftershave, one blue and the other white. "Which one of these you want?"

"Gimme the blue," Karl said. "Don't want to go out smelling like an old man."

"You are an old man."

"But I don't want to smell like one."

Thorsen handed the bottle to Stucki, who rose from the chair. "Here goes nothing," he said, uncapping the bottle and dousing his hands. He clapped them together and then smoothed them over Karl's neck and cheeks.

"Holy cow," Karl said, wincing. "Feels like I'm fifty again."

"Anything else?" Stucki asked.

"No sir," Karl said, then he shifted in his seat and leaned toward the hall and listened for Phyllis. "Unless . . ."

Thorsen put his hands in his pockets and looked at the carpet.

"My old man laid hands on me once . . . must have been seven or eight. I had scarlet fever, temperature of a hundred and six. Should have died. He said a prayer, then I blacked out. In the morning I was out playing in the yard. There were all these neighbors lined up at the fence, watching me. He did it before he broke with you all and left."

Stucki and Thorsen looked at each other for a long time.

"Karl," Thorsen said. "Phyllis won't like it."

"I know it."

"But we can do it if you want us to," Stucki said. "Might not work out like it did before."

"I don't want to hang. I just want to feel calm again. I want to feel like that."

"We'll try," Thorsen said.

Karl pushed himself up and took a deep drag of oxygen.

"Who do you want to do it?" Thorsen asked.

"How about Stucki, if it's all the same to you," Karl said.

"What if Phyllis comes in?" Stucki asked.

"I'll block the door," Thorsen said.

Stucki stepped forward and lifted his hands. They were still as they settled on Karl's head. Thorsen set his hands on top of Stucki's. "What's your full name, Karl?" he said.

"Karl Moroni Ramke."

"Moroni?"

"That's right."

• • •

"I wish I could have told him he was going to be all right," Stucki said.

Thorsen threw the truck in gear and backed out of the Ramkes' place and turned toward town. "I know it."

"Sometimes it burns me when I can't say anything but 'be strong' and 'trust in the Lord,'" Stucki said, turning the heater vents onto his hands. "I get to where I don't ever want to say anything to anyone unless I know it's going to happen."

"That ain't faith," Thorsen said.

Stucki nodded and then looked out the window. The snow came right down to the edge of the road, covering the whole of the valley. They passed a snow-packed car parked under an eighty-five-year-old cottonwood, then a line of wire fence picked up, cutting through the snow drifts. Every fourth post was juniper, lightly dusted with snow. The trees flashed by and then broke for the driveway of Smitty's Welding and Machine Repair. Smitty was out front heaving on the rip cord of a small gasoline generator. Then he was gone.

"Thorsen?" Stucki asked.

Thorsen glanced over at Stucki and then back at the road. "What's that?"

"What in God's green earth are you doing with that Bunker girl?"

"She's got a name."

"You know what I mean."

"If that's the case, you probably didn't have to ask."

"This town's going to explode over this."

"That all it takes?"

"It's not going to seem like charity. You've got to know that."

"I don't care what it looks like. That no-account tossed his own flesh and blood on the street in the dead of winter. Only decent thing was to take her in. And that baby won't deserve any of it when it comes. Didn't do anything except get born."

"It's going to burn out of control."

"Doesn't take much to have her. She cooks and cleans. I'm making out like a bandit."

"I can tell you right now. Folks are going to say you did it to spite the bishop."

"Maybe." Thorsen followed the curve of the road past a cluster of dilapidated outbuildings and a relatively new singlewide perched on a rise at the back of the property.

"What's that going to get you?" Stucki said.

"Peace of mind. Seems the more I rile people up, the more likely it was I made the right choice. Whatever doesn't rile them up turns out to be the devil's business. Angie needs someplace to sort things out. I've got the space. What's the problem?"

"We'll see." They coasted into town, turned on Center Street, and came around to Stucki's shop. Passey's truck was out front next to Angie's car. Thorsen followed Stucki into the shop, where they found Angie, her hands covered in oversized clear-plastic gloves, frozen above Passey, whose head was covered in bunches of foil. He was saved only by the fact that he was clutching an issue of *Field & Stream*. His neck was dressed with a thick white towel, and his hair was slicked back and dark brown, almost mahogany. Passey looked up at Thorsen and then at Stucki. The air in the room began to thicken.

"What's going on, Passey?" Stucki asked. Thorsen pulled off his mittens.

"Well . . . Angie here said she thought—" Passey stuttered. "She thought maybe—"

"He's getting a little gray," Angie said. "He's younger than you two, and he's not ready to turn in his spurs. Are you, Ernest?"

"Well . . ." he said sheepishly, closing the magazine and scratching the side of his face.

"Don't get your paws in it," she said, brushing his hand away.

"Let's leave the young folks to it, Stucki. You want to go down to the IGA and get some prunes?" Thorsen asked. "My bowels are starting to feel like they need a cleansing."

"Before we go, let's find something for Ernest to watch on the television," Stucki said, then he picked up the remote and ran through the stations, stopping on Martha Stewart, who was sewing together two pieces of oil cloth. "There you go, Ernestine."

"You guys are a riot," Passey said.

"Sorry, I can't hear you. Batteries are out on my hearing aid," Thorsen said, cupping his ear.

"Ignore them," Angie said. "You're going to look marvelous."

"You started this," Passey said, pointing at Thorsen, "letting her wash your hair."

"I'm standing right here, guys," Angie said.

"That's right," Thorsen said, staring at Stucki and then looking at Passey. "This is all my fault. I accept complete responsibility for the fact that you are now a sissy."

Chapter Sixteen

The Quik Mart on the south end of Sanpete was already crowded, pickups pulling in and out in the dull morning light. Two men stood next to their trucks, fueling them. One took a last sip from a coffee cup and set it down. The other checked his watch and stared at the road. The first man jerked his receipt from the pump, folded it in half, and then drove off. The second headed into the store, hauling out his wallet. Thorsen and Angie pulled into the empty spot. Thorsen got out and began filling the truck. Angie stayed inside. The second man came out and spotted Angie in the car and looked down at his feet.

"H'lo Larry," Thorsen said, intercepting.

"Jens," Larry said, his eyes flicking briefly again toward Angie in the truck.

"How's the old USDA?"

"She's still there. 'Least that's what my check says," he said, checking his watch. "Sorry to hear about Lila. She was a good person."

Thorsen nodded, and Larry glanced at the back window of the truck. Thorsen followed his eyes this time.

"Sorry to hear it."

"I appreciate the thought."

"I got to get over to Price for a meeting," Larry said.

The nozzle clicked off and Thorsen replaced it and refit the gas cap and closed the door. "Sure," he said, "watch out for them troopers on Highway 6. They'll ticket you for five miles over."

"Got one last month." Larry climbed into his truck and drove off, looking back once and then a second time before darting onto the road. Thorsen came up to the window and motioned for Angie to roll it down. "I'm going to pay for the gas. You want anything?"

"No, but I better make a stop. I'm not much good at holding it anymore."

Thorsen opened the door and let Angie out. They both went into the store. Ammon Seiler was working the register. He was about Angie's age, with two kids, and his mother was president of the Relief Society in Thorsen's ward, which was how Thorsen knew him. She'd been around a lot during and after the funeral.

At one of the tables near the windows, Bill Armour sat with Glade Smith eating donuts. Glade had a Coke, and Bill had a plastic mug of coffee. Both of them turned their heads when Thorsen and Angie came in. Thorsen nodded to Bill. "You working that rotten stretch of 132?" Thorsen asked.

"Sure am. Why anyone needs that road widened is beyond me."

"Maybe the turkey trucks need some turning room."

"Don't know."

During the exchange Glade Smith had cranked his head around, pretending he was reading something on the far wall. Angie folded her arms and leaned toward the counter. "Ammon, can I get the key?"

"Sure," he said nervously, glancing down at the tightness of the bottom buttons of her shirt. "I heard you were . . ." He looked away and then back again and then at Thorsen but not at Angie. "I heard you were back in town."

"Yeah, cutting hair. The key?" she asked.

"Oh, yeah." He handed her a smooth wooden block with a six-inch ring and a key on one end. The block was covered in graffiti, but someone had written GALS on it with correction fluid.

Angie took the key and went past the potato chips and disappeared. Thorsen finished his conversation and got a bottle of V8 out of the refrigerator and returned to the counter. "How you doing, Ammon?" Thorsen asked.

"I'm good, Brother Thorsen. My mom says—well, she says she hopes you know what you're . . . I mean, she says she hopes you're doing okay."

"I'm fine. How are those twins?"

"They're eighteen months now. It's a job keeping after them."

"I got the gas on three and this juice here."

"Okay."

"And I'm going to need a carton of your strongest cigarettes."

Ammon looked around, and then his face screwed to one side. "They don't really sell them that way."

"Which one has got the biggest warning label?"

Ammon looked up and scanned through the cigarettes in the

overhead rack, then stopped suddenly. "They're all pretty much the same size."

By this time Bill Armour was looking over with some interest, and he was tapping Glade Smith on the hand. "You need some help, Thorsen?" he asked.

Thorsen looked straight at Bill and said, "Which of these cancer sticks packs the most punch?"

"Well, that's a complicated question, Thorsen." Bill straightened himself up in his chair and leaned over the table. "You could go for the Camel or Marlboro unfiltered. They'll curl your short hairs. But the Pall Malls are cheap—kind of like a Buick. Now your Lucky Strikes are also something else, they're the Cadillacs, but not quite so popular anymore. But that's probably how I'd go. Lots of versatility there in the Lucky Strike."

Thorsen gave Bill a little salute and said, "Obliged," and he turned to Ammon and said, "Lucky Strikes it is, then." Ammon reached up and pulled a pack down and set them on the counter, just as Angie came back from the restroom and set the key next to the cigarettes.

"That's pretty small. Don't they come bigger?"

"Oh," Ammon said, "that's right, you wanted a carton." He switched them out and swept the key off the counter and hung it behind the lottery-ticket dispenser. He rang up the gas and juice and cigarettes. Thorsen paid with cash and then handed the cigarettes to Angie. Ammon's eyes raced immediately after the cigarettes and then stayed with Angie's belly.

"Tell your mother hello. I'll probably see her Sunday."

"Sure, Brother Thorsen," Ammon said, his eyes still with Angie, who shuttled the cigarettes behind her back. "I'll tell her you were here."

Thorsen said thanks to Bill for the cigarette advice.

Bill tipped his hat and said, "I do what I can to help the faithful."

"Perfect," Angie said. "Now everyone in there thinks my seventy-five year-old boyfriend is trying to fill me full of birth defects."

"I'm not so sure that's what they're thinking," Thorsen said. Angie glared at him and folded her arms. Thorsen drove for a ways, uncapping his juice and drinking from it, fiddling with the heater in between sips. They passed the reservoir and skirted the foothills of the Wasatch mountains. The town of Sterling passed in a blink.

"It's going to get ugly around this town," Thorsen said, "what with the way folks are into other people's business."

"I'm used to it."

"Maybe so, but it ain't right."

They passed a series of large white stones and a fence made of ship chain and poured concrete pilings. A hundred feet farther along was a purple house with an old hand-crank washing machine sitting in the front yard like a lunar lander.

"What's the problem?" Angie asked. "Why do people have to be like this? I thought they were Christians."

"They're people, that's the problem," Thorsen said. "Plus, it's small towns. It's religion. It's the regular grief a person gets around here for not towing the line, but church folks don't have a corner on the small-mind market."

"Or on looking like they're towing the line," she added. "Plenty of people around here play the part."

"And they spout testimony like it's going out of style. I know, I know. But catch them when they're alone, and you've got a different story. A man's true religion is what he does when he thinks nobody's watching."

"They might call it Babylon, but the one thing my friends aren't is hypocrites. Maybe they drink and smoke and listen to punk and don't get married, but they don't pretend to be honest when they're not. They don't pretend to be holier than anyone."

"That ain't a new thing. It got Jesus crucified."

"I've never met a righteous person who said he was. Usually works the other way around."

"Good point," Thorsen said, after taking a swig of his juice. "But the facts are that we still have to live around here. We can't clear them all out. There's nowhere to put them." He watched a jet plane leap from behind the mountains and cross the southern sky. "But with this baby coming and a girl like you out there with an old fart like me, well, it's going to get rough in Sanpete before it gets nice."

"What kind of girl am I?"

"You know what I'm talking about."

"Fill me in."

Thorsen leaned against the door a little and stroked his temple. "Angie, people get ideas. Talk about them long enough and their ideas start feeling true. Once they feel true, they might as well be. You aren't going to change anyone's mind."

"That's pathetic."

"It's people. You ever notice how nobody's watch ever tells exactly the same time, but nobody assumes their watch is the one that's off." Thorsen shifted his weight and then looked at Angie. She was staring out her window at the slope of a low hill as it dropped to the level of the road and then dipped into a wash. "It doesn't matter what kind of person you are. Once people have decided, it's hard to make them change their minds."

"Nice dodge," Angie said. "But I still don't know what kind of girl you think I am."

Thorsen cleared his throat. "Well, you're persistent," he said.

"I know what people think," Angie countered. "And I know what I've done—right or wrong. But it's not a matter of good and evil with me. I just don't believe all this stuff about angels and Joseph Smith and Indians from Israel. I never did. You just can't say that around here."

"Of course not. You can't tell anyone anything."

"It should be live and let live."

"That's right," Thorsen said, picking up the bottle and taking a last drink. "You know, sister, that you don't have any proof about the universe either."

"I don't need proof. I'm not trying to convince anybody of anything."

"You're trying to convince people to leave you alone."

"What does that have to do with your 'does anybody really know what time it is' problem?" Angie made air quotes to mark off her reference.

Thorsen arched his eyebrows.

Angie quoted again. "Get it," she said, "the song?"

Thorsen shrugged. "I didn't think you'd let me win that easy. It's kind of a letdown." Thorsen flashed a fake smile. "But really, doesn't there have to be one big clock somewhere? People used to call time on the telephone."

"Now they just have the time on their cell phones."

"Exactly."

"And who decided which clock they'd use to run the clock phones?" Angie said, with a look on her face that showed she knew her defenses were unraveling.

Thorsen tilted his head a little and thought about it. "That's the point," Thorsen said. "Who keeps the clock? And who set it correctly in the first place? And even if there was one big clock, who's to say it's on time? Maybe my watch or yours accidentally has the right time, but that's not likely, not with billions of people down here. Just as likely to be some fella in the Phillipines."

"Aren't you supposed to be the religious part of this conversation?" Angie asked.

Thorsen nodded.

"Well, if you say that we don't know if any of the clocks are right, then what?"

"If that's the case, then it doesn't matter. We just have to agree that it's nine o'clock and get to work. But if we're going off the one big clock, we'll just have to trust it. If we don't then we're always going to be running around setting and resetting our watches, being late, and always wondering whose fault it was."

Angie fingered a piece of chrome and tried to avoid looking at Thorsen. A crow in the middle of the opposite lane hopped away from some indistinguishable dead animal and then took wing.

"We have to stop talking about clocks, okay?"

Thorsen said, "I'm done," and then he drove, not speaking but not feeling like he was done talking either.

"You know, my dad doesn't talk like this," Angie said.

"He used to," Thorsen said, shifting his eyes toward Angie.

Angie looked at Thorsen, startled.

"He used to be full of ideas, but they called him to something in the church—I don't know what is was. Then he clammed up. I'm sure he thought he was doing the right thing."

Angie picked up a nickel from the dashboard and played with it in her hands as the truck made a long right-angle swing to the west. The prison materialized in front of them: one tall and three short transmitter towers rose up above the institutional buildings and the barbed wire. The lightning-emblazoned globe of the microwave station took the foreground, above the pioneer cemetery that seemed strangely connected to the prison. The only trees in the area ringed the cemetery, and above them rose the single observation tower. It was glassed in and geometrically authoritative, like the tower at an airport. They drove past a log-home builder. One cabin was half built, but there were no workers to be found. They passed the gravel turnoff for the cemetery and slowed.

After they had checked in and parked, Thorsen said, "I didn't mean to say that I thought you were any kind of anything."

"I know it."

"Well, I'm sorry about that," Thorsen said and then slipped the truck key into the ashtray.

"You shouldn't do that," she said, reaching down with her hand. Thorsen froze with his hand on the lip of the ashtray. He blinked once and swallowed, then turned and looked at Angie with an expression that made her pull back her hand and sit up straight and press herself against the door. She said, "I know people who steal cars for a living. They don't usually have to hotwire them."

Thorsen scraped the key out, still watching Angie with a strange vigilance. Then they got out, locked the doors, took the cigarettes and went inside.

The check-in was as they expected, except for the fact that they didn't meet in some glassed-in room where they'd be expected to speak through black telephones. They were ushered into a large room, where men in orange jumpsuits met with their families at small round tables. They stood by the door until a guard brought in Deloy, who was surprised to see Angie. They sat at the table, and Thorsen slid a plastic sack with the cigarettes across to Deloy.

"What's this?" Deloy asked, peeking into the bag. "Are you kidding?"

"We figured they might be worth something," Thorsen said.

Deloy nodded and then laughed a little. "Did you buy these in Sanpete?" Thorsen nodded. "That would have been something to watch." He turned to Angie and just looked at her. "What are you doing with him?" he said, jerking his thumb at Thorsen.

"This is my boyfriend," she said. "I go for the mature type with money." She touched Thorsen on the shoulder, and he shied away. Deloy nodded, then fingered the cigarettes for a moment before he pulled the bag off the table and set it under his chair. The room was full of people at tables. A low murmur filled the spaces, but there was still an institutional emptiness, a barren correctional feeling. Deloy looked thin and hard. A flap of skin on the second knuckle of his left hand was sealed crudely with a black semi-circle of dried blood, and the area around the knuckle was blue and yellow.

"Is this the pep talk my dad said was coming?" Deloy asked.

Thorsen looked at Angie, and she looked into her lap.

"No pep talk, Deloy. I just came to fill you in, let you know Lila passed away."

"I'm sorry, Brother Thorsen," Deloy said, hanging his head.

Thorsen looked around the room. There was a guard in each corner and one roaming between the tables, slapping his night-stick against the palm of his hand, its shaft striking the curve of the guard's wedding ring, giving each sound an extra crispness. Angie crossed her legs and arranged her hands politely in her lap. Deloy watched her without trying to seem like he was.

Thorsen noticed it and smiled. "You know, Deloy, a man can go a long time before he realizes that someday he's going to wake up and the whole house will be empty."

Thorsen saw Deloy fidget with his fingertips and then reach between his legs, grab the chair, and haul it closer to the table.

"You can sure get to the point," Deloy said.

"You've seen how church folk throw this enduring-to-the-end stuff around, but people don't know anything about your life— I don't. I can't even guess at it, Deloy." Thorsen grimaced and scratched his head. "Most people never went through anything like this, and they don't want to. No bishop out there knows what you go through in here." Angie leaned over to Thorsen and asked him what he was talking about. He waved her off and kept talking. "When my wife died, I looked to the scriptures, and I didn't find any how-to section on mourning the dead. When somebody dies in there, people just tear their clothes, the chapter ends, and it's a hundred and fifty years later."

Thorsen looked at Deloy, who was running his thumbnail along the metal edge of the table. When Thorsen stopped talking, Deloy looked up and said, "I feel better already."

"Deloy," Angie said, leaning toward him. "This old man is crazy." She looked over at Thorsen, who had his arms folded and his head down. Then his eyes opened, and he grabbed the end of the table and drew a deep breath.

"Deloy, before you got here, I'll bet it was pretty easy to think you were the one drop of ink in clear water. Probably changed once you got in here. Now they're the ink."

"I gotta listen to this?" Deloy looked around at the walls.

"You can go stand up on the hill in Sanpete and look out over the whole valley, and anything you can imagine has happened at least once," Thorsen said. "I killed someone too, Deloy. No one ever told me it was my fault, but I spent most of my life thinking it was."

"You killed somebody?" Deloy asked.

"Who?" Angie asked.

"A baby. My first one. When Lila and I got married, we lived way out by Orson Wash, maybe thirteen miles from paved road. We were getting by, and Lila went into labor forty days early.

"I was outside under the pickup. She was in the kitchen mending a work shirt when she called out to me, 'Jens, I just lost my water.' I ran in from the front yard with grease on my hands, and she was standing there, her legs bent and tears on her face. Her dress was wet, and so was the chair flipped over on its back.

"She pulled a dishtowel off the counter and said we ought to get to the hospital. I said, 'I don't have those U-joints back in,' but she didn't hear it. She just headed for the truck, didn't notice it was on ramps.

"Then she seized up and fell on the grass. When I got to her, she was laid out on her back with her legs crumpled underneath. She was breathing heavy and quick, and her skin was pale. I asked her if she was all right. She shook her head and tried to straighten her legs. There was some blood on her garments. She said something about wanting to push. Sounded like she didn't have the breath in her to keep talking, but she said she didn't want me to leave her, said it hurt too bad. I told her I had to go call the doctor. She nodded, and I ran into the house."

Both of Thorsen's hands were planted on the table, and he pushed his chair back a little and took a breath before continuing. Angie and Deloy were motionless.

"I went through the phone numbers and couldn't find anything, so I called the operator. 'I have to get Doctor Reed's number in Gunnison,' I said. It took her a while to get it all straight. I wrote the number on the wall, hung up, and called. While it rang, my breath got faster. Nothing on the receiver. Outside, Lila started calling for me again, and I looked out the window, but I couldn't see her. The line was still ringing. I tried it again and again. Finally I called the operator back and asked for the hospital in Gunnison, Salina, Provo, anywhere. She gave me a number, and I called it.

"When somebody answered, I said, 'I think my wife is dying.'

They asked me what was wrong. After I told them, they said to call an ambulance and gave me a number, but the pen rolled under something, and I couldn't think anymore. I heard Lila scream, and I slammed down the phone and ran out to see how she was, and her dress was up around her waist and she had the dishtowel between her legs. I looked under her belly. There was more blood. She was rocking herself and sweating and crying. I stroked her hair back and whispered to her.

"Her breathing slowed down a little. I kept saying she'd be all right, but I was just smearing grease across her forehead. I pulled my hands off her and tried to get them clean. I told her I could get that last joint installed in twenty minutes and then we could get to the hospital, but she'd have to sit here while I did.

"While I was under the truck, I could hear her crying, saying she wanted to push. I yelled at her and said if she pushed, the baby would get born right then, and I wouldn't know what to do. I had just got going on the truck when she screamed out to me.

"I crawled out from under the truck and ran around to where she was. When I got to her, she said, 'The baby's coming.' She could tell. She said, 'It's moving around.' I said, 'Hold on,' and ran back to the truck. I got on my knees and looked for the U-joint. After a second, I found it in there turned upside down, all the pins scattered in the dirt. I tried to clean the pins on my pants before I realized all the grease was coming off, too. Lila had rolled over on one side, holding herself, saying my name over and over. There was more blood on her legs, soaking her garments. I picked her up and carried her into the house. I had to turn her sideways to get her through the door."

Thorsen's eye twitched, and he squinted to disguise the fact. Angie asked if he was okay, and he waved her off. Deloy glanced around the room nonchalantly to see if anyone was looking, but they were all caught up in their own conversations.

"I kicked open the door and set her on the bed. She tried to sit up. I wasn't sure she should have, but she said it didn't hurt as much that way. I asked her if she wanted me to go finish the truck, and she said, 'No, Jens.' I told her I wouldn't go anywhere except try and call for an ambulance again or maybe try the neighbors. 'I'll just be at the phone downstairs,' I said. She said she wished her sister were there to help deliver the baby.

"I said, 'So do I.' She said something I didn't hear. I held her hand and said a prayer, then I laid my hands on her head and gave her a blessing, told her she'd be okay, that she'd have plenty of children. I hated it. I just couldn't say anything about this baby."

Angie nervously adjusted herself. "After the prayer," Thorsen said, "I went down and called around, but I couldn't reach anybody. I was trying to call my friend Lloyd when Lila started screaming for me again. The screams got so bad so fast that I dropped the phone and ran upstairs.

"I tore into the room, and Lila was there holding the baby's head with her own hands. It was slick and blue, but I don't think she could tell what was really going on. I couldn't see the ears or anything, and after all that, I ran to the bathroom and washed my hands. I scrubbed like crazy, but even in hot water the grease wouldn't come all the way clean. I went at it until Lila screamed, then I dropped the soap and ran back to her. Lila was backed up against the headboard with her legs bent. I tugged the sheet out from under her, then dug out my jackknife and laid it open on the bed.

"I whispered to her and took her knees, so I could see in. The head was showing more, and I froze until Lila screamed again. I took her hand and held it for a while until the pain hit her again. When she let go of me, she grabbed onto the blankets. Her screams came right on top of one another. The baby wasn't moving. Nothing went like it should have. I thought maybe the baby had been caught up in the cord. Maybe it wasn't getting its air.

"I tried talking to Lila to calm her down. I stroked her leg and told her I was going to push the baby back up inside. I put my hand on the baby's head and waited for the contractions to pass. I said, 'Don't push,' and pushed him back up inside. What I was doing and me doing it were two different things. I held the head up there for a moment until blood started to drain down my arm. On the next contraction, the baby's head began to show again, then moved out past the ears. It was working.

"Lila said, 'I have to push,' and then she bit into her bottom lip. I told her we were getting somewhere. She started crying again. Then it all went blank. I remember nothing until the baby's shoulder pushed out and he broke the rest of the way through into my hands. He was awful still, and there was too much blood. I told her it was a boy."

A scrambled voice came over the intercom saying that visiting hours would be over in five minutes. The room pressurized, and the pace of Thorsen's story quickened.

"Lila looked up at me with her lips trembling, and I had to look away. It didn't help. I tied off the cord and cut it, then wrapped up the baby. Lila wanted to hold him. I said nothing. She asked me again. I handed her the child so she could have him for a while. I let her do that, but I knew how it would go.

"I took the baby and wrapped him up in a towel. Even though we decided on Arne, she said she wanted to name him Paul. I took him downstairs and looked for something to lay him in, then I went to look after Lila. Once she seemed okay, I got that truck back together and took Lila and Paul to the hospital. He's at the cemetery in Manti."

"You didn't kill that baby," Deloy said.

Thorsen shrugged.

"Jens," Angie said, "that could have happened to anybody. I mean, it does happen. Crazy things like that happen all the time."

Thorsen waved her off. "My point is, how do you put all that together with God and Jesus and heaven and hell and the hymn-book? You can't do it. You just have to keep going. You hear what I'm telling you? You have to keep going. If you start thinking about 'Why me' and 'Couldn't this' or 'Couldn't that,' then you're going to go nuts. The point is not what you did, but what you're going to do. You with me?"

Deloy nodded.

"You take those cigarettes and figure out what it's going to take to deal with things in here, then do it," Thorsen said.

"That's the pep talk?" Deloy said.

"Here am I, send me."

A guard appeared suddenly and tapped the table with his stick.

"Deloy," Angie asked, "do you want us to come back?" Deloy shrugged. "Because we'll come back as long as you want us to. And if Jens can't come, I will," she said.

Deloy looked up and halfway smiled. Thorsen felt like a man who wanted to be three-hundred miles away from everything.

Chapter Seventeen

THORSEN AND ANGIE LEFT THE PRISON and drove to a small diner called Herbie's, which was on Main Street, across from Buster's Birds and Buddies. Angie pushed through the door with Thorsen following. They were both engulfed in the scent of salt and oil. A girl not much younger than Angie was doling out paper-jacketed straws into a dispenser. Her hair was dark brown and heaped nest-like on top of her head with strategically placed coils unspooling past her cheeks. She wore blue-and-white eye shadow, and her neck was thin. She wore a peach tank-top with a white T-shirt underneath. Her small breasts seemed unnaturally high on her chest. She was skinny in a way that looked forced and uncomfortable. When she heard the bell jingle, she looked up at Thorsen and Angie and smiled. Her teeth were clad in clear plastic braces, and it looked as if her tongue was pierced.

Thorsen looked at Angie in comparison. She was fuller from the baby, but she never seemed severe like this girl. Thorsen tried to decide if the difference came from the fact that he knew Angie better, but he couldn't tell. Thinking about it made him feel like an old man.

"What can I getcha?" the girl asked, her attention turned back to the straw dispenser. "Specials are on the board." She gestured to a sign next to a Lions Club gumball machine. Just then a larger girl with a bad pageboy haircut strolled up to the front in a greasy half-apron and filled a large plastic mug with a variety of soft drinks. Once the mug was full, she capped it, drew heavily on the straw, and sauntered behind the thin girl, stopping to pilfer a tray of fries from under the heat lamps. Thorsen was surrounded by girls, and he allowed the thought for only an instant before abandoning it. They were somebody's dream, but not his.

Thorsen asked Angie if she was ready, and she said she wasn't and went on reading the menu. The thin girl turned to the larger one and asked her if Carlos was going to pick her up tonight. The larger girl said that she and Carlos weren't going out anymore on account of his mission, then she stuffed a half-dozen fries into her mouth and disappeared into the kitchen.

"I'll have a patty melt," Thorsen said, "with a large order of onion rings."

"Anything to drink?"

"Vanilla milkshake."

"Pretty cold for a milkshake," the skinny girl said.

"Not in here it's not—you ready, Angie?"

Angie's head was still craned up at the menu. "Are your chicken strips white meat?" she asked.

The thin girl shrugged. "They come out of the freezer. We just fry 'em."

"Could you ask?"

The girl rolled her eyes and then lazily sauntered back to the window that opened into the kitchen and said, "Hey, Lindsey!"

"Huh?" the larger girl hollered, poking her head into view.

"Are the chicken strips white meat?"

She shrugged. "I guess. What else would they be?"

The thin girl came back and said, "They're white meat."

Angie ordered the strips and a Coke. The girl rang them up, and Thorsen paid. Looking down at Angie's belly, the thin girl asked Angie when her baby was due. Angie looked up at Thorsen, who was folding up his billfold, then she cleared her throat. "March fifteenth," she said.

"That's my brother's birthday." The girl smiled.

"Cool," Angie said, stuffing her hands into her coat pockets.

"Plus, my sister-in-law had two babies born on the same day, and they're not even twins." The girl handed Thorsen his change.

"It's neat when that happens," Angie said, then she looked at Thorsen, who was checking the dates on his coins.

"Yeah, it's neat. My sister-in-law didn't even plan it. Dallin—the second baby—he was a month early. It's so weird how off they can be."

Thorsen turned and pocketed the coins and crossed to a table by the window and sat down.

"You got a bathroom?" Angie asked.

"Yeah," the girl said, "just go through the back. Normally you have to go outside, but with the baby and everything, you're okay. Just go through."

"Thanks."

"No problem."

Thorsen set his elbows heavily on the edge of the aluminum-banded tabletop, his back against the vinyl of the booth. He stared across the street at the gray-and-tan buildings and white sky, and then he glanced back, for a moment, at the thin girl behind the counter, who was now making his milkshake. He could hear the food frying in the back, but he had lost his appetite. He looked back outside at his pickup. It was not the one he had in pieces when Paul had come, but it was old like that one, cobbled together. Even once he could afford a newer vehicle, he didn't want one; too many computers inside.

When Angie got back, Thorsen had shredded paper napkins into a pile of confetti that lay between his hands and was drifting off to sleep. "Hey, Brother Thorsen," she said, touching him on the shoulder.

"Your food's up," the thin girl said, sliding the tray onto the counter. "You want fry sauce?"

"Hey, our food's ready. You want fry sauce?"

Thorsen's head jerked slightly. "What?" he said.

"The food's ready. You want fry sauce?"

"No, I hate that stuff."

"Me too," Angie said, then she turned to the girl. "Just ketchup and some honey mustard for the chicken." Angie went and got the food. Once they had it divided up, Thorsen bowed his head and whispered a prayer. When he was finished, Angie said, "Brother Thorsen, all that stuff with the baby and the truck, when did that happen?"

"Nineteen fifty-five."

"He could have been my father." Angie adjusted herself in her seat. "I mean, he would have been old enough now, mathematically."

"I suppose so." Thorsen held his patty melt close to his mouth, but he didn't take a bite, just let his eyes drift out the window. A string of unlit Christmas lights spanning the street swung in the wind. Thorsen shook his head. "Christmas just about got the jump on me," he said, gesturing to the lights with his sandwich.

"They've got Santas all over the place," Angie said, pointing them out.

"I guess so," Thorsen said. "Gets so you don't even see them."

"They started Christmas at the Wal-Mart before Halloween."

Thorsen nodded. "Just making a buck, I suppose."

"I hate Christmas," Angie said.

"There's plenty of people who do."

"The whole thing just makes me think God is no different than all the other men in the world. He gets a girl pregnant and then takes off. If he stuck around, maybe they could have gotten a better place to stay."

Thorsen told her she had a point.

She looked like she was ready for a fight, but Thorsen didn't have it in him. They finished their meals, talking about Deloy and the prison and maybe going back in a few weeks. Thorsen was pleased to get the sense that Angie liked the visit, and he smiled to show her but then lapsed again into silence.

"Everything okay?" she asked.

Thorsen took a last bite of his patty melt and wiped his mouth. "I guess so," he said.

"It's weird how that girl was talking about babies coming early." She tossed her thumb toward the counter. The girl was changing the water for the ice-cream scoops.

"Well," Thorsen said. "Things like this come in threes." He swabbed an onion ring across the thin film of ketchup on his plate and then ate it.

"Is it hard thinking about losing the baby?"

Thorsen looked at her, studied her face. She was beginning to look softer. Her chin was pocked with blemishes caked in beige makeup. When Thorsen didn't look away, she blinked nervously and said, "What?"

"He's got a long row to hoe," Thorsen said, and Angie nodded again. "I know it'll get me thrown out of the Rotary, but I'm starting to feel like guns are more trouble than they're worth."

"You think he's going to make it?" Angie asked, her voice struggling to be cheery.

"Maybe. I don't know the first thing about being in prison. I was in the county lockup overnight once before my mission, but that was small potatoes."

"You got arrested?" Angie asked.

"Sure," Thorsen said.

"What for?"

"Drunk driving."

Angie burst out laughing. "You're kidding, right?"

"No, ma'am. They arrested me for driving drunk, but I was just driving on some codeine pills I was taking for my wisdom teeth."

"You were driving on codeine? I haven't even done that."

"I was coming home from work, popped a couple of those

things and figured I'd make it home before they set in. I was just coming into Manti and started swerving all over the road. A deputy sheriff followed me until I fell asleep and drove up onto the temple lawn."

"How'd they find out you weren't drunk?"

"My mother came with a copy of the prescription. Told them I was getting my wisdom teeth out for my mission, and the deputy didn't want to stand in the way of the Lord's work. He told her to keep me out of cars until my mouth healed up."

"So they just forgot everything?"

"Well, she did wait all night to come down. I had them call as soon as they locked me up, but she thought I had a couple lessons to learn."

"You got arrested for drunk driving." Angie threw back her head and laughed. "Does my dad know about this?"

"Probably," Thorsen said. "We got one more errand to run, then we can get home, maybe try to put on some kind of holiday spirit."

Chapter Eighteen

Lunch sat heavy in their stomachs. The truck was cold, and Angie rubbed her arms and thighs as the truck heater howled open-throated into the cab. They turned off onto a side street in Gunnison and after a block parked in front of a nondescript medical building. A few vehicles were parked out front, but the street was basically empty back out to Main and down to where the road ended in the distance with a three-strand barbed-wire fence. A small black-and-white sign in the window said Free Clinic Mondays.

"This is your errand?" Angie asked, her arms pulled inside her coat.

"Why don't you come in with me? It's pretty cold out here."

"Sure."

As they went into the clinic, snowflakes began to appear on their sleeves and the sidewalks. Thorsen held the door for Angie and judged the weather. "We should be fine getting back," he said. "No emergencies yet." Inside, Angie took a seat while

Thorsen went up to the receptionist. They spoke for a few moments as Thorsen glanced over his shoulder at Angie, who was leafing through a magazine. The receptionist handed Thorsen a clipboard, which he handed back to the woman after gesturing nonchalantly to Angie. The woman nodded and then disappeared into the office. Thorsen crossed the room and sat next to Angie. "It'll just be a couple minutes."

He leaned back in his chair. "What you reading?"

"Baby magazine. I just don't see where they find all these hot expectant mothers."

"California," Thorsen said, leaning over to see the mother in question. "Probably paint the bellies on 'em later."

Angie said nothing.

"Say," Thorsen said. "You felt anything yet?"

Angie looked up at him. She looked upset by the question.

"I mean, if you don't mind me asking."

Angie shrugged. "I don't think I've felt anything but the bigness."

"No kicks or anything?"

"Nope."

"Lila said they all felt like a little fish on the inside."

"Really? Even the one . . . Paul."

"Especially him. Lila said he flopped around all over the place. It's probably how the whole thing got started." Thorsen ran his palms back and forth on his jeans and sniffed.

"I'm sorry," she said.

"That was a long time ago. We're sealed. She's with him now, and that's okay."

Just then the door opened and a nurse poked her head into the room. "Angie?" she said.

Angie dropped the magazine into her lap. "Huh?' she said.

"Yeah," Thorsen said, gesturing to the nurse, "they want to take a look at you and listen to the baby."

Angie threw the magazine on the floor and bolted out of the chair. She grimaced and held her side. "You're no different." Her voice rose in intensity. "Why didn't you just ask me? What's so hard about just *asking me?*"

Thorsen scratched the back of his head and then scrubbed a finger under his nose. "Well, I figured it would end up like this."

"Well, it sure did, didn't it?" Angie zipped up her coat and darted for the door.

The nurse intercepted Angie by stepping into her line of sight. "Angie," she said. "It's okay. You can just go see your own doctor if you want to. It's no big deal. He'll do the same thing we'd do here, but it'll cost you some money, unless you have insurance. Do you have insurance, Angie?"

Angie stopped and thrust her hands into her coat pockets. Her breathing was short and stiff, and her face was flushed. She looked at Thorsen, who was leaning over with some difficulty to pick up the magazine. Angie stormed over, snatched the magazine away from Thorsen's straining hand, and dropped it on the side table.

"Angie," the nurse said. "You do have a doctor you can see, right? A family doctor." Angie pulled her bottom lip across her teeth and gnawed at it. "Because someone's going to have to look out after that baby and make sure things are okay," she finished, placing the clipboard in the opposite hand.

"You could have asked," Angie said.

"I'm sorry," Thorsen said, cradling his head in his hands.

The nurse stepped toward Angie and touched her on the shoulder. "Should we go see the doctor?" Angie let herself be directed through the door, as Thorsen melted into the chair. "We won't be long, Mr. Thorsen," the nurse said.

Thorsen unsnapped his coat and slipped it off and laid it across the arms of the chair next to him. He reached for a magazine, leafed through it absently, then chose another and repeated the process. He went through a half-dozen magazines this way, not seeing anything really, not reading, just letting his hands manipulate the pages. Outside the snow began falling harder. In the pale light of the afternoon, Thorsen saw the darker flecks of snow softly helixing. He set his current magazine aside and massaged the sockets of his eyes with the pads of his thumbs.

The receptionist moved about behind the wall, passing occasionally into view. Thorsen pushed himself up into the chair and crossed his arms. He knew this was a lousy thing to pull on the girl, but when he looked at Angie, he saw Lila moving about in the kitchen of their first house. She was pregnant and slowly gathering the things she would need to raise a child: crib, clothes, towels, diapers, booties, blankets. Lila had prepared the nursery on her own, painted the walls, and made a small, quilted blanket she could use to swaddle the baby. When Thorsen saw Angie and thought of his wife, who was then not much older than Angie, fear swam through his body, as it did with the coming of each of the children after Paul. And with Angie especially, things seemed so finely balanced. The slightest nudge would send everything tumbling.

As the snowfall began to thicken, Thorsen's head dipped and he was asleep. His hands slipped to the ends of the chair arms, and he slumped slightly. His breathing grew deeper, and a low, grumbling snore poured out of his mouth. Soon his head lolled to one side and his jaw slackened, his chest falling and filling, his boots planted squarely on the blue carpet.

"Mr. Thorsen?"

Thorsen started. The nurse was standing over him; she was shaking his shoulder lightly, and he could see straight down into the thin vertical line of her cleavage. "Mr. Thorsen," she said again, "Angie would like you to come back now."

"Back where?"

"Back into the examination room."

Thorsen looked disoriented. "Can't you just put her on the phone?"

"The exam is over," she said. Thorsen looked relieved. "We just need some information, and she wanted you to come back."

The nurse led Thorsen through a narrow hall, past a scale and scientific illustrations of an eye and a woman's uterus and fallopian tubes. Angie was sitting on the examination table with her coat across her lap. The doctor was sitting on a small wheeled stool. He rose and shook hands with Thorsen. "Mr. Thorsen, your granddaughter is going to have to see another doctor."

"Granddaughter?"

Angie threw Thorsen a look. "It's nothing," she said. "They just want me to see a doctor up in Provo next week."

"It's not nothing, Angie," the doctor said. "Mr. Thorsen, Angie's a little bigger than we'd expect in a mother's eighteenth week."

"Bigger?" Thorsen asked. "What does that mean—bigger?"

"I'm just a little bigger than normal. It could mean twins."

Thorsen's eyes went wide. "You're kidding."

"It could be a lot of things," the doctor explained, "but we're not set up to tell. She's a little larger than we'd expect, given the timeframe, and I couldn't differentiate a fetal heartbeat from the mother's pulse, which is nothing to be alarmed about either. But she should see an obstetrician up in Provo. They've got equipment up there that's more sensitive than what we've got here."

"That ultrasound gizmo?"

"That and heart-rate monitors. We're just a basic clinic here. They'll be able to see things a lot more clearly up there."

"Jens, they want to schedule an appointment for next Monday. It's Christmas Eve. Is that okay?"

"Sure. It's just to Provo. When you need to be there?"

"By ten."

"Well, go ahead and make the appointment."

Angie closed her door and reached for her seat belt. "I'm sorry I—"

"No, I'm sorry. I should have told you," Thorsen said as they backed out of their parking place. "Are you worried?" he asked.

Angie shrugged.

Snow fell more intensely, a thin film of it building up on the median and the shoulders, covering the dirty snow that lay derelict in the fields and along the fence lines. They turned onto Main Street and followed it through town, past the artillery in the park and past the prison. Angie's head turned as they drove past, and she moved in her seat to keep from breaking her gaze. "This is what you do?" Angie asked. Thorsen looked puzzled. "Visit people in jail and trick girls into going to the doctor?"

"I figure out ways to stick it to your old man," Thorsen said, adjusting his grip on the steering wheel and checking the odometer.

"I'm serious."

"I am too."

"I mean, you're a salvation army of one."

Thorsen shrugged. "I just do what seems right—but once I start talking about it, I don't like how it sounds."

"Am I a charity case or a way to stick it to my old man?" she asked. Thorsen arched his eyebrows and shook his head. "What is it?" she prodded.

"You're too tough to be a charity case and too nice to be a weapon."

"That's no answer."

"Of course it is. It's double-talk for 'I'm not going to tell you.'"

As they drove on, Angie fell asleep with the collar of her coat sandwiched between her face and the window. The snow kept falling, swooping in the wind against the windshield, where the wipers would sweep the dry crystals away. A thin raft of pink light thickened in the clouds above the mountains as the sun went down. Thorsen switched on the lights and drove on.

By the end of the week it would be the shortest day of the year.

Part Five: Epiphany

Chapter Nineteen

As he drifted around the bend and prepared to slow and turn from the road onto the short gravel drive that led to his house, Thorsen saw a great orange glow hovering in the frozen blackness near his barn. He jammed on his brakes, throwing Angie forward against the dash, then he gunned the throttle and lurched up the drive. Police lights strobed on behind them, filling the side and rearview mirrors of his truck.

"What the hell?" Angie said as the siren chirped and Spencer Kimball's voice barked out into the void.

"Jens. I'm coming around."

Thorsen hit the brake again, throwing Angie against the dash a second time.

"You have to stop that," she said. "I'm pregnant."

Spencer tore around them and sped up the road and stopped. Thorsen pulled forward slowly and impatiently until he was right behind the squad car. He checked the house, which was dark, then his eyes raced over to the barn, which was also dark. The firelight seemed to erupt straight out of the darkness. Once Spencer trained his floodlight on the general area, Thorsen began to see the trailers and trucks parked in his front yard. The wide ellipse of light gleamed as it skimmed the oxidized aluminum skin of Stucki's vintage Spartanette 24. Through the thin-slatted windows of the trailer, Thorsen could see sparks and tongues of orange and yellow flame licking the air.

"Well, it's a fire all right, but I think it's controlled," Spencer said, clicking on his flashlight and swinging it into Thorsen's eyes. Thorsen threw up a hand and told Spencer to quit trying to blind him. Just then, Ernest Passey came around the end of Stucki's trailer with a sandwich in one hand and a thermos bottle in the other.

When he saw Thorsen and Spencer in the random ribbons of light, he turned back over his shoulder and hollered, "It's Spencer and Thorsen, don't worry." A burst of voices erupted and then died down. Passey continued on to the squad car and stuck the sandwich in his mouth so he could shake Spencer's hand. After they shook, Passey ripped a corner off his sandwich and swallowed it in a single reptilian gulp and tried to speak. When he failed to make himself clear, he opened the thermos and took a swig. "What are you doing out here?" he asked, his mouth now clear.

"Bill Chamberlain called in, said there was a fire. Once you let them volunteer firemen out of the bottle, it's pretty hard to get them back inside."

Passey fingered the sandwich, then said, "Well, there's a good twenty percent of us here already. Should save a little trouble."

"That's good," Spencer said, shaking his head. "I know I'll sleep better knowing you guys are on duty."

"Thorsen," Passey said, turning away from the deputy. "We got a situation."

"I'm afraid to even ask." Thorsen surveyed the encampment and spat into the snow. The trailers were packed tightly, as if to thwart an attack.

"That ain't the problem. It's the solution."

Angie tugged on Thorsen's jacket. "I'm going inside."

"Go ahead," Thorsen said. Then he stepped closer to Passey and, trying not to be heard, he hissed, "I'm aching to hear about the problem that filled my front yard with a bonfire and a half-dozen RVs."

Passey took another bite of his sandwich and wiped his mouth on the sleeve of his jacket just as Stucki came out the door of his trailer with a lit Coleman lantern hanging from the end of his arm, like a man coming out of a crypt. Behind him, in the house, a light came on in the kitchen and then in the front room.

"Stucki," Thorsen asked, "I hope you have some idea what's going on?"

Stucki looked at Passey, who shrugged. Then he stole a glance at Spencer and then at Thorsen. "The women have gone hysterical," he said. "It's been brewing for a while, but it came to a head this morning."

"Hysterical? People still use that word?"

Stucki fiddled with the knob on his lantern so the shadows that wrapped around his arm and face leapt and fell sharply. "We were all worried about you . . . finding out." On the other side of

Stucki's trailer, the fire popped and leapt, launching a flurry of orange sparks into the frigid air. Spencer cursed under his breath and then excused himself.

"You're going to burn down my house and barn just to distract me from the facts?" Thorsen asked, rubbing his hands together and huffing on them.

Stucki took a step closer and set the lantern on the ground between them, the light scattering their shadows kaleidoscopically around them, a tight ring of brightness on the ground. "It wasn't you we were worried about," Stucki said and tossed his head toward the house. A light came on in the window of the far dormer. "This is pretty much centered on her. We're just collateral damage."

From the fire circle came a small explosion, followed by a cascade of oaths and laughter.

"You didn't punch a hole in it?" somebody said.

"I didn't have it in there very long," somebody else answered.

"Who was your scout master, anyway?"

"Jeez, this stuff is like napalm," another voice complained.

"You're not going to eat it, are you?"

"Once it cools down, I will."

"You're nuts."

Thorsen shook his head at the disembodied conversation and slowly stroked his temples. "Why don't they just lynch her?"

"I can see their point of view," Stucki said. "Don't like it much, but I can see it. Ordinary people are the most dangerous. How many times have you seen that around here?"

Thorsen grunted.

"This thing has been coming for us since the day Angie showed up."

"Makes me wish I was a hermit," Thorsen said.

"You *are* a hermit. Eighty-percent hermit, anyway. That's why you didn't see it coming."

"How did it go down?"

"The way Violet tells it," Stucki said, raising the lantern slowly, "some of the young women started talking about how Angie was a kind of hero, coming back to Sanpete and making it on her own. Lanelle Comfrey reminded the girls that Angie had gotten herself in a whole heap of trouble and that she wasn't any kind of hero to anyone but harlots. Well, the girls start sticking up for her, saying that there was more sex going on in Sanpete outside of families than inside them, not to mention abortions, and that most girls would rather kill their babies or claim they were raped than have anyone think they were fooling around. So Lanelle slaps one of the girls—I think it was Shawnee Adamson—for saying the Lord could find it in his heart to forgive a prostitute, so maybe Sister Comfrey needed to think about that."

"You're kidding."

Stucki raised his arm to the square and gave the scout salute. "God's truth. I can see why those women are in an uproar. I don't like the backtalk. It's a sign of something I'd just as soon ignore."

"Backtalk comes with free thinking. Least we haven't run off all the free thinkers."

Stucki granted him the point and went back to his story. "So the women call an emergency Relief Society meeting, and they decide they need some kind of plan to keep their daughters from ending up as brazen as Angie Bunker, said they'll be sassing their parents and bishops and falling into dark paths. Violet said someone even suggested that this kind of early sexuality could get girls hooked on witchcraft."

"And all this happened today?" Thorsen asked.

"No," Stucki said. "This has been brewing."

"How long? Since I took her in?"

"It's more on me, actually. People took note when I gave her the job."

"Charity never faileth," Thorsen said.

"Calm yourself. I don't want to misrepresent anyone. All I know is what Vi told me. So what happens is these women decide they're going to call for a boycott of my shop until I send Angie packing off to Salt Lake or Denver or wherever it is unwanted pregnant girls go. That's when Vi broke with the sisters and came and told me. And sure enough the next morning Lanelle Comfrey is sitting in front of my shop with a clipboard waiting to take names. I saw her while I was in town picking up a vacuum from Nickerson's, so I swung around . . . and pulled in next to her. She looked up at me and started writing down my name and then realized who it was. I knocked on her windshield and pointed out my closed sign. She threw her clipboard on the seat and ground on her ignition. I leaned right up to the window and told her she was just making business for a polygamist and then pointed toward Chamberlain's shop, and she drove off like a crazy woman. Nearly plowed right into a mailbox."

"When was this?"

"Couple weeks ago."

"I don't see how that gets me a KOA in the front yard."

"That was Passey's idea. His wife told him that he could sleep in the rec room so long as he kept having Angie cut his hair and do his nails."

"Does she know about the color work?"

"She has to."

"And she still told him to stay clear?"

"Looks like."

"And Passey told her what?"

"He said if they wanted to get together and practice unchristlike behavior as a group, they could do it without a man in the house, then he hitched up his trailer and drove out here. Chamberlain helped back him up the driveway, then he made a beeline for the dump."

Thorsen sighed. Ashton's conspiracy theories about the women made perfect sense now.

"Next thing I knew it was like someone had called out the militia. Everyone had marching orders. Everyone knows the Relief Society is organized, but holy cow. Before too long some of the fellas decided we'd just give them a taste of their own medicine—and we packed it up. Came out here for, you know, moral support."

Thorsen was breathing heavy. A voice came from the darkness asking if it was okay to drink out of the hose. Thorsen told him that it was untreated and probably frozen solid. The next thing Thorsen knew, the back door was swinging open and someone was heading into the house. "Why here?" he asked.

"Passey thought it might be a good show of brotherhood," Stucki said.

Thorsen said he thought the foundations of human civilization were crumbling.

"Foundations of what?" Stucki asked.

A volley of laughter arced over the trailer like a handful of gravel.

Thorsen asked, "What does Bunker think?"

Stucki's face twitched. He didn't mask his surprise.

"Don't suspect it makes him look all that great," Thorsen said.

"I suppose not," Stucki said.

"It must be twelve degrees out here," Thorsen said.

"It's nine with the wind chill and about forty-five with the fire."

"You people are nuts. I'm going inside. You're in charge of that fire, Stucki. If anything burns, it's on you." Just then a second shower of sparks curled and coiled. Thorsen groaned and tossed his hands into the air.

"They're outdoorsmen, Thorsen," Stucki said.

Thorsen stumbled around the tongue end of Stucki's trailer only to find himself nearly blinded by the corona of the campfire. Passey sprang out of the shadows. "Glory of the sun," Passey said, his coat unzipped and beads of sweat riddling his forehead. "Glory of the sun," he repeated, waiting for a laugh. When it didn't come, he rubbed his hands together and basked in the conflagaration. Thorsen could barely hear him over the hiss and roar of the flames. In the darkness behind the fire, a ring of reddened faces twisted and grimaced. The men held steaming styrofoam cups and laughed at the heat and rush of the bonfire gasses.

"This thing is going to be the glory of my barn going up in flames," Thorsen said, squinting.

"We got this under control, Thorsen. Besides, it's mighty cold, if you haven't noticed."

"Not right here it's not."

"Well, then this is a *real* fire."

Bill Armour butted in. "Navajo buddy of mine once said an Indian man builds a small fire and stands close by. White man builds a big fire and stands far away."

"Shut it, Bill. I'm busy," Thorsen said. Passey laughed, which irked Thorsen so much he spat into the fire. "Passey, I need someone to tell me what's been going on with the women in this town."

A sober expression settled on Passey's face as some of the wood at the center of the blaze collapsed in a shower of sparks and crackling flame. "You don't know?" he said. When Thorsen didn't answer, he said it again, dropping the question. "You don't know." His face became serious. "It's an ugliness, Jens. No other way to say it."

"Stucki says they're on some kind of strike. I disappear for the day and come back to Armageddon."

"This has been—hmm, growing for a while," Passey said, pulling off his stocking cap. "People have been watching you and Angie, getting ideas, getting riled. Bright side, though, you could also say that the fellas are getting in our own little counter-Armageddon, don't you think?"

"Looks like the end of the world to me," Thorsen said.

"Shake off the dust, Thorsen."

"Look, I know this better than anyone. You get the women against you, and it's over."

"Actually they're against *you*, brother," Passey said.

"Looks like you're the ones who got locked out."

"Wrong—we released ourselves on our own recognizance."

"I heard it started with backtalk and face slapping," Thorsen said.

"That's one story, Vi Stucki's version," Passey said. "What I heard was that someone at the gas station told Bill Chamberlain he saw you buying Angie Bunker a carton of cigarettes this morning. Chamberlain said they mentioned it to him because they thought you had maybe picked up on some plural ways and was maybe shopping for a harem."

"Cigarettes? That's the stupidest thing I ever heard."

"So, you weren't buying cigarettes?"

" 'Course I was, but they weren't for Angie." Passey cocked his head and eyed Thorsen, who just told him to forget it. "So how does this get from Bill Chamberlain to my front yard being on fire?"

"Well, this thing has been building for a while. But it came to a head when Chamberlain started sniffing around the whole cigarettes thing. He headed right down to the dump to see what old Bob Ashton had to say."

The clarity came to Thorsen all at once, cleanly, like the snap of a chalk line. Ashton's crazy talk unscrambled in Thorsen's mind, and he dropped his head into his hand.

"Bill goes down to the dump because he's smelling dissent among the orthodoxy. He's hoping to have something to tell his wives about how God will leave you stranded if you live low in the gospel. Bob tells him that it started to come apart when Lanelle Comfrey taught a lesson about girls needing to keep themselves pure in the sexual way, and one of the girls—I think maybe it was Kayleen Larson—said that she didn't think sex was as bad as war crimes, which is why Mormons should really be Democrats. So, Comfrey tells this girl that no man would want a woman who'd already had someone else's baby, and Kayleen says something about Joseph being okay with Mary having Jesus, which gets her mouth slapped. Kayleen's not about to take that from anyone, so she hauls off and slaps Comfrey back and Comfrey says Kayleen's no better than that Bunker girl, after which one of the girls re-minded Lanelle that the scriptures tell us not to judge.

"That's how Ashton breaks it to Chamberlain, least that's how I heard it told. Next thing I know, my wife is thundering through the front room telling me that I'm through letting that two-bit teen mother run her hands through my hair, then she gets on the phone and starts calling her Relief Society sisters, who are suddenly having a meeting of the Anti-Angie League in my liv-ing room, and they decide to get people to boycott Stucki's place until he gets rid of her. I'm no dummy. My wife has been a little torqued about Angie for a while, but this thing went to DEF-CON 1 in a couple of days."

"Well, I wasn't paying attention."

"It's not all bad. Violet Stucki didn't like one bit of it, so she stands up and tells the women whoever is without sin can cast the first stone, and then she glares at Linda Carbolla and says some-thing about her being married in city hall, and then she leaves."

"Vi Stucki is as good as they come."

"Once this news hits the streets, the dominoes start falling. I got guys in the shop, then I'm on the phone, calling around, and we decide that we'll all come out here until the women can cool off. I mean, it's right before Christmas. Shouldn't take but a couple days, right. Everyone just needs to cool off."

"Not sure how you'll cool off next to this fire," Thorsen said.

"It's a pretty tense situation," Passey said, toeing one of the logs until it flared. "And it's not Christian."

"Seems pretty Christian to me," Thorsen said with a sigh. "Look, I'm going to bed."

"We'll see you in the morning."

"Who came up with the fire?"

"Bill Armour."

"Armour," Thorsen hollered into the cave of night. "Ever stop to wonder how all this heat is going to get through the walls of your fifth-wheel?"

There was a pause, and then Armour poked his head into the light and said, "The fire has symbolic value, Thorsen. It brings the tribe together."

Thorsen looked at Passey for a second, turned, and walked into the darkness. From inside the house it looked like Huns were getting ready to sack the place. The eerie orange glow washed over the eaves of the barn and the bare tree limbs. Strange canted shadows crawled through the spots of light, trembling as the flames themselves trembled. Christmas was a week away, but it seemed more like Halloween. A year ago all this would have seemed impossible, Thorsen thought. It was a regular town with regular problems, not this rift running right down the middle of things.

Thorsen removed his coat and hung it on the naked hook and stamped his boots on the coarse woven mat just inside the door. In the kitchen the stove hood light was on, and sitting at the center of its glow was a sandwich and a glass of milk. Thorsen took the food and positioned himself at the table, and after taking a bite, he lowered the sandwich, chewed, swallowed, and then lowered his head. He said a brief prayer over the food and then took another bite.

"Sheep," Thorsen growled to himself, shaking his head.

He took a gulp of milk and then another. Outside he heard a generator fire up and then level off. As he continued to eat, he wondered how in the world he'd ever break this to Angie. There was no good way. He thought perhaps he should just let her go down to the shop and find out for herself. But then he'd have to invent some cock-and-bull story about the RV park in the front yard, which would be a waste of time. Everyone would just end up feeling like they were in a bad television show. It would be everybody's fault and nobody's. Thorsen finished the last of his sandwich and emptied his glass of milk and set the plate and glass lightly in the sink, staring a moment at the line of small glass bottles and doilies on the window sill before switching off the light and heading to bed.

Dawn came weakly, hushed and glowing. Snow had fallen in the night; Thorsen could tell without having to look out the window. Then the crows began screeching. He tried to roll over and go back to sleep, but the cawing grew louder and more boisterous. He heard the slam of a trailer door, which quieted the birds for a second or two, then they were back at it. Thorsen threw off his covers and tromped over to the closet, grabbed his shotgun, and threw up the sash. Without really looking, he poked the barrel out the window and pumped five rounds into the morning. The crows scattered in all directions like blackened fireworks, but one dropped onto the roof of Stucki's trailer, thudding against its snow-coated aluminum skin like an old boot.

The shots echoed against the mountains and scattered with the crows, bringing the portable village below to life. Men streamed out into the cold, dressed in myriad plaids and camouflage from a multitude of seasons. They would have made easy targets—all that contrast and color. But Thorsen set the gun against the bed and dressed himself and went downstairs.

Angie was already awake, surrounded in food. She had two griddles on the stovetop, and she was just placing a baking dish full of link sausage into the oven. Thorsen stood quietly in the doorway watching her as she moved over to the sink and began gathering utensils.

"You should just sit down," Thorsen said, transfixed.

Angie shrieked and dropped a fork, which clattered into the sink, then she braced her arms against the countertop and caught her breath before she spun around. "You scared the hell out of me." Thorsen stood there looking at her, Lila's apron draped across her growing belly. "I thought you were still in the bedroom, hunting," she said. "You look like you've seen a ghost."

"I'm sorry," Thorsen said, shaking his head as if to clear it. "It was those sheep."

"Sheep?"

"Crows, I mean. Always cawing when a body wants to sleep."

"You teach any of them a lesson?"

"One, and I'm fixing to hang him on a pole, as an example."

"For who?" she asked. "The Ex-Scoutmasters Association? Ernest says they don't usually meet this late in the year."

"The what?"

"The ex-scoutmasters—when do they *normally* meet?"

Thorsen squinted his eyes as he pondered her question, until it dawned on him that Passey had lied through his teeth to the girl and saved him the trouble. He thought to himself that there was nothing in this world more endearing and difficult to fix than a lie told out of love, but he gritted his teeth and plowed on. "Scoutmasters, right. We usually meet on the third Saturday of the month and knock off in October, but they've been waiting on account of Lila passing, and—well, they decided they'd bite the bullet and surprise me."

"Oh," Angie said. "Well, I was up and saw Ernest and Brother Stucki throwing out a pan of burned eggs. I figured I'd keep them from starving. I hope you don't mind."

"If they starve?"

"They deserve some reward, for their trouble," Angie said as she ladled batter onto the griddle. She hesitated slightly, lifting her eyes before returning to her work. "The only thing is, I'm not sure I'll have time to clean all this up. I've got to get down to the shop and get some things ready. I'm supposed to be getting an order of samples today, and I want to go through it before we open."

"Angie," Thorsen said before he could stop himself. "You don't want to . . ."

"Want to what?" She edged her spatula under the nearest hotcakes.

Thorsen scratched the back of his neck and then thrust his right fist down into his pocket. "Well," he said.

"Don't want to what?"

"You don't want to be *late* is what I mean." He ground his teeth and squinted one eye. "I can clean up this mess," he said, then followed it quietly with, "I hope."

Angie gave him a look and turned back to her griddle. "Yeah, I don't want to be late," she said, glancing back at him. "By the way, thanks for taking me with you yesterday."

"I thought Deloy might like having someone more like—you know, not old and male coming by," Thorsen said, thrusting his other hand into his other pocket.

"I meant thanks for taking me to the doctor."

"Oh." Thorsen tried to wave her off. "I'm not very smooth."

"It was kind of stupid for me to not go." Her hand slipped around her belly, lightly, and rested there for only a second, but long enough for them both to notice it. Once they did, she went back to her pancakes. "I mean it *is* stupid, not to go."

"Well, you went." Thorsen crossed the room and pulled his coat off the hook.

"I'm just saying." Angie's eyes softened. "You all are doing a lot for me, and I don't really deserve it."

"You don't have to say anything."

"I know, I'm just saying."

Thorsen pulled on his coat but left it unzipped. Angie turned back to her griddle and flipped the pancakes, then moved an empty plate closer to the stove and set down her spatula. Thorsen watched her look out the square window over the sink. Though it was clear that Thorsen was still in the room and the conversation was not over, she continued to stare.

"I'm going to the Ramkes'," Thorsen said, then he zipped his coat halfway to the top and stuffed his hands into his pockets, "Maybe do some chores, check on Karl—see how he's doing."

"Okay," Angie said, lifting pancakes from the griddle.

"I'll be back in an hour or so to clean up, so don't trouble your-self."

Angie nodded.

"It's nice of you to feed these jokers. They don't deserve it."

She shrugged. "Nobody ever deserves breakfast."

Thorsen turned and headed through the mudroom and out the door.

The clouds to the east hung heavy on the mountains, their unvarying pewter cast burnished in places by a yellow wash of sunlight. The valley was dimly and uniformly lit, with the exception of the tops of the Wasatch mountains to the west. The air was bitterly cold, dry and edged. A thin wisp of white smoke streamed upward from the center of the ring of trailers. Bill Armour, teetering on the crest of two loading pallets set one against the other like giant playing cards, tried to retrieve the carcass of the shot crow from the top of Stucki's trailer with a cottonwood branch. After a few failed attempts, Bill simply shoved the dead crow off the far side of the trailer. A few seconds later, Passey came through a gap in the ring of trailers with the dead crow hanging from his hand like a sleeping bat. "Thorsen," he hollered, lifting the crow, "what the hell is going on?"

"I'm educating the wildlife," Thorsen said.

"Well, you just about gave me a coronary."

"Hmm, too bad."

"Thorsen, it's a wonder you didn't send that girl into labor."

"She's used to it—listen, I'm heading over to Karl Ramke's place, take care of some chores and look in on him. Angie's in there preparing breakfast for some outfit called the Retired Scoutmasters Association. I think you all should put together a service project and see to it that the kitchen is spotless. Since it seems like the men and the women of this town have switched places, you should find yourselves at home in the kitchen."

"She's feeding us?"

"I'm feeding you. She's making the breakfast. I don't know why, but for some reason she likes you geezers—"

"Jens Thorsen, good to see you," Andy Pearson interrupted, his hand slapping the shoulder of Thorsen's jacket, raising a puff of dust.

"How'd I miss *you* last night?" Thorsen asked.

"Got in this morning—you know, the missus and I are trying to have another little one. The window of opportunity is pretty narrow."

"I'm sure it is."

"Listen, I like what you're doing out here, Thorsen—Christian service, good old-fashioned Christian service."

"Speaking of Christian service, I got two cows need to be

milked, and some sheep need to be run down into the lower pasture. Pearson, you're in charge."

Pearson's head swiveled about with apprehension. "Thorsen, I've got to get to work."

"Won't take but a half-hour."

"Jens."

"I appreciate your schedule, Andy, but I got to be somewhere, and you fellas got some camping fees to take care of." Thorsen marched off and fired up his truck. Once the truck was warm, he threw it into reverse and picked his way through the crowd of frozen men scattered in camp chairs. As he pulled out, Thorsen could see Pearson gathering people together.

Chapter Twenty

Karl Ramke's truck was gone, and four dirty ruts were left in the snow on the north side of the garage. Thorsen figured Phyllis was in town on an errand. He thought about going in to check on Karl, but he figured if Phyllis was gone, Karl'd be sleeping. So, he zipped up his jacket and pulled on a pair of deerskin gloves and headed into the small barn. He fed the horses and checked their hooves, then he took a small sledge and broke the ice on the water trough. He opened a new bag of turkey feed and hauled some down to the turkey enclosure. All the birds were gone but one, which was pacing the floor of the pen, its wattle hanging limply from its beak. Thorsen shook his head and metered out some of the feed into the galvanized dispenser. "You turkeys de-railed my whole cotton-picking life, you know that, don't you? I'm done telling that story," Thorsen said. The turkey cocked its head and began pecking. Thorsen changed the water and made his way to the henhouse. He removed a glove and gathered the eggs, storing them in the large pockets of his jacket. After feeding the chickens, Thorsen carried the eggs up to the house and let himself in.

"Phyllis?" he said, in case he was wrong about Phyllis being gone, but there was no answer. "I'm done with the chores. You got anything for the burn pile?" Again, no answer. Thorsen put the eggs in the refrigerator and grabbed the wastepaper basket and set it by the door. The refrigerator compressor stopped, filling the house with a great silence that caught Thorsen off guard. He stood in the back entry listening to it, and as he did, a strange thought surrounded him. He began to wonder if there would be, as the world was drawing to an end, fewer and fewer babies. Would things taper off? Would there be a day, a week, a month when the nurses would start saying to each other, "You know, we haven't had a baby in here for a while." *There was a first baby, so it only goes to figure there'd be a last one,* he thought. *Or would there?*

Thorsen was nearly to the point of thinking himself a fool when the wind outside stirred and sounded against the windows on the west side of the house. He headed back to Karl's room and found it empty, the sheets on the twin bed peeled back. Thorsen looked around the room. Everything was still except for the light on the answering machine, which was flashing like a turn signal. Thorsen was tempted to play the messages, but he couldn't bring himself to do it. Instead, nausea flooded through him. He shut his eyes to calm himself and his stomach, but he saw Lila sprawled on the floor, and the shock of that vision forced his eyes open: bed, sheets, answering machine. The room torqued quickly, only a few degrees, but it was enough to cause Thorsen to grab his head and search for a chair. His pulse was racing; his breathing came in quickening gusts. "My God," he said, slumping. "What happened?"

Thorsen sat in the chair immobilized for a long while, catching his breath and trying to orient himself. When his head felt clear, he hoisted himself out of the chair and made his way back to the truck. He knew the other shoe was going to drop, but he didn't know when. The mess in town with Bunker and everything with the women were bearing heavy fruit. He was too busy with Angie and trips to the prison. He filled up his days like water in a reservoir. His fear now was that the dam would give way. As he backed down the Ramkes' driveway, he felt a great sadness, for himself first and then for something he couldn't name. He turned the wheel of the pickup and stabbed the accelerator. He wandered the county roads for an hour, bare trees pulsing by, snow crouching at the edges of all the roads.

Before he noticed, he was turning into Wizenberg's driveway. Two vehicles were in front of the house, and the garage door was up. Wizenberg was standing between the vehicles with a fly-rod case stretching from his hands to the floor. He was removing small objects from his vest pocket and dropping them one at a time into the open end of the tube. Thorsen saw him as he looked up, startled.

Leaning the tube against the yellow SUV, Wizenberg strolled out of the garage, brushing his hands on his pants. As he came closer, he ducked and squinted into the truck until he recognized Thorsen. "Mr. Thorsen," he said, his voice muffled by the window and the heater fan. Thorsen quickly turned off the engine and pawed at the door until it opened. "Is everything okay, Mr. Thorsen?" Wizenberg said, stepping back to make room.

"I was just over to the Ramkes', Doc," Thorsen said. "Karl Ramke, the fella with—"

"I know him," Wizenberg said. "Is he home already?"

Thorsen dragged his sleeve underneath his nose. "Home? No, nobody's there at all. The whole house is empty. Left open. That ain't like Phyllis."

Wizenberg's face fell.

"What's wrong?" Thorsen asked. "Something's wrong, isn't it?"

"Jens, they took Karl to the hospital up in Provo."

"When?"

"Yesterday, about noon. He had respiratory failure. It's pretty common with emphysema."

"Dammit."

"It's pretty common. The chest cavity fills with fluid and the patient can't move the diaphragm. Phyllis called an ambulance, and they put him on oxygen and brought him to the clinic. I turned them right around and sent them to Provo. We're not equipped for that kind of thing."

Thorsen stared down at his boots and shifted his weight from one foot to the other. "How is he?"

"I haven't heard anything."

Thorsen turned and began to climb back into the truck.

"I could call. You want me to do that?"

Thorsen stopped.

Wizenberg pulled out his cell phone and punched the keypad twice with his thumb. "Hello, this is Dr. Wizenberg from the Sanpete Clinic. I'm checking on a patient, Karl Ramke. An ambulance brought him in yesterday with pulmonary edema." He looked at Thorsen and grinned. "I speak the lingo," he whispered. "Thank you," he said into the phone, then he looked up again. "Someone's checking."

Thorsen closed the door of the truck and unzipped his jacket. The morning air was dry and cold as iron. He blew into his hands.

"Okay . . ." Wizenberg said. His eyes lifted skyward, then he frowned. "All right, thank you." He switched off the phone and slipped it back in the pocket of his vest.

"Jens."

"You don't have to tell me."

"I'm sorry."

"I knew it."

"It's not uncommon for this kind of—"

"I mean, the light on the machine was going. The house was empty. It's obvious what happened."

"I tried to see him," Wizenberg said, "but his wife—"

"Phyllis—"

"Right. His wife wouldn't let me talk to him. She called me a Jewish atheist and told me to get the hell off her property. Jewish atheist? She's a prize."

"You didn't hear me say it," Thorsen said, scratching the back of his head. "But that woman's on her own program." Thorsen put his hands in his pockets and strolled around the truck and stepped out onto the hard snow covering the front yard. The trench he'd dug with the backhoe was neatly covered with snow all the way from behind the house to the road. "That ditch still working for you?" Wizenberg nodded. "Good," Thorsen said. "And those sandbags?" Wizenberg told him it was all perfect. Thorsen walked a little farther out into the snow and craned his neck around the edge of the house and then nodded and crunched back and stood again in front of his truck on the bare driveway. He extended his hand to Wizenberg, who took it lightly and shook it. "Thanks for trying. Thanks for everything. Karl knew his number was up. He just didn't know when they were going to call it."

"I don't think anyone does."

Thorsen nodded. "Maybe not."

"If it's any consolation, this kind of thing is common with emphysema. It's just how the disease works."

"Sure," Thorsen said, climbing back into his truck. "Thanks."

Chapter Twenty-One

Thorsen had been working on a section of fence that ran parallel to the road running to town, when a pair of travel trailers roared past him, bucking and rattling on a cold hump of asphalt that straddled the road where he was working. Thorsen followed them with his eyes as they grew smaller and disappeared on the shallow downslope of the road. As they did, snow appeared in the air, curling only slightly in its descent.

Thorsen hammered a last nail into an ancient juniper post and tested the tension of the wire, then he climbed back into his truck and drove into town. He swung past the Main Street shops and the city hall, and he pulled in front of Stucki's shop and got out. Two women in a small, cream-colored sedan looked suddenly at each other, and then the one in the passenger seat began scribbling something on a clipboard. Thorsen squinted, but the snow built up on their windshield so he could barely see them. He wondered how they could possibly see out. As he watched, their windshield wipers pushed the snow away in a single sweep. It was

Sue Ellen Barclay and Anita Bennion. Thorsen brushed off his coat and went into the shop.

Stucki stood behind the farthest chair, his clippers starting up with a snap and buzz. Wayne Blitch sat in the chair, half his head clipped and the other half still wet and combed back. Passey sat in the closest chair in new work overalls already stained with oil and grease. He was carefully leafing through a copy of *Esquire* magazine, stopping for a moment to lower his nose and sniff at one of the pages. Passey's brother-in-law, Glade Smith, sat in a side chair with his jacket stuffed underneath. He was watching *The Magnificent Seven* with the remote control jammed in his fist and tipped back against his lips like he was studying the film.

"Hello, Jens," Stucki said, gesturing with the comb.

Thorsen said hello back.

"Nope," Glade said, "I think that dude is something Buchholz, maybe Hans or Heinrich."

"No, it ain't," Passey said, "It's Trini Lopez."

"Trini Lopez sang 'Lemon Tree.' He wasn't in *The Magnificent Seven*," Glade said and then turned back to the movie.

"Who cares?" Blitch said.

Passey lowered the magazine into his lap and said, "Those watchmen out there get you on their head count?"

"Looks like they did," Thorsen said and climbed into the vacant seat.

"They've been counting all day long," Stucki said. He returned to the other side of Blitch's head, his hands still and sure.

"Hurting business any?" Thorsen asked.

"Nope," Stucki said, "might be helping a little."

Passey just glared at Glade and then turned his attention to Thorsen. "I came in here to have Angie look at my eyebrows, but she didn't even come in this morning. Stucki hasn't seen hide nor hair of her either. Isn't that right, Stook?"

Stucki shrugged and gestured to a box sitting on the floor. "She had some samples here she was waiting on, and the box wasn't even open. And when I got here, there was some broken glass in one of the parking places."

Passey rolled up his magazine and leaned forward in his seat. "One of the kids working in my shop said he saw a couple of women driving through town with a busted-out windshield in their SUV. I told Stucki about it, and he told me about the glass out front, and we decided the best way to find out what was what was to call old Bob Ashton—"

"Keep him out of this," Thorsen said.

"Ashton said he'd heard some chatter on his scanner about Angie apparently throwing a thermos bottle through the window of Lanelle Comfrey's Ford Explorer," said Passey.

Thorsen started laughing.

"What's so funny?"

Thorsen shrugged and glanced over at Stucki, who lifted his eyebrows and changed the guard on his clippers.

"I don't know," Thorsen said. "Just seems funny, that's all— pregnant girl throwing my thermos at that Comfrey woman. You know, hell hath no fury and so forth."

Passey shook his head and started uncurling his magazine and laughing as well.

"You know, you're turning into a sissy," Thorsen said. Glade erupted into laughter and dropped the remote skittering onto the floor. Passey glowered him to silence. Each man glanced at the other until the room felt cobbed and tangled with trepidation. Just then a church bell on the television started clanging and the kid began his discourse on cowardice. Glade dropped to his knees and began rummaging under the far seats for the remote. When he found it, he hit the mute.

"That's what I've heard," Passey said. "And we haven't seen her all day."

Thorsen looked at his watch and then turned and squinted out the window. "Well, she likely ain't at my house, but then again it would be hard to tell, what with all the derelicts on my property."

"We've got cold war going on, Thorsen," Blitch said, kicking the smock and setting his boot back down on the foot rest. "We can't have any fraternizing."

"How can you have fraternizing with women, anyway?" Glade asked. "I mean, isn't a fraternity all guys?"

"Fraternizing doesn't mean having sex," Blitch said.

"That's what they told us in the Navy," Glade quipped.

"Of course they would—that's how it goes in the Navy," Blitch said. Glade fumed.

"Well, I don't know where she is," Thorsen said.

"I sure hope she's not out in this mess," Stucki said.

Just then a pair of headlights appeared in the window glass and then switched off.

"Look sharp," Stucki said. "Speak of the devil." Everyone tried to settle in and look natural. Angie pushed through the door, shaking snow off her coat.

"H'lo, Angie," Passey said without looking up from his magazine.

Angie was bent over slightly as she slipped her coat off. Her eyes flicked up at Passey and then her lips hardened.

"How you been doing?" Stucki asked as he spread talcum on Blitch's neck and whisked it away with a small horsehair brush. Angie's eyes skewered Stucki and then ratcheted around the room. When they came to Thorsen, he just turned his lower lip out slightly and then asked if he was in the way.

"Ex-Scoutmasters Association?" Angie asked.

"Now listen, Angie—" Passey said, straightening himself.

"You should have told me," she said.

"We were going to." Passey hoisted himself a little higher. "It's just—"

"If you had any character, you would have told me. I knew there was a reason I left."

"Did Spencer just pull up?" Stucki asked, gesturing toward the door with his brush. Everyone froze and turned toward the window and saw the red-and-blue lights just above the hood of Passey's pickup truck. Spencer got out of the car, his large white cowboy hat jutting into view. He went around the back of his own car and stooped next to the cream sedan parked out front. Angie immediately flushed and started looking from side to side, as if she just realized she'd lost her purse.

"Holy smokes," Thorsen said. "What's eating you?"

"All right," Angie said, "I'm not here, okay?"

The men shrugged. Angie rushed past Glade and slipped into the back room, slamming the door behind her. A moment of silence boiled in the shop, and then Glade took up the remote and unmuted the television. Passey went back to his magazine and Stucki to dusting off Blitch's neckline. Thorsen took out his jack-knife and began cleaning and paring his fingernails. Spencer's white hat appeared again, and he came through the door.

"H'lo Spencer," Stucki said. The men seconded Stucki, lifting hands and nodding. Glade said something about the snow.

"Howdy, fellas," Spencer said, removing his hat and cracking the door to shake the snow from it. "Say, you seen Angie Bunker today?"

Stucki froze and stared toward the top of the south wall of his shop, pushing his lower lip out slightly. He turned to Passey, "Angie been in today?"

Passey lowered his magazine. "Can't say that I've seen her. Jens, seen Angie?"

Thorsen tugged at one ear and told Passey that he'd seen her at about seven, "But that was at the house. Ain't been there since eight-fifteen. So . . .she could be in Ephraim, for all I know."

Spencer scowled and then eyed the men. "That's funny," he said, shifting his weight, "because her car's right out . . ." He jabbed his thumb toward the door. The men in the shop were quiet and still, except Glade, who nervously fingered the remote. Spencer's eyes shot to the screen. "Is that *The Magnificent Seven*?"

Glade nodded.

"I love this movie," Spencer said.

Spencer hung his hat on the rack and maneuvered himself for a better view of the screen. "It's just on regular TV?"

"Nope, cable," Glade said.

"Say, Spencer," Thorsen said, gesturing with the point of his knife. "Passey here thinks Trini Lopez was in this picture. What do you think?"

"Who's that?" Spencer asked.

"Everyone knows who Trini Lopez is," Blitch said, smiling.

"Isn't she that golfer?" Spencer asked.

"That's *Nancy* Lopez, Spencer," Stucki said. "Your father would be ashamed."

"*Trini* Lopez, the singer?" Passey asked, arching his eyebrows.

Spencer shook his head.

"Let's figure this out," Passey said. "You've got your Yul Brenner and Steve McQueen."

"That's two," Thorsen said. "Starting with the easy ones."

"Then there's Charles Bronson?"

"He was in *The Magnificent Seven*?"

"Sure was. He's in the blue shirt." Glade pointed to the screen.

"What about that guy from *The Rifleman*?" Spencer asked.

"He ain't in this picture."

"You sure?" Spencer scratched the side of his nose.

"You're thinking of James Coburn," Glade said.

"Okay, that's four," Thorsen said.

"That guy from *The Man from U.N.C.L.E.*, the dandy with the gloves."

"Robert Vaughn," said Glade.

"He's weird looking."

"You got two more." Thorsen craned his neck toward the street to check on the women in the sedan. "You think they might want to get out of the cold?"

"Leave them," Stucki said. "You guys are forgetting Eli Wallach."

"He played the bandit," Spencer said.

"They've got a Jew playing a Mexican?" Thorsen asked.

"That's how they did it back then," Passey chimed in.

"Still got two more." Thorsen folded up his knife.

"I told you," said Passey. "It's Trini Lopez."

"Listen, Trini Lopez was *not* in *The Magnificent Seven*." Glade threw up his arms and dropped them with a smack.

"Are you sure?"

"Positive."

"He didn't play the kid?"

"No, that was some German guy."

"He looks like a Mexican."

"They got Jews *and* Germans playing Mexicans? What the hell is wrong with these people?" Thorsen said.

"That's why they call it acting, Thorsen," Glade said. Thorsen waved him off and reopened his knife. Glade continued, "I'm serious. The guy's name is Buckminster or Buchholz or something."

"Glade's right," Spencer said. "They got a thing on the DVD about it."

"*Horst* Buchholz," Glade erupted, gesturing grandly. "It's Horst Buchholz, not Trini Lopez. Ha!"

"Okay, so that's six. What about the other guy?"

"Which one?"

"That one," Passey said, pointing at the television. "The one who's always asking about treasure."

Spencer shrugged. They all looked at the television. A line of

Mexican girls in white dresses paraded by. Steve McQueen, who was fiddling with a pinwheel and watching them, said, "You know, I've been in some towns where the girls aren't very pretty. And, in fact, I've been in some towns where they're downright ugly. But this is the first time I've been in a town where there's no girls at all—except little ones."

Spencer jerked and stepped away from his spot in front of the television and slipped his thumbs down into his belt. "All right, you almost got me there, but it won't work."

"What won't work?" Stucki asked.

"You know what I mean. I came in here looking for Angie Bunker." Spencer was fuming, his head nearly shimmering with heat and vapor. A dull thud sounded from the back room, and Spencer lurched for his pistol, pulling the snap off his holster.

"Hold on there, Barney Fife. Keep the gun where it's at," Thorsen said.

Everyone in the shop erupted into laughter. Spencer reddened and wiped his mouth with the back of his hand. "What did you call me?"

"Doesn't matter," Thorsen said.

"He called you Barney Fife," Glade said. "You know, that guy from *Andy Griffith*."

"Don Knotts," Passey said.

"Wasn't he also Mr. Limpet?" Stucki asked.

"That was on last week," Blitch said. "Man, that show was almost as good as *McHale's Navy*."

A second bump came from the back room. "Okay, you're doing it again," Spencer said, pushing past Blitch and Stucki. "Get out of my way." He threw open the back-room door and charged down the short, narrow hallway.

Stucki leaned toward the door and said, "Don't suppose you've got a search warrant." The rest of the men crowded around the door, craning their necks. They watched Spencer move around the small table and three chairs of the room like a dog checking luggage. He picked up one of the twenty or thirty bluish paper-towel rolls that were stacked on the tabletop and set it down. "Any other way out of here?" Spencer asked.

"Nope," Stucki said. "Except for the mouse holes. Seems like they can come and go as they please." Passey snickered and lifted his magazine and pretended to read it.

Spencer came out and checked the bathroom with a quick flick of the door and the lights. "This is pretty fishy." He pointed toward the door. "Those women out there say they saw Angie come in here not ten minutes ago. Plus, her car is outside. Plus, you all tried to trick me."

"You can check under my apron here," Blitch said. Snorting, he lifted the edges of the apron and kicked his feet.

"She might be here under one of the seat cushions," Glade said, rising.

"Shut up."

"Spencer, why would you trust those women in the first place? They've done nothing all day but try to drive away this brother's fine, upstanding customers," Thorsen said, crossing one leg over the other.

"She smashed in a windshield this morning, Thorsen. I know she's here. I'm going to sit right there in that car, and I'm going to watch this door." He shoved open the door and headed back into the snow.

"He forgot his hat," Stucki pointed out.

The door exploded inward and Spencer snatched his hat from the rack and headed out the door again without looking at anyone.

Glade went back to his movie, and everyone else acted like nothing had happened, but all their eyes ticked back and forth between the back-room door and the front door.

"Where do you think she went?" Passey asked.

Stucki glanced into the back room furtively and said, "I think she's inside one of the toweling boxes."

"Well, we can't leave her in there," Passey said.

"We can't go get her—he's watching," Thorsen said.

"We've got to get her out of there," Stucki said and began taking off Blitch's smock.

"Hold on a minute, Stook," Blitch said. "Go ahead and lather up my neck."

"You sure?" Stucki said, looking around the room. "I got you pretty good before."

"Just lather me up, and start on my right side so you're right between me and John Law out there."

"Okay," Stucki said and loaded his fingers with lather from the hot dispenser and began dabbing at Blitch's neck. Then he stropped the razor and moved into position, running a screen for Blitch, his hands trembling as they moved closer to his neck. As soon as the blade edge settled on skin, the trembling was gone, and Stucki took a single upward stroke.

"Hold on right there, Stucki." Blitch rifled around under his smock and brought out a small wireless phone, upon which he stubbed a couple of numbers before bringing it up to his ear. "Bill Chamberlain? Good to talk to you. You driving that new truck of yours? Nope. Well, I didn't think so, because I'm out here west of town and, sure as shooting, I thought I saw some kid driving your truck out toward the dump . . . No, sir . . . No, sir. That's right. I'd call the cops right now, get 'em to pull that son of a bitch over . . . Sure, Bill. No problem. You say hello to Lucy, Emma, and Verlene for me. All right." Blitch ended the conversation with a beep and slipped the phone back under the smock. "Did he see me?"

"Nope."

"You can get the other side now, Stook."

Two minutes later the lights on Spencer's squad car switched on. He backed into the street, his tires spinning in the snow, and he headed west.

Chapter Twenty-Two

"WHAT ARE WE GOING TO DO with my car?" Angie asked. She was lying down on the bench seat of the truck, covered in a heavy red-and-black-checked wool blanket.

"We'll pick it up later, when the heat is off," Thorsen said. "Keep your head down."

"You know, this is a lot harder than it looks."

Thorsen pressed down on her head and said, "Quit squirming, will you? We're just about out of town."

"I'm getting up anyway," Angie said, kicking her legs. "Let go of me." She sat up and pulled the blanket off her face. To either side of the truck, snow-covered junipers flashed by. "What are you talking about? We're nowhere near town. It's like you *have* to lie or your pants will fall down or something."

Thorsen cocked an eyebrow. "Don't you mean my pants will be on fire?"

"Shut up."

"Angie, come on."

"Shut up. I mean it."

Angie arranged the blanket across her lap, then aimed the heater vents so they blew on her face and hands. Thorsen turned his head slightly and tried to watch Angie out of the corner of his eye. She was sitting plumb, her back only slightly leaning against the seat. Her chin was extended, and her lower lip bunched together like a sack with its drawstrings pulled tight.

"They didn't think of it as lying," Thorsen said quietly.

Angie glowered. "Hitler didn't think of it as killing."

"Angie, I've tried not to play the old-man card with you, but I've lived a long time, and I've figured out a couple of things. One, men are like dogs, dumb as the face of a shovel. And two, women are like cats, smart but they—"

"Like cats?"

"Sure. So you put them together, and you get howling and bits of fur flying around. But a man, as stupid as he is, has got one redeeming quality—he's loyal."

Angie laughed out loud. "Loyal like my little one's daddy? That kind of dog?"

"That's right—no, not that kind of dog."

"And what's a woman's redeeming cat quality?"

Thorsen looked out the driver's side window.

"Is it that she's proud?" Angie's eyes narrowed, and she planted her feet on the floor of the truck. Thorsen shook his head. "How about self-possessed?" she asked. Thorsen pulled the seatbelt away from his chest and let it snap back into place.

"Well, it's not something I had all the way worked out," he said, then rubbed the side window with the sleeve of his jacket.

Angie slid her hands under the blanket and chuckled to herself.

"Listen, Angie," Thorsen said. "Those geezers didn't do anything they wouldn't have done for their own daughters or granddaughters. And besides, in this whole thing, those women were just running scared. Can't blame them, even if you wanted to. They've been trained for this. It's reflexes."

"I'm okay with blaming them," Angie said.

"Okay, forget it. These guys might be old, but they think the world of you. And they're out at the house because they're on strike, but they didn't want to break it to you. They didn't want to be the ones to say—"

"That I was right. That church people are all hypocrites waiting to cast the first stone."

"I won't argue that. What I'm trying to say is, these fellas didn't want to admit that their wives were the ones trying to burn you down. They took a stand, which is something—look at this snow." He hunched a little and gestured across the road, his old hand cupped slightly like a docent's. "They wouldn't rough it like this for just anybody. It's stupid to say it like this, but you won their hearts, and that isn't easy to pull off. A lot of these fellas haven't had to use them in a long time."

They drove on for a while, snow falling, seeming to swoop toward the truck monochromatically. A pair of headlights appeared ahead of them, dim at first but growing larger. Almost immediately a truck appeared, a hand waving madly, then the sides of a fifth-wheel passed. "Was that Bill Armour?" Thorsen asked.

"Who?"

"In that truck? Was that Bill Armour? Shoot."

"What, are your ex-scoutmasters flying the coop or something?"

"Two of them left this morning after you were gone."

"What is it you were saying about men being loyal?"

"I'm just going to drive the truck," Thorsen said.

"Why don't you do that?" Angie said.

"I'm going to."

Angie folded her arms above her belly, and she let her head bob a little with the dips and swells of the road. Her eyes narrowed, then she tossed her head almost invisibly to one side. Thorsen reached down and scratched his calf through his pant leg. Angie leaned toward the dash and turned down the heat.

"That okay?" she asked.

"Go ahead."

Snow was falling so thickly that the wiper blades could barely keep the windshield clear. The air between the junipers had grown thick, and the snow blunted the sound of the tires.

"Karl died," Thorsen said. "The funeral's in a couple days."

"Oh, no," Angie said, sitting up. "You want me to go with you?"

"No, I wouldn't wish that on anyone. I suspect Phyllis is going to crack, and when she does, smart folks will head for high ground."

Thorsen braked and turned the truck slowly and carefully from the road. The snow was deeper, and the tires slid a little as the truck crested the hill. "These fellas are going to have a pretty tough go getting their rigs . . ." His words trailed off as he saw two trailers harbored in solitude, the whiteness of the snow like an ocean. "They sure enough caved, didn't they?" he said. Angie rustled around under her blanket. Thorsen parked the truck and craned his neck around. "Left a fire going, though—Judas Priest."

"Whose trailers are left?" Angie asked.

"Stucki and Passey's. Don't mean they're coming back, though." Thorsen spilled out of the truck, cursing, and slogged through the snow to the fire pit and kicked at the blackened logs with the sole of his boot. The fire flared orange, the only color anywhere. Then he cursed again. Angie quietly slipped from the truck into the house. Thorsen grabbed the hose, shook snow from it, and yanked up the lever on the stand pipe. After twenty seconds the hose end was still dry. Thorsen shook and inspected it, and still nothing, so he hobbled back over to the fire and began heaving armloads of snow onto the fire, where it hissed and spat. Enoch poked his head out of his stall to watch, his head enrobed in vapor.

When Thorsen went inside, Angie was writing an elaborate message on a notepad.

"Uhh, Phyllis Ramke left a message for you," she said.

"Oh, no."

"Actually, she's been pretty much calling all day. Remember what you said about heading for high ground?" Angie raised one eyebrow. Thorsen shut his eyes and breathed out a slow, steady stream of air through his nostrils. Angie set down her pencil. "I think you should start heading."

"I can't do this on an empty stomach."

Chapter Twenty-Three

Thorsen made a late lunch for himself and Angie and ate it in a chair next to one of the large double-hung windows on the east side of the house. The two vigilant trailers nearly disappeared in the gathering snow. The twin back windows of Stucki's Spartanette had been lidded with snow, which had slumped down the glass until the trailer seemed nearly asleep. When he was finished eating, he took his plate to the sink and clicked the button on the answering machine. Angie told him to prepare himself.

The machine rewound and beeped, and the voice of Phyllis exploded into the room. *"Thorsen, I want you to call off the dogs. They've been raining down on me for two days straight. I'm about ready to drown in hairspray and casseroles. They have no respect for a person's privacy. And besides, when have they come out before? Do they just perch in the trees waiting for folks to die so they can swoop down and start baptizing the dead with Velveeta and mushroom soup? They've got no respect. You tell them I've got Karl's shotgun right here with me on the kitchen table, and I can put a load of shot in a girdle just as fast as I can put it in a pair of jockey shorts. And one more thing, you tell that girl of yours she should tell those women to go to hell—I have maps, but I don't think they'll need them. The hornets swarming around that poor thing don't represent this town. There's some people who don't—"* Then a beep.

Thorsen and Angie looked at each other.

"She's just warming up," Angie said. Then another beep.

"I don't know where that cut off, but you tell that girl she should not spend a single second worrying about those hypocrites. I've been around enough to know that there's plenty of women in Sanpete have families before they have husbands, and saying otherwise is lies on top of lies. Motherhood has made more liars out of people than the government has. You all would make more progress in this world if you'd figure out that you can't just drive people into heaven like a bunch of cows. Even if you could manage to get them there against their will, they'd hate it, and they'd spend their time breaking the windows so they could breathe. You all can't scare a person into religion either. What you get out of that is hypocrites, and there is nothing I hate more than a smooth hypocrite who claims to be Christian. I'm sick of the dropping by and the friendliness with strings attached. In the thirty years me and Karl have lived here, we ain't been tempted to take up with you people. I don't suspect a couple of relief visits are going to turn the—"

One last beep.

"See what I mean?" Angie said.

Thorsen grabbed his coat and stopped at the door. There was an inch and a half of snow covering the truck, and his tracks had been almost completely filled in.

"You're not going back out in that," Angie asked.

Thorsen rehung his coat on its hook and walked slowly and stiffly through the kitchen and down the hall. Dropping heavily in his chair, he sat there motionless until he fell asleep.

The urn rose slightly from the small draped dais in the center of a draped table. It was flanked by lilies in narrow crystal vases, and a small folded card that read KARL MORONI RAMKE sat in front of the dais and to one side. The type was not raised. A few people moved about the room quietly. Phyllis sat to one side, her head lowered, and her hands, like cracked wooden paddles, lay folded in her lap.

Stucki walked stiffly and stood next to Phyllis. His head was trembling slightly—his hand trembled as well, but stilled as he set it on Phyllis's shoulder. Thorsen watched Stucki bend down and whisper to Phyllis, who nodded. Stucki went to the table and picked up the urn and cradled it in the crook of his right arm, then walked carefully to where Thorsen was sitting.

"I'm going to take old Karl up to the Kaiparowits, see if we can't find that saber-toothed cat of his, lay him to rest."

"You going in the snow?"

"Might not have to. They say we got some high pressure moving in. Plus, we can always get in on sleds."

"You'll kill yourself, is what."

"I hear freezing to death is a nice way to go. Visions. Beautiful girls. I wouldn't mind it."

• • •

The snow had stopped before the funeral and then started again, and as Thorsen parked in front of the hardware store, the clouds broke a little and a scrap of sunlight fell crosswise along the State Farm offices and the street and the corner of Zions Bank. Still clad in his suit, Thorsen passed the pallet of deicer and a thirty-gallon garbage can full of snow shovels. The Cannon girl at the register looked up at him, pulled the long curl of bleached hair behind her ear, and then looked back down at the tray of hardware she was sorting. He walked past the bins of cheap tools and clamps and past Wilmer Anderson, who seemed to be meditating in the caulking and tape aisle. He walked past the brushes and brooms aisle and then heard Mrs. Dalton ask where the brooms and shovels were. He crossed in front of a Shop-Vac display, and Bill Armour appeared out of nowhere in a red vest with his name embroidered on it.

"What can I help you with, Thorsen?" he asked.

"Looking for some felt weather stripping and one of those aluminum and vinyl wraparound jiggers that slips around the bottom of a door."

"I think we're out of the felt."

Thorsen cursed.

"We got the foam."

"Don't want it. What you doing here, anyway? Don't you work for the state?"

"Just trying to make Christmas fly. Whining taxpayers don't make it easy on a civil servant."

Thorsen nodded.

"Let's go look at that foam," Bill said, turning toward the back of the store.

"I know where it is." Thorsen started to move past him.

"Hey, Thorsen?" Bill said. Thorsen stopped. "You know, I'm really sorry about that buddy of yours—Ramke. It's a shame."

"I appreciate that," Thorsen said.

He walked past a display of Christmas lights, and he realized that he had forgotten to put up any this year. He stopped and picked up a box and then, out of the corner of his eye, he saw power tools suspended from the pegboard display. He set down the lights and stepped into the aisle and picked up a red Milwaukee Magnum hammerdrill. The specs and price were listed on a card. Thorsen perused them and then set the Magnum back. A few steps down was a yellow Dewalt half-inch. The amps were higher on the Dewalt. "No Porter Cables," he said to himself. "Burn up one of these in five minutes."

At the far end of the aisle, a light came on. Thorsen glanced up to see a display of motion-sensitive floodlights. He waved his hand, but no other lights lit up. Thorsen picked up the Dewalt hammerdrill and turned it over in his hands and then looked over at a blue Makita just as another bank of floodlights switched on. When he glanced over, he found Darrell Bunker examining a plunge router.

"Dewalt's got nine amps," Thorsen said.

Bunker's head lifted and slowly turned. "Dewalt don't plunge." Then he sneered and turned away.

"True."

Bunker gestured to the hammerdrill in Thorsen's hand. "You got Dewalt stock or something? You sound like a shyster."

"Give me a break. I'm thinking about upgrading. You might know something about that."

Bill Armour appeared at the far end of the aisle, became alarmed, and disappeared.

"It's about time. That Porter Cable of yours was on its last legs years ago," Bunker said.

"It was fine until somebody borrowed it."

Bunker looked down at the routers and then put back the one in his hand. Bill Armour's head reappeared, followed by Andy Pearson's. Both of their faces were split between concern and amusement.

"Make sure you get a dual mode—and the half-inch chucks'll take the large bits," Bunker said.

"What's the router for?" Thorsen asked.

"Making some furniture—a little dresser, some other doodads. Old guys do that sometimes."

Thorsen nodded. "They do, don't they?"

"It's gotten out of hand, don't you think?" Bunker said. He moistened his lips briefly and then set his jaw. "I thought you were gonna sic the law on me for selling land in the open market. I got ready for you, but you never came."

"Must have felt like prom night," Thorsen said.

Bunker looked like he was going to take Thorsen's head off, but he breathed through his nose a few times. "Look. I told her this would happen. That's why I suggested she just get out of town."

"Suggested?" Thorsen slammed the hammerdrill down. "You've got a way with words. You can get them to mean whatever you want."

"I'll bet she said I threw her out."

Thorsen tried to remember his conversation with Angie when

he found her in Stucki's shop. He couldn't recall her saying the words, *He threw me out.* But the message seemed clear. Thorsen gripped his forehead and then skimmed his hand over the top and back of his head.

"Thorsen, I don't have to explain myself to you. But I told her things would go south if she stayed here. I told her she should go live in Reno with her aunt. A pregnant girl wouldn't attract as much attention there. Nobody in Sanpete was going to give her a break—and, well, I was right, wasn't I? We pretty much had a natural disaster around here the last few days."

"I gave her a break, and so did Stucki. Passey. Glade. Plenty of people did."

"And plenty of people didn't. I figured it would be better for everyone if she just left."

Thorsen was silent. He looked at the displays behind Bunker: router bits, jigsaw blades, circular-saw blades, wire wheels, buffers, and grinding wheels. At the end of the aisle he saw the toe of a work boot that vanished as soon as he looked at it.

"We've got company," Thorsen said.

Bunker looked down the aisle. The floodlights came on all at once, and small percussive footsteps sounded in the adjacent aisles.

"All I'm saying is I'm not sure you fixed things."

"Go ahead—you got the First Amendment behind you. Should I tell her I saw you?"

Bunker shook his head.

"She's been going to the doctor," Thorsen said.

"Good."

"I'm taking her again tomorrow—up to Provo."

"You don't have to do that."

"Is that because you're gonna take her?" Thorsen said. Bunker toed the linoleum. "They need to run some kind of tests or something." Thorsen sniffed.

"Anything wrong?"

Thorsen shrugged. "They're a lot more careful than they used to be."

"About some things," Bunker said. "Other things, important things don't even come up."

Chapter Twenty-Four

THORSEN LOOKED AWAY AS Angie's blood leapt into the small glass tube. The nurse calmly worked the needle and then covered it with a small square of cloth and withdrew it. "It's not so bad as you think it's going to be," Angie said.

"Just a little prick," the nurse said, untying the rubber tourniquet.

"What's this test for, anyway?" Thorsen asked.

"It's a test for beta human chorionic gonadotropin," the nurse said. Thorsen's eyes crossed. "It's a hormone we find in a pregnant mother's blood."

"It's pretty easy to tell she's pregnant," Thorsen said.

"It's a marker for a lot of other things, too."

Thorsen looked at Angie and shrugged.

"If you'll follow me, the doctor will be with you shortly," the nurse said, rising. She led them into a room two doors down, noted something on Angie's chart, and then slipped the chart into a rack on the door. When the door closed, Angie hoisted herself onto the examination table, the paper crinkling. Just to the side of the exam table was a computer terminal on a rolling cart. Surrounding it were pieces of beige equipment connected together with shiny black cables.

"I can wait out there if you'd be more comfortable," Thorsen said.

Angie lifted her eyes, her thin lips like a single wire. "If *I'd* be more comfortable?" She smiled and rubbed her palms along the length of her skinny thighs. "I'm sure they don't think *you're* the father."

Thorsen rolled his eyes and planted his boots one at a time on the carpet. "That's not what I meant."

The door opened and another nurse came in. She set Angie's chart on the counter, tore open the blood-pressure cuff, placed it around Angie's biceps, and began inflating it. "Am I going to have to, you know . . ." Angie asked, gesturing to her clothes. The nurse raised her eyebrows, removed the stethoscope from her ears, and deflated the cuff. She wrote Angie's blood pressure on the chart.

"I'm sorry?" she said.

"Am I going to have to strip down or anything?" Angie asked.

"Oh, no. The doctor will just lift your shirt a little."

Angie flipped a look at Thorsen. "Can you handle that?"

Thorsen had buried his face in his left hand. With the other, he gave a gesture of resignation. The nurse smiled and began asking Angie some questions. "When was your last period?"

"Labor Day," Angie said. "Pretty ironic, huh?"

The nurse smiled. "Are you having any cramps or spotting?"

"A little—spotting, not cramps."

"What color is it?"

"Kind of dark, but there's not very much."

"Like a period?"

Angie shook her head. "Lighter than that."

"Any nausea?"

"Other than the morning sickness?"

"Yes."

"No, nothing really. I mean, I can't stand spicy food anymore."

"Thanks. Your feet swelling?"

"Yeah, a little."

"Have you ever had a miscarriage or an ectopic pregnancy?"

"What's that?"

"A pregnancy that starts in your fallopian tubes."

"No, I've never had that."

"How about a miscarriage?"

Angie lowered her head and brushed her hair out of her face. "Yeah," she said softly. Thorsen lifted his face from his hand.

"How long ago?"

Angie sniffed.

"It's okay, honey. How long ago?"

"March."

"How far along were you?"

"I don't know. Maybe ten weeks. I wasn't even sure I was pregnant until it happened." Angie sniffed again and lightly scratched her face.

"It can be pretty scary, huh?" the nurse said. Angie nodded. "Okay, Angie. The doctor's going to come in and give you a little sonogram. It'll be a few minutes." As the nurse opened the door, the doctor came in, having just given another nurse a set of instructions. "This is Angie. She's up from the Gunnison clinic."

"Hi, Angie, I'm Doctor Cannon. Let's see what we've got here." He looked over the chart, set it down, and washed his hands. "Can I get you to pull your shirt up a little, just to where your ribcage starts?" Craning his neck around, he asked, "Who's this?"

"Thorsen. Jens Thorsen," Thorsen said, standing briefly and awkwardly.

"This is my grandpa," Angie said. "I'm living with him right now."

"That's right," Thorsen said, and then sat back down.

"Nice to meet you, Mr. Thorsen."

The doctor stepped up to Angie and had her lie back on the table. His hands moved diagnostically across the tight skin of her belly. When he was done, the nurse handed him a small measuring tape. One end he snugged down just inside the top of Angie's pants, the other end he smoothed across her belly. "Nineteen point five centimeters. That's pretty big for nineteen weeks."

"Yeah," Angie laughed. "Maybe it's twins."

The doctor gathered up the tape and handed it to the nurse. "Twins is one way to do it," he said. "Angie, we're going to do an ultrasound, which'll let me take a look inside."

"It that the same thing as a sonogram?"

"Same thing. I'm going to sit down here and run the machine. Jackie is going to have the wand, and she'll be moving it around on your belly."

"Angie," Jackie said, "I'm going to squirt a little jelly on you—helps us get a better picture. It might be a little cold." She shook a bottle of bluish gel onto Angie's stomach and placed the transducer on the near side of her belly. The doctor was clicking his mouse and moving through different windows of a complex-looking program. A weak pulse came through the speakers mounted on either side of the cart.

"Is that the baby's pulse?" Angie asked.

"That's yours. When we get the baby's, you'll know it," the nurse said.

"I need to get a sagittal view," the doctor said. The nurse moved the transducer. "I can't get a fetal heartbeat."

"What does that mean, no heartbeat?" Thorsen asked.

"Hang on, Jackie. Will you trade me places?"

"Is something wrong with my baby?" Angie asked.

"Hang on," the doctor said, taking the transducer and sliding it around. He moved methodically from one side of her belly to the other, pausing and pressing one edge of the transducer a little more deeply and easing up on the other. "What are you getting?" he asked.

"Snowstorm," the nurse said, her voice low and even.

"No grapes?"

"No grapes."

"What's wrong?" Angie sat up. Thorsen was stunned. "What's wrong?" The pitch of her voice was rising.

"Angie," the doctor said. The nurse was carefully wiping off the gel with a paper towel. "How much did they tell you at the clinic?"

"Just that I was a little bigger—maybe it was twins. What's going on with my baby?"

The doctor took Angie's hand and looked her in the eye. "Angie, there's no baby," he said.

"How in the world can she *not* be pregnant? Open your eyes," Thorsen boomed.

"Yeah, I mean I'm pregnant. Obviously. Look at me. I mean, what's all this?" Angie grabbed her belly.

The nurse moved the transducer off the examination table and onto the ultrasound cart while the doctor continued to speak. "I know this is going to sound strange, but you *are* pregnant. Your beta-hGC levels are through the roof. You've probably felt pregnant, morning sickness, the whole nine yards. The thing is, there's no baby." Angie sobbed. The nurse handed her some tissue. "You've got a gestational trophoblastic neoplasia," he said. "Sometimes we call it a molar pregnancy."

Thorsen slumped in his chair and stared at his boots. Angie rustled the paper. "What does that mean?" she asked. "Is the baby dead?"

"There's no baby. Judging by your beta-hGC levels and the ultrasound image, you've got a complete mole, which means when your egg was fertilized its DNA disappeared or switched off or was damaged somehow. We call that an empty egg. There's no baby inside you, no placenta. That's why you're spotting a little— should be more than what you describe, but not always."

"What do I have to do?" Angie asked, shocked, not crying any longer. "Do I have to have it?"

"You can't go through a normal delivery. That would probably kill you. We'll have to do a dilation and curettage. It's a surgical procedure. You'll be under a general anesthetic."

"Do I have to do it today?"

"No, but we should get you in here right after Christmas. Cure rate's about a hundred percent. It's a pretty well-worn path. The longer we wait, though, the harder that D and C will get. I'm sorry."

"There's no baby," Angie said, shaking her head.

"Correct. There's no baby."

Angie was asleep when they pulled back into the drive at Thorsen's place. Snow had been falling steadily the whole trip back. When he came to the house, Thorsen noticed that Stucki's Spartanette was gone, and Passey's truck was hitched to his fifth-wheel, exhaust billowing from under the hitch. Angie's car was back, too. Thorsen parked, and Passey stepped out of the trailer with a large blanket-wrapped bundle in his arms. "We're home," Thorsen said.

Angie stirred, rubbing an eye with the back of her wrist.

"Passey's here."

Passey crossed around the front of the truck and motioned for Angie to roll down her window. Thorsen braced his arm against his door and clutched his temples.

"Hey, Angie. Hope everything went okay up there."

"Yeah, sure," she said. "Just fine."

"I got something here for you—a little Christmas gift or something," Passey said, peeling the blanket corners away. "I made it myself. It's not much, but I think it might be nice. You know they're all made of plastic and MDF these days—bunch of garbage." Passey unveiled a small cradle built of cherry, a dozen or so spindles lined up along either side. The head and foot were solid, with hearts scrolled into the top at each end. "I turned the spindles on my lathe. It looks a lot like the one my mother used to put us kids in."

Angie crumpled onto the dashboard, buried her face in her arms.

"What did I say?" Passey asked, his eye twitching once and then a second time.

"It's okay," Thorsen whispered. "Just set that crib on the step there. It's nice work, Passey. Nice work. Don't worry about it. She's had a hard day."

"All right," Passey said, covering the cradle. "Merry Christmas." He walked slowly through the snow and set the cradle down by the door, then motioned to Thorsen that he was going to head home. Thorsen nodded and waved and turned his attention to Angie.

"He didn't know," he said.

Angie nodded but kept her face hidden.

"I'm going to go inside and start a fire and get some dinner together. You want me to take these pictures the doctor gave you?" Angie nodded again. "Okay, just don't freeze to death out here."

"I won't," she said, rolling up the window.

Thorsen walked around the living room straightening things, then he built a fire in the woodstove and closed the doors. He took a flashlight from a drawer in the kitchen and went into the basement. The flashlight beam cut back and forth through the darkness for a few minutes, then Thorsen disappeared into the darkness and came out with a large box with dog-eared flaps and one side stove in. He hauled the box upstairs and began pulling out strings of Christmas lights wound carefully around split cedar shakes. He hung the lights from the exposed heads of small painted brads driven into the window sills and molding. When he was finished, Thorsen stooped down and plugged them in.

He switched off the overhead lights and flopped in his chair, staring across the room, his brow creased, his body slumped, his knuckles hanging off the ends of the armrests. He noticed the rise and fall of his chest and scanned the room, which did not feel festive.

Thorsen rose disgusted and went into the kitchen, where he prepared two identical meals: ham and mustard sandwich, carrots, glass of milk, brownie. He ate his meal standing over the sink and set the other meal on a plastic tray with a plaid napkin and took it upstairs. Thorsen rapped on the door, but there was no answer, so he set the tray on the floor and went downstairs.

At the base of the stairs, Thorsen stopped to look at a family picture. He and Lila were at the center. She was wearing large glasses with a blue cast to the lenses and a flowered blouse with a wide, triangular collar. Thorsen was wearing a red-and-black work shirt with a white-agate bolo tie. Lilly and Ammon stood behind their mother. Lilly's husband, Hunter, was behind her. Ammon had already been divorced from Carol. Jens Junior and his wife Kaylyn stood behind Thorsen. In the empty space next to them was the barn and garden.

Thorsen closed his eyes and then opened them.

After a half-hour of rummaging through the decorations,

Thorsen cleared space on the coffee table and set up the nativity: manger, Mary, Joseph, Christ child, livestock, kings, shepherds. He wadded up the newspaper the nativity had been packed in and tossed it in the open box. The miniature scene was strange surrounded by copies of *National Geographic*, one showing the weathered face of Sir Edmund Hillary, the other picturing a desiccated Incan mummy wrapped in wool, a shock of blue and orange parrot feathers lying across one eye. Next to the magazines was a letter mailed from the missionary training center in Provo. Thorsen started to open it but set it back down. He took another look at the nativity, snatched up the baby and placed it in his shirt pocket, then rose and brought Passey's crib into the house and took it to the basement. He returned and carefully wrapped a small wooden hand mirror in the Sunday comics. Then he fashioned a small card from some paper he found in a kitchen drawer and addressed it to Angie. Since there was no tree, he set it next to the childless nativity and went upstairs.

The tray was in the same place he left it, but the food was gone. He didn't knock this time, just picked up the tray and went downstairs to stoke the fire. He sat in the dark for another hour, running his thumb along the carved edge of the baby Jesus he had slipped into his pocket. A Guy Lombardo Christmas album played in the background. At midnight he set the baby back in the manger, shut everything off, and went to bed.

In the distance, Thorsen saw a woman crouching in a garden. Her back was turned, and she worked next to a tree with three large roots. The branches were filled with white blossoms, and the air around them glowed with the bodies of pollen-encrusted bees. A narrow stream ran next to the tree, and along that stream laid a path. Behind the woman and the tree, a building rose from the landscape. It was large but vacant. The woman worked without pausing. Thorsen walked toward her. As he drew closer, he noticed her hair. It spilled to the ground and pooled about her like golden bushels of wheat.

Thorsen was about to speak when a man stepped from behind the tree and placed a finger to his lips.

"Paul?" Thorsen asked, and the woman turned her head.

When she saw Thorsen, she smiled and pivoted, using a small basket for balance. The basket was full of beans and squash. "Jens, I'm going to need the rest of that corn," she said, then gestured to a section of the field where corn stalks grew suddenly from the ground, unfurling leaves, ears, tassels.

"Lila?" he asked. A hawk landed in the branches of the tree.

"Hurry," she said and turned back to her work. "They won't be there forever."

Thorsen awoke into the low gray light of the morning. His hand moved across the sheets, and in the dimness he saw his clothes thrown carelessly across a chair in the corner and the reflection of a second window in the mirror above Lila's dressing table. He pushed himself up with some difficulty and pivoted on the edge of the bed until he was sitting upright. Grabbing the same clothes he had on yesterday, he dressed himself and laced up his boots, the dawn gathering only the slightest intensity. He pulled open the window shade and peered out.

A great fog drifted about the roof of the barn and the cottonwoods, which were clad in hoarfrost. Its brocade was barely visible, but the silver-white filigree covered everything: branches, fence and power lines, weather vanes, vehicles, grass, eaves, rooflines. The window itself was cold to the touch, but not painfully so. As Thorsen watched, the fog shifted, filling in an open spot next to the barn and revealing the space in the hedges at the road end of the drive. From there the faint blue shadow of tire tracks ran toward the house, unbraiding as they went, until only two sets of tracks were visible, one of them faint and the other sharp, stopping at a blank spot next to the barn.

Thorsen burst into the hallway, knocked once, and went in. The bed was made, and a few towels and linens were neatly folded and stacked and set on the corner of the dresser. Thorsen tore open the drawers; they were empty. The hangers in the closet were bare.

He pulled up the window shade and saw the same set of tracks ending in open snow, but from this vantage point he could see a line of footprints in the snow leading from the terminus of the tracks straight to the house. Next to the tracks, Angie's frost-encrusted car was parked. The wheels were dug down into the frozen ground and snow was crammed into the wheel wells. Thorsen's truck was nowhere in sight.

As he came downstairs, he saw the comics page balled up on the table and an elegantly wrapped gift sitting next to the nativity. He picked up the gift and shook it. A dull rattle came from inside. A small card tucked under the ribbon said *To: Jens, From: Thanks.*

He tore off the paper and opened the small, stiff box. Inside was a simple pocket watch. A tag hanging from the stem read *Now you don't have to wonder.*

Thorsen dropped the box on the table, took note of the time, and slipped the watch into his pocket. Next to the box lay the odd-sized envelope containing the ultrasound pictures. "Stupid, stupid," Thorsen said to himself, imagining the roads of Sanpete County hovering in front of him like a large transparent map. He chose and eliminated her routes by illuminating them in his mind, deciding finally on a route that would take her through Las Vegas. He imagined her traveling in his truck along the interstate, finding little open but the self-serve gas stations, and then at the state line his map dissolved and Thorsen again stood alone in his living room.

Chapter Twenty-Five

Hoarfrost covered everything—shaggy, husky, delicate. The whole stretch of road between Thorsen's home and Bunker's was transfigured, even in the pale light of the morning. Occasionally a small flurry of frost would drop, sprinkling from a fence wire or a power line. Weak dilapidated outbuildings seemed an outgrowth of the bleakness of the winter landscape. The colorlessness of the sage and junipers somehow ennobled them, and the strange, conjoined homes of the polygamists seemed to signify something profound.

Thorsen pulled Angie's car carefully into Bunker's driveway next to three crude snowmen in the front yard. One was scarved, one had three eyes, and the other had a piece of red licorice for a mouth. Thorsen looked at them for a moment, then picked up the ultrasound pictures and walked up to the dark door. He knocked three times and then stood back.

When the door opened, he saw no one but heard the light thud-scratching of pajama feet on the floor. "It's not Santa," a child called out. More running.

"Nope, it's just Jens Thorsen," he said, then he came closer to the door and stooped down. "Is your grandpa here?"

The door slammed. Thorsen stood up and looked back at the road and his car. The sky had lightened some in general and had gone pale orange to the east. He turned back to the door and knocked again, but there was no answer. Thorsen peered into one of the narrow side windows, and through the lace curtains he could see three small children scatter from around the tree and fireplace. Thorsen knocked again.

Alice Bunker opened the door. When she saw Thorsen, her eyes narrowed and her mouth became gravely thin.

"Alice," Thorsen said, nodding.

"Jens Thorsen, you have a lot of nerve. It's Christmas morning." Alice turned quickly to her grandchildren and hushed them. "You can go into the kitchen and get your breakfast."

Thorsen leaned into the storm door and lowered his voice. "Alice, listen. Is Darrell here?"

"He is, and he's asleep. Don't you think you've done enough damage?"

"Well, no," he said, then he tried to retract it. "I'm not trying to do anything but talk to Darrell. Could you get him please? I just need a minute."

"Who do you think you are, Ebeneezer Scrooge? You've seen your ghosts and now you want to make amends?" Alice folded her arms and shifted her weight to let a child slip past her. "Sorry's not going to undo the hurt you've caused this family."

"No, Alice. I don't think it will," Thorsen said, huffing twice into his hands. "Sorry won't fix anything. Never does. But I do need to talk to Darrell." He turned and gestured toward the road. "I can wait in the car if you think that would be better." Behind Alice, the children had reconvened. They huddled together behind the spindles in the stairwell. "Just send him out to the car, if you would," Thorsen said.

Thorsen turned and walked down the front steps with the envelope clutched in one hand. He scratched the back of his head with the other. When he got to the car, he fished the key out of his pocket. He got in, took another look at the watch, and tried to wind it.

A knock sounded at the passenger-side window. It was Bunker.

Thorsen leaned over and unlocked the door. Bunker climbed in. "This hers?"

"She's got my truck," Thorsen said, then he tossed the envelope onto the seat next to Bunker.

"What's that?"

"Open it."

Bunker took out the pictures and examined them. "Is this the baby?"

"There's no baby," Thorsen said, grasping the wheel.

"She lose it?"

"No."

"Then how?"

"There's no baby. They call it a mole."

Bunker squinted at Thorsen and then looked through each of the grainy pictures again. "She okay?"

"She's fine, but they're going to have to go in and clean her out," Thorsen said, staring straight ahead. Bunker tightened his jaw, the thickness of his neck swelling. "It's pretty much the same procedure as an abortion, except—"

"There's no baby."

"Right."

"You said they're *going* to have to clean her out. When's that going to happen?"

Thorsen shrugged. "Probably right after Christmas, except . . ." Thorsen considered the road in his mirrors, then let his eyes sweep across Bunker's yard.

"Except, she's run off again," Bunker said. "Stole your truck?"

Thorsen nodded.

"Well, that's par for the course."

Thorsen shrugged.

"You can keep the car," Bunker said. "Don't know if it's a fair trade."

"It isn't."

"Any way this could hurt her?"

"Don't know. The doctor said something about it turning into cancer if she waited. So if she talks to you—"

"She won't."

"Okay, then *if* she talks to you, you need to make sure she's been to a doctor."

Bunker nodded, then the two men sat in the car silently, watching their breath. After a few minutes, Thorsen cranked on the engine and opened up the heater.

"Can I keep these?" Bunker asked.

"That's why I brought them."

"I hope you're doing okay without Lila," Bunker said.

Thorsen nodded. "I appreciate that."

"What was it?"

"Heart attack."

Bunker shook his head, then opened the door. "I got to get in there. Grandkids are probably running riot."

"Make sure you ask her."

"If she calls, I will."

When Bunker closed the door, Thorsen put the car in gear, checked the road, and pulled away. In the mirror he saw Bunker close the clasp on the envelope and head into the house.

Dawn had finally broken, and Thorsen headed into town and drove methodically through the streets of Sanpete, slowing as he passed the still houses of the Meeks family and Noreen Hafen. He considered checking on them but couldn't bring himself to stop. He was consumed by the thought that if he stopped, the car might never start again. He would slow to a creep and then begin rolling only an inch at a time until the car was frozen to the road and he was frozen to the wheel.

He drove past the darkened windows of Passey's shop and Stucki's, then he drove out to the Ramkes' and found unbroken snow leading from the road to the house, so he continued on until he reached the Wizenbergs'. Both garage doors were down, and the orange *Sanpete Gazette* box was full. Church parking lots were empty, the streets too. Thorsen continued to prowl through the pale-blue morning until the sun crested the mountains. Then he noticed that the air was beginning to scintillate as if a mirror had shattered high up in the atmosphere. But with the sunlight, the frost began to disintegrate almost before his eyes, sloughing from the trees and roofs and traffic signals and signs. Only a nudge, Thorsen imagined, and the whole world would splinter into dust.

Epilogue

Deloy Meeks strolled calmly into the visiting area, climbed over the short bench, and sat down. Jens Thorsen slid a plastic bag across the table and then pointed after it. "Got you some more cigarettes and some other things in there, tooth brush, word of God, et cetera." Deloy pawed through the bag, then set it aside, pulled a postcard from his breast pocket, and, with a slight grin, slid it across the table. Thorsen picked it up. The picture showed a marina full of sailboats and cruisers, blue sky, darker water, a few clouds just above the horizon. The text said Mission Bay.

"San Diego, huh?" Thorsen said.

"She's got a job in a hair place down there. Says she's making good money, has a couple roommates. They sound pretty cool."

Thorsen flipped over the card and read. "Tests are all good?"

"Perfect."

"She feeling okay?"

"Perfect."

"Good. You know, Deloy, you should write your mother."

Deloy nodded and grinned and looked around. "I know. It's just . . ." He gestured vaguely and then relented. When the guard returned, Thorsen shook Deloy's hand and told him to tell Angie to drop him a line. He agreed, and the guard led him away.

Outside, the sun flared white in a cloudless sky. Somewhere in the parking lot a cicada screamed, and the heat loosened Thorsen's bones, made him remember what it felt like to be young. He walked to where he thought he parked Angie's car, but it was gone. He looked around, then cursed. He held the keys up to the sky and shouted, "I took them with me this time."

At the far end of the lot he saw a truck that was just like his. He took a few steps closer and squinted in the light. The plate matched. He looked around the parking lot, but it was empty. He thought for a minute that he might be on *Candid Camera*. When he got to the truck, he saw that it was clean, a San Diego Community College parking sticker on the back window. The doors were unlocked, and he climbed in. Everything inside was clean as well, as if it had just been vacuumed. His hand went down to the ashtray, and he opened it. Inside were a single key and a small piece of paper, folded in half. Thorsen looked around again and, seeing no one, he read the note. It said: *I owe you.*

He leaned back against the seat and set the note back into the ashtray. The sky was clear and blue, one set of contrails unfolding in a path westward. He watched the horizon for a few minutes, afraid to change anything. Then there was a buzzing in Thorsen's pocket. He took out a small black cell phone and opened it. "Really?" he said. "Well, don't do that. Tell them I said not to." He got the note from the ashtray and read it again. "I can be there in a half-hour," he said. "No, it'll be okay. Don't listen to them. They don't know what they're talking about. Really. I can fix it. It's not a bother. I don't have anything else going on." Thorsen closed the phone and looked at it, then he put the key in the ignition and turned it on.

He drove out of the prison parking lot and turned onto the highway. Two crows jumped up from the road and flew across the open end of the valley. The last of the snow was fading on the mountains, and in that clear, dry light, Thorsen felt as if he hadn't failed after all.

Todd Robert Petersen was born and raised in the Pacific Northwest and currently lives in Cedar City, Utah, with his wife and two children. He has a Ph.D. in English with an emphasis in creative writing and critical theory, and he teaches fiction writing and visual studies at Southern Utah University. Petersen is the author of a story collection titled *Long After Dark*.

ACKNOWLEDGMENTS

Thanks to Ken Brewer, who read an early unfinished draft and helped guide this novel onto the right path, also to Carol Houck Smith, who was an early champion of Jens Thorsen. Her attention kept me driving through the dark and helped me realize that *Rift* was worth doing. May they both rest in peace.

Thanks also to William Morris, Kyle Bishop, and the Pretenyrds at Southern Utah University. Their insights were paramount to the last major transformations of this project.

Special thanks to my wife, Alisa, who listened patiently and critically as I worked out the details of five revisions of this novel over the last seven years. Her insights are on every page.

"What a pleasure to read the work of a writer who understands and can accurately portray the small, out-of-the-way parts of this world where honor, generosity, and sheer cussedness are still operative principles. With *Rift*, Todd Petersen has written a funny and tough-minded account of a place where family, faith, and community still come first."

—Brady Udall, author of *Letting Loose the Hounds*
and *The Miracle Life of Edgar Mint*

"Todd Petersen is a master at capturing small, authentic human moments in charismatic characters. Jens Thorsen, the big-hearted, short-tempered, shrewd, and persnickety troublemaker at the center of *Rift*, is a rift-maker. He'll call out a hypocrite, stand by an outcast, and spur a sleepy throng into action when the cause is just. He married Lila, the only woman in the valley as stubborn as he. A vibrant love story fuels their old ornery marriage, and they will steal your heart. In drawing characters, Petersen is both unflinchingly honest and compassionate; in drawing western landscapes, he's got an eye for original detail. A natural storyteller, a native son, he wields a reliable pen when it comes to capturing the true contemporary West in fiction."

—Ann Cummins, author of *Yellowcake* and *Red Ant House*

"Attention readers of literary fiction: a stunning and richly imagined character has entered our congregation. Jens Thorsen, protagonist of Todd Robert Petersen's striking debut novel, is an aging patriarch and incurable curmudgeon—strong, wise, and ornery. Interestingly flawed and utterly irresistible, Thorsen is a true saint for these latter days. Read his gospel!"

—Aaron Gwyn, author of *Dog on the Cross*
and *The World Beneath*

"You might think you already know Jens Thorsen—the rural Utah Mormon, the ornery old man. But Todd Robert Petersen has created a character who transcends easy stereotypes. Thorsen is a jumble of contradiction: generous and judgmental, impatient and long-suffering. In short, he is fully, deeply human, and I missed him after I turned the novel's last page. Petersen is a terrifically gifted writer, and his keen understanding of the vagaries of human nature, coupled with his ability to craft one gorgeous sentence after the other, makes *Rift* a novel worth reading, and reading again."

—Angela Hallstrom, author of *Bound on Earth*